"Alternately funny, sad and thrilling . . . [a] stellar super-natural crime novel."
—*Publishers Weekly,* starred review

"*Headstone City* is a seamless and wholly believable blend of the supernatural with hardboiled noir. Razor-sharp characterization as the dead and the damned play out their violent destinies in a modern-day Dante's *Inferno.*"
—Bill Pronzini, author of *Nightcrawlers* and *Mourners*

More praise for the Novels of Tom Piccirilli

NOVEMBER MOURNS

"A sustained and unnerving evocation of the dark side of Appalachia . . . Piccirilli tantalizes with hints of awesome mysteries that defy complete understanding."
—*Publishers Weekly*

"*November Mourns* is dark, ambiguous, strange, and sometimes surprisingly sweet. . . . The taint in the land brings William Faulkner to mind, while the taint in the people is pure Flannery O'Connor. Piccirilli has taken Southern Gothic imagery and woven it with his own po-etry to create something uniquely his own, a book of ter-rible beauty and beautiful terrors."
—*Locus*

"If Victor Frankenstein had stitched together pieces of Flannery O'Connor, Stewart O'Nan and James Lee Burke, his creature might have risen from the slab to write Tom Piccirilli's haunting new novel. Piccirilli

"If you go down to the woods with Tom Piccirilli, make sure you have eyes in the back of your head. Scary, engaging, this story gives a totally new meaning to the phrase 'cliff-hanger.' "
—Graham Masterton

"*November Mourns* is a mesmerizing, one-of-a-kind backwoods meditation on death, madness, and moonshine. Tom Piccirilli's voice is unique, and his fever dream storytelling is spellbinding and surprising."
—Mick Garris, director of *The Stand*

"No one else *writes* like Tom Piccirilli. He has the lyrical soul of a poet and the narrative talents of a man channeling Poe, William Faulkner, and Shirley Jackson."
—T. M. Wright, author of *A Manhattan Ghost Story*

"Piccirilli creates a burgeoning sense of unease, and his lyrical writing and insightful characterizations make *November Mourns* as intoxicating as moonshine."
—Tim Lebbon, author of *Dusk*

"A novel of supreme and mesmerizing power that reads like a head-on collision between Flannery O'Connor and M.R. James. . . . This novel is—in the correct, dictionary sense of the word—a masterpiece."
—Gary A. Braunbeck, author of *In Silent Graves*

A CHOIR OF ILL CHILDREN

"A wonderfully wacked, disorienting, fully creepy book from which I never once reeled in revulsion even though as a reader I am admittedly a bit squeamish. I didn't reel because the poetic nature of the prose and seriousness of intent carried the day in every scene."
—Dean Koontz

"Riotous, surprising, and marvelously gruesome."
—Stewart O'Nan

"A searing portrait of twisted souls trapped in a wasteland . . . Will appeal both to genre fans and to readers of Flannery O'Connor and even of William Faulkner. James Lee Burke and Harry Crews devotees should also take note."
—*Publishers Weekly*

"Lyrical, ghastly, first-class horror."
—*Kirkus Reviews*

"*A Choir of Ill Children* demonstrates the author's versatility and penchant for the bizarre. . . . Piccirilli has created a world that is disturbing and compelling."
—*Rocky Mountain News*

"*A Choir of Ill Children* is a full-on Southern Gothic . . . a surreal melange of witchcraft, deformity, and ghosts."
—*Fangoria*

"A narrative puzzle as intellectually challenging as it is slap-your-knee entertaining. Piccirilli creates a geogra-

phy of pain and wonder, tenderness and savageness. There is as much poet as popular entertainer in his approach."
—*Cemetery Dance*

"Tom Piccirilli writes with a razor for his pen. *A Choir of Ill Children* is both deeply disturbing and completely compelling."
—Christopher Golden, author of *Wildwood Road*

"A resonant title for a resonant, powerful, lyrical, and disturbing piece of work. I enjoyed *A Choir of Ill Children* enormously."
—Simon Clark, author of *Stranger* and *Darker*

"Tom Piccirilli's work is full of wit and inventiveness—sharp as a sword, tart as apple vinegar. I look forward to all his work."
—Joe R. Lansdale, author of *The Bottoms*

"*A Choir of Ill Children* is spellbinding. Piccirilli writes like lightning, illuminating a dark landscape of wonders."
—Douglas Clegg, author of *The Hour Before Dark* and *The Infinite*

"This book is brilliant. Surprises abound on every page, and every one of its characters is unforgettable and sublimely imagined."
—*Flesh and Blood Magazine*

"Brilliantly grotesque, beautifully written, and yet shockingly morbid, pulsing with blood that seems a little too real for fiction. This is not just another genre novel, it's a macabre work of art."
—Edward Lee, author of *City Infernal*

"*A Choir of Ill Children* is effing brilliant—Carson McCullers by way of William S. Burroughs.... A powerful meditation on isolation, pointless anger, and familial obligation that ranks right up there with *Geek Love* and *Tattoo Girl*."
—Gary Braunbeck, author of *In Silent Graves*

"Tom Piccirilli's *A Choir of Ill Children* is rich with poetry, his characters are vivid and sharp, and his writing peels away layers of everyday reality. Like all the best authors, he leads readers into the strange and dark places inside themselves."
—Gerard Houarner, author of *The Beast That Was Max*

"Piccirilli courageously walks a dangerous line, telling his story in a fast-paced stream of consciousness narrative that drops the reader into fascinating circumstances with the very first sentence. You won't be able to stop reading."
—David B. Silva, author of *Through Shattered Glass*

"Better start revising your favorite author list—Piccirilli deserves to be at the top."
—*Book Lovers*

OTHER BOOKS BY TOM PICCIRILLI

NOVELS
November Mourns
A Choir of Ill Children
Coffin Blues
Grave Men
A Lower Deep
The Night Class
The Deceased
Hexes
Sorrow's Crown
The Dead Past
Shards
Dark Father

COLLECTIONS
Mean Sheep
Waiting My Turn to Go Under the Knife (Poetry)
This Cape Is Red Because I've Been Bleeding (Poetry)
A Student of Hell (Poetry)
Deep Into That Darkness Peering
The Dog Syndrome & Other Sick Puppies
Pentacle

NONFICTION
Welcome to Hell

HEADSTONE CITY

TOM PICCIRILLI

BANTAM BOOKS

HEADSTONE CITY
A Bantam Spectra Book / March 2006

Published by Bantam Dell
A Division of Random House, Inc.
New York, New York

All rights reserved
Copyright © 2006 by Tom Piccirilli
Cover design by Craig DeCamps

Bantam Books, the rooster colophon, Spectra, and the portrayal of a boxed
"s" are trademarks of Random House, Inc.

ISBN-10: 0-553-58721-8
ISBN-13: 978-0553-58721-0

Printed in the United States of America
Published simultaneously in Canada

www.bantamdell.com

OPM   10   9   8   7   6   5   4   3   2   1

For my wife
Michelle

ACKNOWLEDGMENTS

A debt is owed to the following for their friendship, support, encouragement, and inspiration over the writing of this novel. My thanks need to go out to: Gerard Houarner, Linda Addison, Adam Meyer, Matt Schwartz, Ed Gorman, T. M. Wright, Dallas Mayr, Lee Seymour, Bill Pronzini, Giovanni Arduino, Tom Monteleone, Jack O'Connell, John Skipp, Brian Keene, Jim Moore, Chris Golden, Thomas Ligotti, Thomas Tessier, Patrick Lussier, Mick Garris, and Dean Koontz.

Extraspecial thanks go out to my editor Caitlin Alexander.

HEADSTONE
CITY

ONE

They came after Dane in the showers while he had soap in his eyes.

It was pretty much how he'd expected the hit to go down during his first six months in the can, but by the end of the first year he'd dropped his guard and started to grow a little comfortable. You'd think it was impossible, getting used to a place like this, but it had slowly crept over him until now he nearly enjoyed the joint. The crazy sounds in the middle of the night, the constant action, and the consoling security of having bars and walls on every side.

He'd gotten some of his edge back after the fire, but it hadn't lasted long enough. The Monticelli family held Dane in such low regard that they'd contracted outside their usual channels and hired one of the Aryans.

A guy called Sig, who whistled old Broadway show tunes only Dane recognized. Usually from *South Pacific*, *Fiorello*, and *Oh, Kay!* It got your foot tapping. Sig had

Joseph Mengele's profile branded into his chest. He used matches to singe away his body hair, the black char marks crossthatching his body. This Sig, he was a masochistic pyro who'd hooked up with the skinheads because you could get away with searing yourself to pieces with them. In the name of racial purification.

Dane was in his cell reading when Sig walked down the D-Block aisle holding a little plastic bottle of gasoline he'd filched from the workshop. Unable to contain himself, Sig let out a squeal of wild joy and Dane looked up to see a liquid arc flashing through the air. He rolled over and yanked his mattress on top of him just as Sig tossed a lit match, his eyes full of love and awe. The cell burst into flames and Dane squeezed himself behind the toilet, pressed his face into the bowl to soak his hair, and used his hands to cup water and splash himself down.

This Sig though, he had some issues. He cherished the fire so much that, standing there, he grew jealous of Dane being in the middle of the flames. Tugging at his crotch, he stepped into the cell, spritzing gasoline from his bottle left and right. It was a good thing the mental institutions were even more overpacked than the prisons, or maybe the Monti family wouldn't have wound up with such a schiz.

The flames bucked and toppled over Sig. He flailed, spun, and took a running leap off the second floor D-Block tier.

Dane sat with toilet water dripping down his face while he tried to take in the whole moronic situation. The bulls worked fast with their extinguishers. When they found him he was laughing on the shitter, thinking about how Vinny would react to the news when it got back to him.

It had been funny more than anything, so he grew

complacent again. He kept waiting for the family to pay off a pro who would do the job right. There were at least five guys on D-Block that Dane would never be able to take on his best day. But instead of doing him in, they let him read his books, play chess with the old-timers, and even spotted him when he worked the heavy weights in the gym.

Dane had grown especially sloppy these last few weeks, with his grandmother and the dead girl always on his mind. He should've known the hit would happen today, since it was their last chance to make a play while he was still on the inside.

But he'd been worried about getting presentable and smelling fresh for when he saw Grandma Lucia this afternoon. He thought about her slapping him in the back of the head, telling him that just because he was in prison didn't mean he couldn't still look nice.

Dane thumbed the suds off his face and tried to clear his vision as they came at him from the front, standing shoulder to shoulder. They weren't pros. They had the jitters, hands trembling as they held out poorly sharpened shanks.

Mako stood about five-one and suffered from short-guy syndrome. Always getting into everybody's face and tackling the biggest cons just to show them he wasn't afraid. He loved to scrap but never went in for anything much heavier than that. Put a weapon in his hand, and he didn't know what the hell to do with it. Even now he held the shank wrong, high and aimed back toward his own belly, so it would be easy to twist his wrist and get him to fall onto the blade. He looked like he was going to either scream or cry, and Dane felt a sudden wash of pity for him.

Kremitz was an insurance investigator who'd sign off

on almost any suspicious claim so long as he got a kick-
back from it. He'd done all right for himself for a couple
of years but finally got nabbed in a sting run by the fire
marshal. Kremitz was muscular but gangly, with an ambiguous temperament. He'd used a shiv on his Aryan
cellmate a while back but only after being sodomized for
about a year. He was known as a wild card on the block.
You never knew which way Kremitz might jump.

Dane had never gotten used to being naked in front of
other men. Not in the high school showers, not in the
army, and especially not here in the slam. And now he
had to stare down these two with his crank hanging out.

They gaped at his scars, the way they wove up and
twisted around to the back of his neck. Dane could brush
his hair to hide most of the metal plates securing his
skull, but under the showerhead they came up polished
and gleaming. The shiv started to dance in Mako's hand.

"How'd they get to you two?" Dane asked, genuinely
curious.

"The same way they get everybody," Kremitz said.
"They want something done, they put the pressure on
until it's done. Me, they reeled me in through my
brother. He owes twelve grand to their book. Likes to
think he's going to get off the docks by winning on college basketball. He used to get out from under by jacking a few crates, but this time, he gets caught. The other
longshoremen kick the shit out of him because he hasn't
given anybody a taste. He's got no other way to pay off.
So it falls to me to save his worthless neck."

"Sorry to cause you trouble."

"It's not your fault. Just bad luck all around. Except
for my brother. He's just an asshole."

Turning to Mako, though, Dane could see the little
guy had no excuse except he was scared.

Water swirled madly down the drains. A shadow moved at the front of the showers, where someone was standing guard to keep others out. At least one bull would've been paid off, possibly more.

Dane touched the scars and felt some of the tension leave him. There was power in your own history, in the stupid traumas you'd endured.

"I ain't got nothin' against you," Mako said.

Kremitz agreed. "Me neither. Really."

"I know it," Dane said. He just kept shaking his head, thinking how ridiculous it would be to buy it now, only a couple hours from being on the street again. "I'll be out of here this afternoon. When I'm gone, the heat'll be off you."

"Lis—listen—" Mako had to cough the quiver out of his throat. "The Monticelli family won't forget us if we foul this up."

"Yeah, they will." It was true. This wasn't Vinny's serious play anyhow. It was him having fun, breaking balls, keeping Dane on his toes.

"Those bunch of goomba pricks don't forget nothin' about nobody," Mako whined, shuffling his feet so they squeaked. "If they did, they'd have let you ride out of here."

"It's a different situation."

"And I'm supposed to trust what you say? That they'll fade back?"

"Yeah."

"I get told I got a visitor. First visitor I've had my entire nickel in the joint. My pa don't come, my old lady, not even my kid, the little bastard. This visitor's a big guy in an Armani suit, one eyebrow, hands like he goes around slugging brick walls for fun."

That'd be Roberto Monticelli. It took Dane back

some, wondering why Berto had come himself instead of one of the family capos or lieutenants.

"Guy tells me I do this to you or I get it done to me. Goes into all this bullshit about blowtorches and meat grinders, how he's gonna mail me to six cities all over New Jersey. Except with him, I know it's not bullshit."

Dane couldn't really help but argue the point. "Most of it is."

"It's the part that's not that worries me."

"Maybe I can help."

"The hell you gonna do that?" Mako groused. Thinking about Berto had gotten him all wired up, given him the shakes. The point of the shiv danced against his T-shirt. "Even if you get out the front gate, you'll be dead before you hit the corner."

"Don't believe it."

"We got no choice."

Kremitz started to steel himself. Jaws clenched, leaning forward on his toes, he was jazzing himself up to attack.

Dane had been a pretty poor soldier overall, but he'd liked the hand-to-hand combat training. His drill instructor would use him all the time as a practice dummy, flipping Dane over his hip and throwing him down in the dirt. Kicking his feet out from under him over and over. The DI would demonstrate how to drive the knife in, how to keep the blade from getting stuck in bone.

Without fully realizing it, Dane had absorbed a lot, and would pull the moves when he got drunk, beating on the loudmouthed Irish officers who called him a greasy guinea. But he never got used to the stockade the way he did the slam, and he couldn't figure out why.

Mako and Kremitz weren't going to be too tough so long as he didn't slip on the wet tile. They didn't know how to work as a team, standing too far away from each other. They swept out clumsily with their shanks and both of them tightened up, lurching, wanting to end it fast. Faces growing more grim, but with a hint of pleading in their eyes.

The drill instructor would call Dane and another guy over, tell them to charge at him. He had this one routine where he'd maneuver past Dane, grab hold of him by the elbows, and use his body like a shield to block the other soldier's attack. Dane would be standing there like a bag of potatoes, getting the crap beat out of him while the DI let out a brash chuckle.

Dane had never tried the move and decided this might be a good time. He dodged past Kremitz, hooked him by the elbows, and swung him around into Mako's face. Mako let out a grunt of surprise and jumped back, under the steaming force of the shower. Dane kneed Kremitz in the thigh from behind, brought him low, and shoved. The sound track from a Stooges short couldn't have made it any more perfect. Kremitz and Mako clunked heads and dropped their shivs, slid to all fours in the soapy water.

Dane couldn't help himself and let out a chuckle of his own. He hated the sound of it, but there it was. You were nothing but an amalgam of your influences. He grabbed one of the shivs and stabbed both men in their upper legs, in the thick meat of the muscle where it wouldn't do a lot of damage. He twisted the blades just enough to make the wounds look especially ugly. Mako and Kremitz both started to scream, and Dane said, "I'm doing you a favor, so shut the hell up."

While they writhed on the shower floor Dane ducked back under the showerhead and rinsed off the rest of the soap. Blood swirled near his feet. When he was finished he toweled off and got dressed, listening to them groan through their teeth trying to swallow down the pain. They rolled and squirmed across the tiles.

"Sheezus shheee-it!" Kremitz hissed. "Y-you crippled us!"

Moaning, Mako stuck his face in the drain, blowing bubbles as he gripped his leg to hold in the blood.

"You're both going to be fine. Say that you got into a fight with each other."

"Jeezus!"

"You'll be in the infirmary for three or four weeks. You're not hurt bad but they'll want to keep an eye on you for infection. After that, the bulls will toss you into solitary for at least another month. By the end of your run, I'll either be dead or this shit with the Monticelli family will be cleared up."

"You sure . . . about that, Johnny?" Mako whimpered.

"Even if I'm not, you're better off than I would've been, right?" Dane let out a slow smile. A part of him wanted Mako to end it now. Cut their throats, finish it the right way. You don't injure the enemy, you eradicate him. His fingers twitched. A small, sharp fury nearly broke free from the center of his chest, but as he felt himself about to take a step forward, it receded. He almost wished it hadn't gone. "Don't fuckin' complain."

Mako grabbed him by the ankle and squeezed once, as a sign of thanks. Dane combed his hair back, checked himself in the mirror to make certain his grandmother wouldn't give him a rough time.

He walked out past the guards on the Monti payroll, gave them a grin and a little salute. He felt good, stronger than he had earlier in the day, more settled. He'd been half wondering if he'd had a death wish, and the answer seemed to be no. Still, it was the kind of thing you couldn't be a hundred percent sure about.

When he got back to his cell, the girl he'd killed, Angelina Monticelli, was sitting on his cot.

"Oh Christ," he said, his scars suddenly burning.

She wavered for a moment, fading and reappearing, then vanished, leaving an old man sitting where she'd been—Aaron Fielding, a neighborhood grocer and fish seller buried a couple of rows from her in Wisewood cemetery. The guy was always smiling and letting the kids steal cheap candy bars from the wire racks at the front of the store. He'd let out this heavy, booming laugh whenever something hit him just right.

But old man Fielding had a wild and desperate look to him, colorless eyes flitting all over the place, hinges of his jaws pulsing. He raised a hand to Dane in a gesture of pleading. "Johnny, I need—"

"I can't talk to you right now, Mr. Fielding," Dane said, his voice hard, flat. "Later."

His gray face filled with terror. There was none of the joy and peace the nuns taught you about when you were a kid, what you hoped for when you hit the other side. "Please!"

"No."

"Just for a little while."

"No, Mr. Fielding."

"A minute. Only one moment more!"

"No!"

Angie snapped back into focus. She let out a soft laugh, like it was funny the shit she had to go through to talk to Dane. Or what he had to do to bring her in.

She said, "Berto says they're going to let you go home and visit your grandmother first, then they'll clip you on your second or third week out."

"I guess he's not as eager as I thought he was."

"He wants to build up tension, make it spectacular."

"He doesn't have the imagination or style for that."

"I know, but it's what he tells his crew."

"Does the Don agree with all this?"

"No, but Daddy doesn't really stand up to Roberto anymore. He's old and in a lot of pain."

"What about Vinny?"

"He's waiting for you."

Fifteen years old when she'd bought it two years ago, but still appearing so full of life, with that overwhelming hipness of youth. She was dressed the way she was the day she OD'd: oversized black sweater and blue jeans, no makeup, her dark hair falling straight back over her ears, the slightest curl of bangs up front.

Heat flooded his stomach and got his skin dancing. He started breathing heavily, and when his breath reached her she closed her eyes and lifted her face to meet it. Her bangs stirred and wafted. She smiled and he swallowed thickly, again and again.

Jesus. He realized he still wanted her. What the hell did that say about you, when you were aroused by the dead? Or was it only because she looked so much like her older sister, Maria?

"Angie—"

"You don't have to be embarrassed with me, Johnny."

"I'm not."

"There's no shame in it. You keep me sane in hell."

It made him chew his lips, hearing that. He sat on the floor across from his bunk, staring at her. If only he'd driven faster, or hadn't run over the cop.

But why stop there? If you're going to go back, go farther. If he hadn't given in and agreed to take her to Bed-Stuy in the first place. She'd talked circles around him until he'd cracked. It hadn't been difficult. If only he'd cared a little more and been a lot smarter. He shouldn't have been so pathetic, but that's what the familiar streets had done to him. What he'd allowed them to do. What they were still doing, even in prison.

"Will you visit me in Headstone City?" she asked.

"I don't think so. It's best if I'm not seen there."

"You live there."

"I mean at your grave."

"Nobody visits. They act like they miss me so much, but nobody takes the time to say a prayer or bring a shitty plastic flower."

"I'm sorry, Angie."

"Johnny, I need you."

Something began to soften in his belly then, and he felt himself going with it. A weakness that had always been there but was broadening, intensifying. Maybe he was about to cut loose with a sob. Twenty minutes ago he was almost ready to cut throats, and now this fragility and brittleness. He wanted to ask her if she held him responsible the way her family did. It was a question he'd never asked her before. She didn't appear to want to make him feel guilty, didn't try to get her claws into him, the way she had in life.

Dane heard the bull coming for him, turned to watch as the guard stepped up to the cell door. "Danetello. Let's go."

He stood and the guard escorted him down the tier, through the gen pop, across the courtyard, and back into the visitation quad, where all the new cons first set foot in the can. The warden was nowhere to be seen. They handed him a ream of paperwork, but nothing for him to sign. The clothes he came in with had been pressed and folded into a pile that lay on the counter. He reached for them, and another guard said, "Hold it."

"What's the matter?"

"You've got a phone call, if you want it."

"Why wouldn't I want it?"

"Most cons who get this close to the outside on the day of their release don't turn around and go answer the phone."

Dane figured it was his Grandma Lucia, jonesing for sugar. He went back and took the call. His grandmother said, "Stop off at the bakery and get some *cannoli* and *biscotti,* will you, Johnny? And don't let the girl put you off. She's dead, that one. She doesn't know what she's talking about."

TWO

This town, it took your blood and replaced it with cement, asphalt, and pigeon shit. You became a part of it as much as the steel and iron, all the bone meal sprinkled into its cornerstones. No matter who you were, you got hard.

Brooklyn, New York.

Fourth largest city in the United States, cradle of roughnecks and Nobel Laureates, center of America's most diversified gathering of angry cultures.

You knew it, and it knew you. Every dark corner, edge to edge. Handball and knock-hockey in Highland Park. Nights sleeping in a tent under Stoney Bridge out near the reservoirs. Stickball on Schenck Avenue, the street tar on top of the old cobblestones getting soft in the August sun. You could lift it with a spoon. Watching a parade curbside on Flatbush Ave. Playing pinball and having an egg cream at Louie's candy store. A shot of syrup, a dollop of milk, and a steady stream of seltzer.

The foam would rise to the rim of the glass but never overflow.

Louie wearing a black merchant marine wool cap, even in the summer, never taking any shit off the kids. Once, Roberto Monticelli walked in and, because his voice had changed and he'd grown a few inches that year, tried to get protection money out of Louie. Kept making vague threats about arson, using a big word like "accelerant" and asking, *Hey, anybody smell smoke?* Louie smacked him in the mouth, took him outside, pried up a manhole cover with a tire iron, and threw Berto down into the sewer. About the funniest thing Dane had ever seen in his life.

The Don never came after Louie for retribution. You didn't fuck with the corner candy stores. They meant too much to the neighborhood.

A century ago Headstone City had been known as Meadow Slope, one of the richest areas in Brooklyn. Industrial-age barons, moguls, and merchants pursued their brazen luxuries in the new era of abundance. They'd ride their carriages from Manhattan to Outlook Park and attend masquerade balls thrown along the Mile, where the wealthy built their extravagant Victorian mansions. You could see it if you put your mind to it. The fashionable elite strolling the vast gardens and embracing the celebrated performers of the day.

Politicians and businessmen wanted a hub for cultural pursuits, where the masters of fine art could lord it over the laborers who greased their axles or fetched their tea. Local entrepreneurs constructed Grand Outlook Hall, an Italian Renaissance gallery. Five lavish stories and 150,000 square feet, a shrine to the arts that became the jewel of the Meadow Slope community. Back in the day it was considered the equal in beauty to the Academy of Music, Botanic Garden, and Grand Army Plaza.

The marble corridors, rich oak and mahogany paneling, ballrooms, opera house, chandeliers, and terrace nurseries brought the rich and prominent flocking. They'd come in their top hats and tails, ladies dressed in Parisian gowns, to hear the star entertainers.

During prohibition, opera connoisseur Al Capone frequented the Hall and had his own balcony seat in the ballroom. One of Al's cronies from Chicago, guy with the stupid name Peachy Fichi, tried to whack him in the loge, but Al hid behind one of the brass statues until he could get his pistol out and return fire. You could still see the bullet holes in the garlands of gold-leaf molding. Neither Al nor Peachy could shoot worth a shit. After reloading three times each, they both ran for it.

The bus let Dane off at the corner in front of the Grand Hall. The mid-October wind braced him, leaves skittering against his ankles. He allowed two teenage couples coming out of the parking lot to precede him onto the street. Guys in tuxes and the girls in silk dresses and mink stoles. Dane asked, "Who's on tonight?"

"Kathryn Mondiviaggi," one of the kids said, his bow tie just a little askew. His cheeks sprouted crimson from the chill. "In the revival of *La Traviata*."

"I heard Sophia Campescio sing it on her last tour, about twenty years ago," Dane told them.

"Really?"

"Michael Finelli played Alfredo Germont."

"Oh, he's so handsome," the kid's date said, moving closer and speaking with a hushed tone, as if to a conspirator. This was how the real fans talked about opera, in close, like it was somehow gossip. She had a smile that caught Dane low and almost made him flinch. Her hair flowed back and forth, reaching for him. "Even more so now, with the white patches in his beard. Truly debonair."

"He was still new on the scene back then, before he'd made any movies."

"I saw *Venice in the Morning* seven times."

"He threw a rose to my grandmother in the fourth row. She rushed the stage and nearly tackled him."

"I would've too. Did she save the flower?"

"Yeah. It's pressed in the front of her Bible, where the family history is filled out. All the vaccinations my father had back in the fifties, stuff like that."

The guys turned a deaf ear, put off by the intrusion. Dane understood, so he watched them escort their girls off without another word. You never knew who might be moving in on you, even in the opera house parking lot. Dane called out, "Have a good night!" He grinned, turned, and began to walk home.

The neighborhood had been going to hell on the inside track for the last four decades and looked like it'd just about gotten there. Even the graffiti lacked style, none of that old, cool flair of the seventies. Now it was just a lot of fuck you's and Freddy + Boopsie on the brickwork. Kids didn't know what to do with themselves, no creative expression at all. More bars on the windows, but the small lawns still perfectly manicured and just as many people in the street, walking store to store. The old Italian ladies in black heading to the cemetery.

Wisewood cemetery had been inspired by Central Park landscaping, laid out in the middle of Meadow Slope. It was meant to be a retreat where visitors could ponder death, guilt, and redemption.

Trunks of stunted oak broke the hilly terrain. Rutted

paths channeled through the area, cutting around knolls. The afternoon sun glazed the battered, blunt faces of granite saints and martyrs. Tombstones—rounded, sharp, or opulent—jutted at odd angles. Some less than six inches from each other.

There were miles of the dead. Sixty thousand supposedly in Wisewood, his mother and father among them, but Christ only knew how many more had been dumped in the ravines and sumps bordering the highway. Or like they did it in Naples, four to a casket when nobody was looking.

There was a church within three blocks' walk in any direction. The rich and fashionable would wander the paths and picnic, playing charades on the vast lawns while funerals were being held just a few feet away. The cemetery's most prominent feature was its Gothic-style front gates. They stood wide and inviting just down the block from Grandma Lucia's place.

Dane had been to four wakes before he was nine years old. No one would ever tell him how anybody died, just that they'd had an accident. It scared the hell out of him, thinking that all these people were croaking from falling off ladders, running with scissors, slipping on the stairs.

It brought him together with strangers in an obscure, shared grief. Funeral processions moved through town every weekend with a fierce and forbidding commitment.

One night he'd gone out to Wildwood with his first girl and made a mad, quiet love to her on a sheet of marble tomb. When they were finished she had the name of a dead guy pressed into her back and an ugly bruise from a bas-relief cherub.

Dane stood in the middle of the street, staring off to the north, where the Monticelli mansion could be seen at the top of the rise, the waves in the bay breaking gently in the horizon. The surrounding woodlands of Outlook Park seemed to clutch at the skyline.

He walked around the corner and down three blocks to Chooch's Lounge. He hung back against a nearby stoop, watching the door.

Lit a cigarette and thought, by the end of this smoke, I ought to just do it.

There was a reason why the big mob families were fading fast. They weren't as sharp as they used to be, not as careful anymore. In the old days, the bosses lived in their little houses and watered their tomato gardens and hid their big cash offshore or under their mattresses. Now their grandkids drove Mercedes and flashed black diamonds and didn't even bother to come up with a cover story for where the money was being filtered in from. A twenty-five-year-old in a Jag wearing suede and silk, partying at the fanciest clubs in New York, telling people he bussed tables in his uncle's pizza parlor for a living. No calm, no cool, and no code.

The Monticellis weren't quite as sloppy as some of the others, but Vinny and Berto had cut their crews too much slack. It used to be if you spent too much out in the open, the capo would take you for a drive and stick a knitting needle in the back of your head. Then go and gather up the wife's mink stole, the Caddy, the $1,200 Italian shoes, and burn it all out in the pine barrens. The families had a quiet class and knew how to keep it under wraps.

Nowadays, the goombas were mostly fat and slow, but they could still play pretty rough when it came down to it. You had an edge if you moved fast and didn't pick their pockets. So long as money wasn't involved, they all had to sit back, hold meetings, and have discussions on what should be done. The organizations gathering to-gether in drunken cabals down in Atlantic City.

Then the bosses talking to the capos, and the captains to the crews. Then more dinners and gatherings and councils to figure out who would do whatever had to be done. Maybe the verve had drained out of the process be-cause so much of it was legal on paper now, all stock market reports and swanky coffee shop investments.

Dane saw how it would go down.

He'd walk into Chooch's and they'd give him the slow turn, the slick smiles, until he got up closer. The muscle would lumber to their feet, try to straight-arm him. He'd buck past and tight expressions of worry would cross their heavy faces and crinkle their bloated features. Now they'd have to move faster, reaching inside their jackets and going for their pea shooters and popguns.

. He'd known them all for most of his life. In Brooklyn, your neighbors were as much your family as your own blood. The fact that they'd had his father killed only brought them all closer together.

By the time Dane hit the table they'd have two or three pistols in his face. Vinny would hold out his grace-ful hands, the thin alabaster fingers patting the air like the symphony conductor his mother always wanted him to be. He used to practice violin when they were kids, Dane riding his bike to the estate and calling up on the guardhouse phone. Vinny standing there in the high window with a look of superiority on his face. Seeing all the things that would be coming to him one day when he wouldn't have to play the fucking violin anymore.

Back then, Dane didn't fully understand their differ-ences, though his dad had tried to warn him.

So he'd be at the table and Vinny would pat the air, his head angled but with that patronizing grin, as if prepared to listen to the excited musings of a child. The glass eye fixed and rigid, the fake teeth not very white so they'd look more real.

Dane would have the chance for a beautiful uppercut if he wanted to take it. Lift Vinny right up out of his seat, snap him four feet into the air, and maybe even break his neck. In the excitement he might even be able to run, but then the whole mess would just keep following him around forever anyway.

It would leave him only the chance to get off a wiseass insult or two. Vinny would smile, then chuckle and cock his head again, this time the other way. Like he was listening to the whispers of angels, then he'd let out his hyena laugh.

Vinny wouldn't say much, just something innocuous and meaningless. "Welcome back, how you been?" Three or four thugs would grab Dane's arms and pull him away, rough him up a little before shoving him against a parked car. You couldn't toss people in the gutter anymore, there was too much traffic.

This little meeting, it would hold them both until later, when one of them would have to die.

So Dane decided to walk in, just to see if he could rush things along, get the ball rolling. For two years in the can he'd been pretty calm, but now it seemed like he just didn't want to wait anymore. It could be fun.

THREE

Dane had taken a step toward the front door, feeling the possibility of his own murder about to come down, when Phil Guerra, his father's old partner, drove up in a sky-blue Cadillac.

"Oh man, beautiful."

Dane took a step back and nodded his approval. The car had been waxed to perfection, radiant and gleaming. He could see his reflection in what they called the Magic-Mirror acrylic lacquer finish. Looking really uptight and more than a little lost.

It was a sin to be that uncool around a '59 Caddy.

Sixty-two hundred Series. The dream car and pinnacle of success for every man in Headstone City around Phil's age. And their sons and grandsons.

Outrageous rocket tail fins and jet pod taillights. The grille was a glittering partition of chrome. Dane checked and saw there was even a dummy grille across the lower rear deck. The parking and turn signal lights were paired at the outer ends of the massive front bumper. The rear bumper had huge, chrome outer pods with recessed backup lights. It got his pulse thrumming just to see the car in such cherry shape.

Phil lowered the driver-seat window, leaned over, and asked, "You like it?"

"Oh yeah. I know it's what you've always wanted."

"Me and everybody else. My old man had one of these, right off the line. Same color. I was thirteen and he never let me drive it. Not once, the prick. But he'd make me wash it twice a week after school until I had soapsuds coming out of my ass."

"Looks like retirement's been good to you."

Grinning now, posturing a touch. Phil had a self-satisfied smile that just kept going and going until you could see all the way down the back of his throat. "You ought to get something for your thirty years besides a gold watch." Some acute bitterness there, but not like the cops who'd really gone to the wall. "Putting your life up against it every day, in the street with the garbage. I would've been better off in sanitation with the rest of the mooks."

Dane's father had been proud of his badge, never bitched once, and had died on the job. So Dane didn't have much sympathy for Phil. "You get a full pension, insurance, and benefits. Then you take a security position in a warehouse someplace, sleep on the job, and draw another check."

"Why don't you get in, Johnny? Before some wiseguy decides to shoo you off the sidewalk."

Dane thought about it. Maybe he should take care of this first. When you had accounts to square going all the way back to your childhood, it was tough to prioritize. They all threaded together and snarled into the same web. There'd be time enough for the showdown after he'd cleared up a few other matters. He took another look at the front door of Chooch's, imagining blood on the ceiling. He grinned at Phil and climbed in. "Sure."

Fifteen years ago, when he was seventeen, he could've stolen and sold this car for maybe twenty grand cash. Now, he couldn't even guess what it might run.

"You know why the Caddy has such ludicrous fins?" Phil asked.

"Yeah."

"You do?" Like he was afraid if he said some kind of bullshit now he'd get called on it.

Dane looked at him. "Yeah. The designers were fascinated with rockets and space missions. Before man walked on the moon, but they knew it was coming soon. You take a look at the rear, it resembles the exhaust ports of a jet, right? Even when it's sitting in your driveway, it's still cruising. Cadillac was going head-to-head with Chrysler at the time. They put a rush schedule to get the 1959 draft completed. The entire lineup flaunted visibility. Spaciousness. You can see all four corners with this windshield."

"I like how it curves."

"Nice. They did a good job refitting it." Dane ran his hand over the seat. "You got burned on the fabric though."

Phil froze, the proud smile going rictus. "What?"

"The interior isn't original."

"You fuckin' with me, Johnny?"

"No." Dane felt good, showing off. A couple hundred hours stealing cars and working in chop shops came in handy for conversations like this. "You've got the metallic fabric used on the Fleetwood Sixty Special. It trapped the hairs of women's mink coats so the manufacturer switched it out. Weird that your restorer would put this in." Stroking it, enjoying the feel, like petting the back of a sleeping woman's head. "Same period . . . even more rare, really, when you get down to it. But not the high-class stuff." Dane tried to think which mob garages might've had the old Fleetwood fabric tucked away for fifty years.

Phil turned, expressionless, but seething beneath the false composure. He didn't mind being ripped off half as much as being alerted to the fact.

Guerra. The name meant "war" in Italian, and Phil liked that. It gave him an extra measure of poise, especially when he was a cop. He said his name—the word—like he practiced it, putting everything he had into it.

Voice firm and smooth as a character actor in some noir movie from the thirties. Phil had porked up about fifty pounds since he'd retired, but he'd been working on everything else. A pretty good rug with the right amount of silver in it, a nice tan from spending half the week in an ultraviolet booth. Stylish clothes, expensive leather shoes. He was pushing sixty but looked ten years younger. The extra weight hit him mostly in the face, filling out his cheeks and making him look jolly and generous.

Phil drove badly. Way too fast, riding bumpers all around town. He circled Wisewood and sped under the highway. He barely slowed for the stop signs and always gunned it during yellow lights.

Years ago he'd had the moves to back up his break-neck driving, but with age the man's reflexes had slowed considerably. Dane remembered Phil and his wife Mabel taking Dane and his parents out on long drives across Jersey and Pennsylvania, to the Poconos. Upstate to Albany to see the Capitol Building. Mom would be in the backseat petrified as Phil gunned it across bridges, swinging through lazy small-town traffic and nearly clipping cattle that had wandered onto the road. Mabel would scrunch down and pour herself a gin and tonic from the Thermos she always brought along. Dad occasionally laughing, watching, always with too much on his mind. Dane would sit on his mother's lap and giggle like crazy, shouting, "Go faster, Uncle Philly! Go faster!"

He could remember, very clearly, but without being able to feel it anymore, just how much he used to love Phil Guerra.

"Who picked you up?"

"Nobody," Dane said. "I took the bus."

"That's terrible. That's just awful. I'm sorry about that, Johnny. If I'd known you were gonna do that, I would've come by. It must be awfully hard walking back into the world and not seeing a friendly face the minute you step outside."

Actually, it was a lot tougher never seeing a friendly face on the inside, but Dane didn't want to cloud the issue. "It's all right. The ride was fine. Two other guys I knew from the joint were being released the same time, and they had their whole families on board. It was like a tour bus. Wives and mothers, their sisters, kids. One guy, he's thirty-seven and has three grandchildren."

"Gotta be a spic then."

Dane took out a cigarette while Phil eyed him, trying to hide his anxiety. The thought of ashes falling onto the fabric, even if it wasn't original, put a crazed gleam in his eye.

"Don't light that."

"I won't."

"So was he a spic or a nigger?"

Sometimes you had to let the old-school bigotry go

by, and sometimes you didn't. Dane said, "His name's D'Abruzzi. Stefano D'Abruzzi. His kids brought a laptop with them, playing DVDs on it. I watched the first half of one of the Harry Potter movies. Pretty good for a kid's flick. Anyway, Stefano's father's got a restaurant on the Upper West Side."

"Oh yeah? Let me think. *D'Abruzzi's,* that's right. I ate there a few times. They had to order their *tiramisu* and *torrone* from the Jewish bakery down the block. What proud Sicilian is gonna do that, I ask?"

"The grandfather was from Naples."

"That explains it then."

Phil had already pulled Dane's trigger and made a harsh association, so now he had to ride his hate out. It was usually like this when you talked to the old-world Italians in the neighborhood. The old cops, the old-school mob guys. You couldn't get away from it. Their attitude was ingrained. No way to ingratiate or back down, you just had to shoulder past. Dane nodded passively, like he did whenever the bulls started to pull this sort of crap. Trying to start a race war because they were bored.

Phil's brow unfurrowed. He knew he was getting off track and didn't have a lot of time to make whatever play he was going for. "Hey, don't light that."

"I won't."

"You see Grandma Lucia yet?"

"No."

"She's gonna be worried. You should've gone straight there to say hello."

"I talked to her before I left the prison. She wants me to get her some *cannoli* and *biscotti.*"

"Go to *La Famiglia.*"

"I will."

"They still know how to bake. Their *amaretti* are the best."

Were they really talking about cookies?

But then Phil Guerra, patting the side of his silver rug, finally managed to get around to it. "You shouldn't be hanging around this part of the neighborhood, Johnny."

"That right?" Like you could be in the neighborhood without being in every part of it at the same time. When you were back, you were in all the way.

"It's not the safest place for you."

"Think it's safer than the can?"

"Maybe not."

Phil took the next turn so wide that they wound up in oncoming traffic, tires squealing. He let out a wild guffaw and swerved back into his lane, tapping the curb. Dane shifted uneasily.

"What, you scared?"

"No."

"You look edgy."

"I always do."

It still got to him, after all these years. He hated being in a car with anybody else driving, no matter who it was or how good they were behind the wheel. Dane was a driver. He always wanted to be in charge of the machine.

Rummaging through the glove compartment, he came up with a pair of thick glasses in dark plastic frames. He figured they'd be there, the man too vain to use them. "You sure you don't need these for driving, Phil?"

"Ah, them optometrists, whatta they know?"

"That you can't see?"

"I see fine."

Dane put the glasses back, imagining how tough it

must be on Phil's wife, Mabel, living with him now that
he was retired, refusing to think of himself as any different than when he was twenty-five. She probably had gin
bottles stashed all over the house, in the toilet tank, behind the insulation in the attic, in back of the cabinet
under the kitchen sink. One of these days she'd grab the
drain opener instead and that would be the end of her
consoling, sneaky sipping.

Now the guy was getting a little crazy. Phil nearly
sideswiped a bus making a tight left turn from the opposite lane. Dane fidgeted again, knowing this was a weakness he couldn't hide, and it had taken the man all of five
minutes to find it out.

"Well, at least you've got a hard head," Phil said. He
let out a slow, low, counterfeit laugh that went on for too
long. He tapped the inside of the windshield...one,
two, three...then reached over and did the same to
Dane's forehead...one, two, three. Phil even grabbed
him by the neck so he could lay his fingers on the scars
and check if they were still there.

Knocking at the metal doors of his skull.

On the day Dane and Vinny stole their third car, they
went joyriding down to the Jersey Shore. They spent the
day swimming, lying out on the sand, and moving the
car around to different parking lots whenever a police
cruiser came by. They met a couple of girls, freshmen in
college, who spent equal parts of the afternoon snubbing
them and aggressively flirting with them. By sunset they
lay wrapped in their beach towels in the dunes, drunk
and mostly naked. As with all the worst troubles in his
life, Dane missed his chance at an easy escape by only a
few seconds.

Vinny spoiled the night by putting on his pants, taking out his wallet, and offering the girls money. Not

even much at that. He was still a little steamed about his girl initially rebuffing him, even though she'd eventually hauled his ashes. He could carry a grudge to the bottom of hell.

Pissed off and humiliated, the girls threw their beer cans at Vinny's chest, gave him the finger, and fled. Dane actually had to grab him by the arm to keep him from giving chase, like he was going to smack them around, make them take the cash. He was just starting to show the Monticelli temper, the resentments that he'd never shake.

By the time Dane and Vinny finished another six-pack and got back to the car, they were buzzing pretty good. Dane took it slow out of the parking lot, driving carefully, but suddenly the exit was blocked by two screeching cop cars.

Instead of pillow talk or discussing the violin, Vinny had told his girl all about boosting the car. Showing off, starting to swing his weight around, mentioning the Don. After he'd embarrassed her, she'd gone up to the boardwalk and called the nearest precinct.

Dane said, "Uyh," shook his head, and tried to assess the situation. He saw an escape route clear and distinct in his mind. He could stand on the gas, cross a couple of rows of parked cars, slip around a streetlight, and jump the curb. It came down to about thirty seconds' worth of real action. If he could get a fifth of a mile head start, he knew he could lose the cops, dump the ride, and pick up another. But only if he could get that fifth of a mile.

He turned to Vinny to ask him what he wanted to do, but Vinny was already hissing under his breath about the girl, laughing to himself and sneering. Saying how he was going to kill her, stick a filleting blade in her kidney.

Dane had never seen Vinny like that before, nearly fucking foaming.

The longer they sat around the worse it would be, so Dane threw the car into drive, ready to turn the wheel and try to make the curb. With a crazed, grating screech of eagerness Vinny screamed at him to bust through the roadblock instead. It was the kind of nutty crap that would never work. Making a death run at the cops would only get them aggravated assault, attempted vehicular murder.

High beams filled the stolen car and another siren blasted behind them. Megaphone voices snarling and ordering them out, onto the ground, facedown. Interlace your fingers and put your hands behind your head.

So, it was over before it had started. Dane went to shut off the engine and Vinny let out a yelp of joyous rage. Maybe he was happy, thinking he wouldn't have to play the violin in the joint.

He sort of dived up against Dane, giggling madhatter-style, like it was all a bad joke that would somehow end pleasantly. Suddenly he was trying to wrestle himself into the driver's seat, shoving Dane up against the door, jamming his leg across Dane's, and stomping the gas pedal. Vinny had a death grip on the wheel that Dane couldn't break.

They hit the blocking cruisers going about fifty and they both went headfirst through the windshield.

Dane had been lucky. Just one bad gash along his front hairline that took forty stitches, all the other trauma happening in back of his head, where nobody could see so long as he grew his hair long. A couple small metal plates to reinforce his cracked skull, about a hundred staples holding his brains in. Nothing that would show until he started to go bald in another eight or ten years.

Vinny hadn't been quite as fortunate. He'd landed face-first against the curb, shattering his nose and taking out most of his teeth. Crushed one cheek, burst his right eye, and caused a long dent in his brow. It was almost deep enough that you could fit your pinky in it and your finger would be flush with the rest of his face.

The court took more pity on them for that. The Monti attorneys were slick and got both of them off with probation.

"I just don't want to see you wind up like your dad," Phil Guerra was saying.

Dane frowned, and asked, "How so?"

"You know. Dead before your time."

That tickled Dane so much that he had to suppress a chuckle, leaving it under his tongue. Jesus, Phil sure could push a point home.

"You ready to visit your grandma?"

"Drop me off at La Famiglia. I still need to get her some pastry." The bakery was two blocks away from Chooch's. They'd circled the neighborhood and were pretty much back where they'd started.

"Sure." Phil let him out on the corner and shook his hand. "Give Lucia my love. Good luck, Johnny."

"Thanks."

"Give me a call if you ever need anything. I mean that. Anything at all."

"I will."

"And don't steal my car!" he shouted, letting out the sham laughter again. Dane sort of chuckled with him, thinking he just might have to boost the Caddy before this was all over.

Then he smiled and let his cigarette hang loose from

the corner of his mouth, knowing that when he hit that pose, he looked exactly like his father.

Phil stuck his index finger out, cocked his thumb like it was a gun, and pretended to shoot Dane. Jesus, if these guys were always this subtle with their stupid threats, it was a wonder that anybody ever got bumped. Dane let his smile widen, showing teeth, squinting, the way Dad used to do when he was on the edge, ready to take somebody down.

Dane stood there and watched his father's partner drive away, knowing with real certainty for the first time that it was Uncle Philly who'd shot John Danetello Sr. in the head with his own service pistol.

FOUR

The impatient death angel, circling overhead, having waited long enough for another chance.

So here we go.

Dane walked around the block to Chooch's and stepped inside. The place was empty, which took him back a little. There were always a couple of muscle boys around and a familiar face or two at the back tables, even this early in the day. Nobody at the bar, not even a bartender.

The lights were on though. He cocked an ear, listening for noise in the back rooms, but there was nothing.

Dane moved farther into Chooch's, remembering the first couple times he'd been here with Vinny when they weren't even in their teens. Big Tommy Bartone setting up a couple of shots for them, thinking it was funny to let them drink themselves sick, dragging them both out in the alley to puke. Tommy laughing his ass off while they turned a deeper green and stumbled home.

Dane's scars began to burn, his skull abruptly pounding. He saw a slight blur of motion in the mirror and turned. Vinny was behind him, moving across the room to an empty table. He sat and stared at Dane expectantly, waiting like bait in the center of an ambush. His graceful hands folded easily in front of him. The glass eye pinning Dane, just a little off. It had a few flecks of green in it that the real one didn't have. He'd filled in the hairless section of his scarred eyebrow with an eyebrow pencil.

You wait so long for the moment to come, imagining what it'll be like and how you'll feel about it, and when it finally arrives you feel nothing. Even staring at the man who, out of everybody in the world, still knew you the best.

"It's good to see you," Vinny said, and he sounded like he meant it. "Let's put this meeting off for a different day, all right?"

"Any time in particular?"

"Yeah, a rainy afternoon out in Wisewood. There'll be a hot-air balloon outside St. Mary's. I'll let you know when."

"If that's a threat, it's a little cryptic." Dane wanted to sit across from Vinny, lean across the table, and meet his eyes up close, but there were no other chairs around. There was always something that fucked up your big dramatic moment. "You want a guy's knees to tremble, you ought to be clear about it."

"I'm telling you the truth, Johnny. I always do."

"Your truth has a way of changing," Dane said.

"That's not my fault. I just try to make the choices from the three I've got."

"Is that all you have, Vinny? Still?"

"Yeah."

Dane glanced around. "Why's the bar empty?"

"I knew you were coming, so I gave everybody the day off and told my crew to stay away."

"I didn't think you ever closed up Chooch's."

"It's only for a little while."

No anger showing through, no upset or anything else. Vinny looked almost bored, maybe with a touch of regret, like he knew what was coming and had heard it many times before. Dane expected him to get a little hot, squeezing more juice out of the scene, but he only shrugged. Maybe both of them were hoping the other would just pack up and move away.

Vinny had taken something extra away from the accident too, the way Dane had done. A new kind of burden laid across their backs.

Three years after the crash Vinny became a lieutenant for his father, Don Pietro. It wasn't the usual way of things to have a blood relative of the big boss being a capo so early on, but it's what Vinny wanted, and the Don tried to play into everybody's strengths.

Vinny's first serious job had been to whack a guy named Paulo Cruz, who ran a Colombian crew over in south Jersey. They were hijacking trucks full of casino equipment from the Monticelli hotels in Atlantic City, causing lots of heartburn for everybody.

When Dane heard that Paulo Cruz had taken two in the head, and Vinny showed up at the bar wearing a glow of distinguished confidence, Dane knew Vinny had killed his first man.

It took the Jersey mob about a week to counterattack. It wasn't a particularly well-thought-out plan, just Paulo's brother Baldo and one of his soldiers walking down 82nd Avenue with their hands in their pockets, coming toward the bar.

Dane and Vinny were stepping up the curb together.

"This doesn't have anything to do with you, Danetello," Baldo Cruz said, which surprised Dane. Most wiseguys didn't care who they took out, so long as they got the one they were after. Classy.

A strange sound filled the air. It took Dane a second to realize it was coming from Vinny

This wheezing cackle, like he'd been laughing for hours and could barely catch his breath now.

"The hell is so funny?" Baldo asked.

"You!" Vinny shrieked. "Thrashing around on the ground like that!"

"What the hell you talking about, man?"

"The look on your face! Like you just got a bad piece of ass. Oh Jesus Christ, and ... and ... you're pissing yourself!" Vinny shook with laughter like a complete maniac. The fake eye never moving, staring straight ahead.

It made Dane's scalp tighten and a chill form at the base of his spine. His scars began to heat, the knowledge spreading through him that the entire world was shifting just an inch to the left. He felt dizzy and nauseous, like everything around him was reeling. Not him spinning, but the rest of existence. The metal in his head felt like it was tearing loose.

Baldo and the Jersey shooter made their move. Dane spun up the sidewalk and tried to get behind a lamppost, scared but not all that worried. The apathy had already taken hold by then. It was a bad feeling to have at a moment like this.

But they were slow, much slower than Vinny, who drew his .32 and pointed it at Baldo's legs. He fired twice and did this little dipping, zigzag motion that looked silly as hell. Like a nine-year-old girl sort of skipping along.

The Jersey shooter had drawn a .45 and pulled the trigger, aiming for where Vinny had been an instant before. But the bullet struck the sidewalk and shards of cement exploded toward Dane. There were moments when you realized how ridiculous you looked in flight.

Vinny capped the shooter in the face and stuck his gun back in his jacket. He stared down at Baldo Cruz, thrashing in the street, pissing himself, an expression on his face like he'd just been poorly laid.

Then Vinny got a firm grip on Dane's arm and ushered him down the block and into his car without a word. They circled the neighborhood twice, Vinny grinning the whole time, proud of himself. But there was something more there. Dane asked him what was going on, and Vinny explained about the three trails of reality he occasionally saw and could slip into, fuck around with, decide upon, and even sometimes return from again. He could walk into a different version of the world in midstream, and just keep going. Dane laughed like one of them was crazy, not knowing which. Vinny laughed the same way.

Afterward they'd gone to Aqueduct to watch the races. While Dane stood around thinking about what it might be like to walk into a different reality and walk out again, Vinny lost fourteen thousand bucks.

"So why didn't you bet the winner?" Dane asked.

"I didn't see the winner. He wasn't one of the three choices."

"The hell good is foresight then?"

"I didn't say it was good. Not always." Smiling, the false teeth too fucking white. "Not at the track today, but pretty good on the street with Baldo, eh? How about you? You come away with anything from the accident?"

"No."

"You're lying."

"No."

Dane, unsure how to say that Baldo was right there behind Vinny while he was talking about the guy, staring at Dane with dead eyes, whispering, "He hates you too, Danetello. He's going to want your head on a platter. He'll get it, someday, unless you get him first."

Since then, Dane had been trying to figure out which of them had a greater burden. He still wasn't sure.

"Why don't you just let it go?" Dane asked.

"It's you who won't let go. You're resistant now, but that's okay. We'll get there together."

"Where?" Dane tried to grin but he could tell it just came off sickly, his features contorting. A ripple of vertigo spread from the inside of his head outward, his vision clouding as it throbbed through him. It felt like Vinny might be toying around with his alternate tracks even now, taking Dane along with him for a step or two. "I just want to be left alone."

"Nobody pushes you, Johnny. Whatever happens is because it's set in motion the way it's got to be. You stand or slump on your own."

Dane figured that after all these years he was as hard and strong as Vinny. That if they were going to do this thing, they might as well do it now. Vinny wasn't packing. Hand-to-hand, Dane could kill him without half trying, if only he could make himself do it.

"Don't make me kill you."

"I won't," Vinny said, and let out a sort of sad smile. His lips squirming on his face. "Death is nothing anyway."

"It's something."

"We beat it a long time ago, when we went through the windshield. You didn't know that?"

"You *pazzo* fuck." Dane spun and headed for the door, and the nausea washed through him again. He doubled over but didn't hit the floor. His metal skull rang like a church bell. Vinny was toying with reality again, changing tracks in midmotion, and somehow dragging Dane along.

"Don't forget the *cannoli*," Vinny told him, patting him on the back and walking out the door.

Dane looked up and the bar was full of people. A few of the Monticelli muscle boys and a couple of familiar faces at the back tables, staring at him oddly. A brute of a bartender looking like he was about ready to jump over the bar and toss Dane out.

An orange-lipped waitress carrying a tray of screwdrivers leaned over him and said, "You okay?"

"Didn't Vinny give you the day off?"

"He never gives us the day off." She helped him to straighten up, hand on the back of his neck, but after a second she yanked her hand away, like her fingers had been singed by his scars.

FIVE

His daddy, large in Dane's mind but not in his life, took on a greater shape and made himself known again. The man, wherever he was, looking at Dane from the other side of the void and giving him a *run along now* pat on the ass, just so he wouldn't forget there was unfinished business to be taken care of.

The past gained greater momentum, reckless in its approach but carrying him along, bringing him up to speed. If you don't fight this kind of current, it would take you wherever you had to go. He could feel himself catching up a little more, fitting back in. The trouble was making sure you didn't jump the track and completely derail.

Dane walked the mile to the Olympic Cab & Limousine Company. Looking through the window of the inner office, he saw that Pepe Morales had been promoted to manager.

Pepe was sitting at the back of the office chattering on

the radio, huge pictures of his wife and kids on the large metal desk. He was telling a story that Dane had heard maybe twenty-five times, about the night when Pepe picked up the two lesbian hookers over by Sheepshead Bay and one went crazy with a straight razor on the other. The laughter grew so loud on the speakers there was feedback.

Pepe had been the only one from the neighborhood to visit Dane in the slam. You could count on him making the holidays something special even behind bars. Pepe would show up on Easter, Thanksgiving, and Christmas Eve, bringing a bunch of gifts. Books and magazines mostly. He'd spread them around to the nine or ten buddies and relatives he had in the joint, and sometimes even brought something for the bulls. Keeping everybody in a good mood, even the guards drawing the shit shifts, who couldn't be home with their families.

Dane moved to the counter, where a harried young brunette with mussed hair fidgeted in a chair, filling out blue forms and chewing a toothpick to splinters. Without glancing up she said, "Yeah?"

"I'd like to talk to Pepe."

"He's busy."

"I'm a friend," Dane said. He grinned but she still hadn't lifted her head. Maybe he was starting to lose some of his charm.

"All his friends are locked up."

"I know, but I just got out."

"Well, isn't that just fuckin' great for the rest of society."

"It made my grandmother happy," Dane said, giving the smile all he had even though his lips were starting to get tired.

"A respectable woman."

"Yes."

"Upon whose house you bring shame."

"Actually, I bring her a lot of *cannoli*."

She flipped through more papers and spit the shreds of toothpick on the floor in front of Dane. "I told you, he's busy."

"So are you and you're talking to me, honeybunch."

It got her attention. She swiveled in her seat and glowered from beneath a jumble of loose curls. Bloodshot eyes, the seething tension there sharpening into instant hatred. At least she was looking at him.

"You a mouth?" she asked.

"No."

"You got something you want to say? Am I going to have trouble with your ass? You think I'm putting up with that shit?"

Dane could never quite figure out why everybody was always so pissed, showing disapproval over any small thing, ready to jump into a stranger's face. Everybody in the joint was much more relaxed.

"I'd just like to speak to Pepe."

"I already told you twice now, he's got work—"

It was already too late to defuse the bad atmosphere. Dane stared beyond her and tried to make eye contact with Pepe. He was up to the part in the story where one of the working gals is slashing like wild, her girlfriend screaming with her cheek sliced open, blood everywhere, and while Pepe is struggling with the slasher they wind up driving off the pier. He couldn't swim and almost drowned, sucking down half the East River, shouting for somebody to save him. But this version of the tale had a happy ending, because the whores made up while they were giving him CPR.

She reached under the counter and got hold of something heavy, maybe a bat or a tire iron, gaze locked on Dane the whole time, getting ready to pounce.

Willing to kill him but not willing to go knock on the goddamn door. People drew very strange lines in the sand.

Pepe turned around and spotted Dane, and let out a cry of delight. He walked out of the office and stopped short, frowned, and made a pleading gesture to heaven. "Fran, put down the nine iron, will you, please?"

"No."

"C'mon!"

"I don't like this one," she said.

"Almost nobody does, but I'm still sending you for stress management courses. You don't even drink coffee, what's the matter with you?"

"He's got those smirky eyes."

"He thinks he's being charming."

"He's not."

Smirky eyes? Did he really do that? Dane thought he knew just what she meant, but he'd never heard it about himself before. It was the kind of thing he despised.

"Take over for a while," Pepe told her. "All right? I'm going for a fifteen-minute smoke."

Lips tugged out of whack like they were being yanked by fish hooks, Fran caterwauled, "Fifteen minutes! Like hell! What're you smoking out there? Cubans? Be back in five, I've got enough shit to do around here."

"Ten."

Pepe came around the counter with his arms open. He clenched Dane around his waist and picked him off the ground. The guy still weighed under 120 but it was all sinew and muscle. After a quick twirl in the air, Pepe set him down gently and gave him a quick hug, rubbing him softly on the back the way Dane's mother used to do when he was a kid. They walked out to the back of the garage together.

The stink of grease, oil, and transmission fluid struck Dane like an old lover embracing him.

"You need to cut her hours back some," Dane said. "That one in there."

"Ah, it's her just her office personality."

"You ever get any repeat customers?"

"Franny's a sweetheart, but she's got an instinct for trouble. In this place, it comes at her from all sides, makes her a little paranoid."

"Okay."

Pepe had been a lightweight champ and still moved like he was stepping into the ring. Light, fast, and with his arms loose in case he had to snap a jab into somebody's face. He'd been born in Spanish Harlem, back when there was such a thing. When he was about thirteen his family moved to Headstone City and Pepe fell in with Dane and the other Italians of the neighborhood. He had no Puerto Rican accent anymore, and spoke with the same hand gestures that Dane used himself.

"I'm off at six. We'll go out and have a few beers and get you laid."

"I've got plans tonight," Dane said.

"What?" Drawing his chin back and peering into Dane's face, taking a good look, trying to see what could be seen. "You've been in the bucket for two years and there's something else you wanna do on your first night out?"

"It's sort of a matter of necessity."

"So's getting your pipes cleaned. Okay, so you're not in the mood for fun, you fuckin' killjoy." Pepe squared his shoulders, a sign that he was serious. "What are you after? A gun? You know I'm not your man for that."

"I already have one."

"I should've known."

"I need a job," Dane told him.

"You got to have a license first."

"I do."

That threw Pepe, made him twist around. His hands started moving all over the place. "How's that possible? You ran over a fuckin' cop!"

"Yeah, but he was only a traffic cop."

Dane's father had always told him to stay clean because the first bit of dirt he got on him would just keep growing. He'd been right. Dane had been nabbed stealing cars a couple of times in his teens, then got tagged for vehicular assault the day he bumped the traffic cop while Angelina Monticelli was dying in the back of his cab.

Pepe dropped his chin, gave Dane the look he was starting to get used to. "Listen, maybe you shouldn't stay in the neighborhood for too long. For your own good."

"Did Vinny tell you not to hire me?"

"Not exactly. A guy came around who likes to talk out the corner of his mouth and clean his fingernails with a butterfly knife."

That'd be Joey Fresco, the big hitter.

Playing with his fingernails, Pepe mimicked him pretty well. "He tells me that if I see you, I should give the Monti crew a call, it would be in my best interest. They'd consider it a favor. If I didn't, it'd be a show of disrespect. Since Puzo's book, that word hasn't had the same meaning for you guineas. So he wags the knife around for a while, scrapes it along his throat like he's shaving. Not even doing the slit slit *you're dead* motion, no, this guy's too hep for that." Pepe broke out of the performance, stood there smiling again. "He didn't give

me the number though. Like I'm going to walk up to the
front door of the Monti mansion and knock. Ask for the
hitter who shaves with a butterfly blade."

"Okay," Dane said, and started to walk by.

"Wait a minute, I didn't say I wouldn't hire you.
Jesus, you're as neurotic as Franny! You should both be
in group therapy. I was only explaining the situation."

"I know, but you don't need to deal with their shit."

"You're still too sensitive. How the hell did you survive twenty months in the bucket, man?" Pepe thought
about it, rubbing his chin, trying to figure every angle
the way he always did. "How about this? I'll give you
eastern Long Island, all right? The Hamptons and Montauk run."

It was a straight ride at a specified price, $99 to the
end of the Island, nearly three hours one-way with no
fare back. He could make five times more driving for any
other cab company in the five boroughs.

"No," Dane told him.

"What?"

"The season's over. Nobody's even going out to the
Hamptons this time of year."

"They still go. Plenty of them."

"Besides, I want to stick closer."

Getting brash now, getting paternal. "You take what I
give you or you can go throw fish down at Fulton's."

He knew Pepe was doing it to help him, to keep him
out of the neighborhood and on the road. Like he didn't
have to go home at night.

"I need to earn a living."

With the fingers again, this time ticking off each point
he had to make, Pepe said, "You live with your grandmother, you got no rent. She feeds you four-course meals,
you don't gotta pay for your food. You got no kids, you

got no wife, you got no ex who wants alimony or child support." Now on to the left hand. "You got no habits, no vices. You don't drink, you don't throw dice, you run away from the whores. In fact, you run away from the nice girls too. The hell do you need money for?"

"A stake."

"A stake? What's that mean, you want a stake? For what?"

"To get things rolling," Dane said.

"Jesus." Easing out this grumble from the back of his throat, showing dissatisfaction without actually having to pull a face. "Fran's right, you know it? I never noticed it before but you do have smirky eyes. And it's not so cute."

He was really going to have to do something about that. "When can I start?"

"You got a suit?"

It was a dumb question. Every guy in Headstone City had a black suit for funerals. "Yeah."

"Tomorrow if you want. So long as your hack license is actually up-to-date."

"It is."

"Christ, you got off easy. Except for, well... for the mob wanting your ass and all."

There was still that. "One more thing. I need a car."

Pepe doing his classic freeze, the head cock, the eye roll. More like a Jewish mother than a Puerto Rican grandfather. He should be doing dinner theater. "You expect a lot."

"Anything will do."

"I got an '87 Buick GN. A junker I fixed up pretty good. It's not the most gorgeous thing on the road but it'll get you around. I can let it go for a grand."

"Take it out of my pay."

It got Pepe's chin firmed up, his lips crimped. He was having trouble holding himself back from putting it on the line. Saying that Dane might not live long enough to pay him the money.

"If I catch two in the head, you can have it back," Dane told him. "Where's the keys?"

Pepe grinned at that, his own eyes kind of smirky. It really was ugly.

"How about if we just call it a loaner for now? And don't run over any cops while you're in it, okay?"

SIX

There are sections of your own history that you've gone through many times before. A track that's become a trench that's become a pit. You just keep going around and around, but each time you're in a little deeper. A pattern so deep-rooted that you fell into it without knowing it was happening. After you took the first step, then the next had to follow, and the next. Laid out before you the same way it had been from the beginning, no matter what.

In the mostly quiet streets off the central plaza, rows of residences towered above the memorial arch to fallen soldiers of both world wars. A broad, tree-lined parkway led straight to the granite arch. Dane drove the GN around Grand Outlook Hall and along Outlook Park, gravel walks flanking the rolling grassy hollow.

He wanted to visit his parents in Wisewood, but with the gardens dying at the approach of autumn, the

scent of rotting roses and carnations eddying through
the busted floor vents, he found himself passing the entrance leading to their graves.

Instead, he took the long way around and drove the
GN down the half-mile square between Outlook Park
and the rest of Headstone City. It seemed to be the only
way he could move through the neighborhood, this direction, every time.

Staring up at brownstones carved with the faces of
the seven deadly sins. Before he'd joined the army he
used to see himself in lust. Afterward, more like envy.

Now it was the hang of sloth's relaxed face that reminded him of his own features, the nearly grinning
mouth, the semidazed eyes.

He had to do something about that too. His list was
getting longer. He had to get moving.

It felt right being back behind a wheel, the thrum of
the engine working through his chest. A union of precision between reflex and skill and tuned machinery. As
always, he thought about taking it up onto the highway. Imagining the open miles of parkways leading to
the Verrazano Bridge, Staten Island, and from there to
Jersey and the rest of the world.

But if he got rolling he might never stop. The urge
to run was powerful but futile, and it was always there.

Coming around the far edge of Wisewood, he turned
the corner, passed the gates, and parked in front of his
grandmother's house.

Soon, he hoped, he'd be able to visit his mother and
father again. At least on foot. But it wouldn't be for a
while yet, and he'd probably never be able to drive it.
He was a neurotic bastard, just like Pepe had said. The
pattern was too powerful, always drawing him the same

way through the neighborhood. No matter how many times he tried it, he always passed up their graves, then had to lie about it later to whoever might ask.

The heady aroma of fresh-cooked pasta swept over him on the front stoop, and he walked in without knocking. He was home, and with the place came another embedded pattern he would never emerge from.

"That you?" Grandma Lucia yelled from the kitchen.

"It's me."

Like if it wasn't him somebody else could just say, It's me, and that would be all right too.

She plodded out into the living room, carrying seventy-eight years of brass and reliability. Thick and stoop-shouldered, but with large, powerful arms that had spent sixteen-hour days toiling in post-WWII sweatshops down in lower Manhattan, scrubbing factory floors. She'd buried her father, her husband, and her son—all police officers who'd died in the line of duty before they hit thirty—and she just kept struggling forward year after year despite the assaults of the world.

Her presence drew up against him as inflexible as a natural force of the earth, like a thunderstorm. She'd dyed her hair pink and he couldn't stop looking at it. Holy Christ.

"Where the hell's the *cannoli*!" she shouted.

Eyes wide, feeling that tickle of anxiety he always got when Grandma Lucia used that voice. It was about the only thing that could really get to him anymore. "I forgot."

"You get so many calls in prison you can't remember me talking to you?"

Mother Mary, that hair, it was searing his retina. "It's been a busy day."

"Fine, they were for you anyway." She pulled the drapes back and stared at the Buick. "That an '87?"

"Yeah."

"It's garbage. You got it from Morales, didn't you."

"Yeah."

"What'd you pay?"

"It's kind of a loaner, but he wanted a grand for it." Saying it with a quiver of shame, knowing Pepe was his only friend, but the guy had still tried to rob him. "I'm working at Olympic again."

"You got ripped off. He probably gave you the shit Long Island run too. Didn't you learn anything in the slam?"

He thought about it. "No."

"Come sit down in the dining room, I made ravioli."

There wouldn't be any small talk. There never had been in the Danetello household. You said your piece, told your story, made your point, then shut the hell up. The silence tended to throw visitors off, especially around the holidays. They'd come in and nobody would be talking, and they'd think the family had been fighting.

Instead, there'd been a precision of conversation. Clipped and sharp, but usually funny. Brutal in the way it carved away the fat and got to the heart of matters. Little laughter when he thought about it, but that didn't mean there'd been bitterness. Or even anger, really. At least not before Ma got sick.

Dane found that there had always been a strange equilibrium between calm and violence. Or maybe it was just him.

Grandma cleared her throat, and he could tell she had subjects to broach. Things she needed to get out, but hoping he'd be the one to start.

It wasn't easy. The house already felt like it was pressing in on him. He could sense the remaining tensions of those who'd lived and died there. Mostly in stillness, but with loud, abandoned thoughts.

His father, a hard man of imperfect justice. His mother, a mere suggestion that dwelled in the house, unseen but still obvious, often coughing. His grandmother, a Sicilian witchy lady of sorts, a soothsayer who didn't soothe. It was her way. At nine, she'd seen the Virgin Mary in an olive grove outside Messina, in the shadow of Mount Etna. She told her local priest, who had burned her with sulfur for speaking with the devil's tongue. You heard about stuff like that and you understood why she loved chapels but hated churches.

Since then, she'd had dreams that gave her a glimpse through the thinnest part of the veil. They informed her of what was happening, who might be visiting Dane from the other side. She called it the burden but didn't treat it as such. It had been passed to him like a rock. Now he had to find out how much she already knew.

Dane still couldn't stop looking at her hair, thinking, Jesus, the hell did she do to herself?

She noticed him staring and slid a hand over the bangs, primping them. "It's magenta."

"Oh," he said. "Is that right?"

"Matches my nail polish. You look like you've got something to say."

"It just takes a little getting used to."

"You shut up."

She uncorked a bottle of red wine and poured two glasses. He ate, sipped, and looked around the table at the remaining chairs, empty except for the muscular weight of memory.

"So, this is what I changed your diapers for?" she said, trying to sound heartbroken but not even coming close.

"What?"

"Raised you for? Fed you for all these years? So you could sit and not say a word to me, like I was the DA?"

"You told me to shut up."

"I didn't mean it."

"I'm just gathering my thoughts."

She pressed a piece of sausage onto his plate, motioned with her fork for him to eat more. "You put that girl out of your mind yet?"

"It's not about that so much, at the moment," he admitted.

"What, then? All the talk about Vincenzo Monticelli coming to put a double tap in your brain"—reaching over to thunk him twice on the head, where the scars lay hidden beneath his hairline, everybody clunking him in the head—"you can forget about it for now. You take it one step at a time, plan it through, then when you start moving you don't stop until it's finished. You can do it."

Telling him, pretty much outright, that she expected him to go against the mob and clean house. Take them all out, one way or another. That easy. Come home afterward and she'd have garlic bread waiting.

She didn't say it without reservation, or fear, or even

love. But there was a controlled fervor in her voice, the
same kind that had been in his father's voice, often de-
void of sentiment. His old man used to put it down on
the line, with an acute conviction, and once you figured
out what you had to do, no matter what it was, you just
went and did it.

"It's only him and his brother and maybe a little extra muscle," Grandma continued, spooning more ravioli onto his plate. "Three or four guys maybe. No more
than, say, six. Joey Fresco and Tommy Bartone are the
only old-school hitters. Maybe ten guys. You're not going up against the whole family, think of it that way. A
dozen, tops."

He used to wonder if he could do what she'd done,
cleaning factory floors all day long, every day, for years.
Raising a kid by herself. His father, just a toddler, told
to be quiet, don't move, wait until Mama's done, staying there for sixteen hours with nothing to do. His own
father dead on the job, whacked by upper brass because
he didn't take enough graft, busting ass and spoiling
the take for them. Under investigation, found posthu-
mously guilty, no pension.

Every time Dane thought he was hard, he just
thought about shit like that and realized how listless
he truly was. The army hadn't shaken his apathy, and
neither had the can. Now she's saying he's gotta go
take out the local mob when all he wanted to do was
flatten Vinny onto his ass. One nice shot, and then the
rest, whatever happened afterward, wouldn't really
matter.

"Vinny's got the edge," he said.

"Why? Because he says he can see the future?"

"He can."

Grandma Lucia's hands in the air, like Pepe, like Dane himself. How would they communicate if they ever broke a finger? "That he can walk three different trails and decide which to follow? Go back and forward in time? He can't see anything, Johnny. If he could, you think he'd still be in Headstone City, leading a fading mob family?"

"Grandma, I've seen him do it."

She didn't hear him. "The Monticellis went legit and lost most of the money they made from all the illegal action. What his father earned on trucking hijacks and prostitution, him and that Berto lost on mutual funds and junk bonds."

They drank another glass of wine together. Dane had a question he needed to ask, but his grandmother was in a fierce mood. That threw him, made it even harder to keep focus. "Has she ever spoken to you?"

"Who?"

He stared at her.

"Your mother?"

He hissed air through his teeth, thinking of Ma in the back room, seeing angels, choking on cancer, calling his name.

"Oh, that other one? Angelina? No." Shaking her head, the pink curls bobbing left and right. Her voice lost some of its edge and took on a delicate quality. "Sometimes in dreams I hear the two of you talking, but I can't always hear the words. Only that she's giving you a hard time."

Dane finished his dinner, picked up his dirty dishes and took them into the kitchen, put them in the sink and poured some soap and ran the hot water tap so the sauce wouldn't crust. When he got back to the table she was having more wine, her cheeks covered with red splotches. It was the histamine in the wine, it made her face turn beet red.

He asked, "Is my gun still here?"

"I cleaned it this morning and put it on your bed, wrapped in a clean rag."

Some kids had little old grannies who did nothing but go to church and crochet. Vinny's grandmother used to listen to him play the violin and accompany him on the piano.

Dane's—she's breaking down and oiling a Smith & Wesson .38 with a four-inch barrel, laying it out on his pillow. Overhearing him talking with the dead.

SEVEN

With the night came a heavy, abiding fog rising off Long Island Sound.

The kind that seemed intent on action, wanting to chase Dane down. Throbbing as it coiled against his tires, calling him along the expressway mile by mile. He could race into the heaving clouds and hide his crimes, hunt for the ambitions he'd set aside until no one was looking. This was the living darkness that matched what was locked inside his rib cage.

Swirling gray threads swallowed the headlights, laid across the road to snare his front end. The nimbus of twin beacons looked like burning souls wandering lost in purgatory, side by side down the road. Maybe him and Vinny, after they'd finally done each other in.

Dane drove over to the warden's house out in Glen Cove, right on the north shore. He wheeled past million-dollar estates that compelled men of meager salaries into jealous rages and flipped them over the big edge.

All you had to do was stare up at the third-floor windows, look at the wide expanse of lawn and trees in the yards, the three-car garages, to know why there were guys guzzling whiskey in the local hole in the wall. Their bitterness crawling over them like heat rash, a loaded shotgun in the trunk. It had nothing to do with women or champagne or even money. It was a balance of power.

Some Wall Street whiz with capped teeth changing the fate of the economy, and you over there with your finger on the trigger.

The warden's place was huge. One of those new, moderate mansions built to look like some Georgian manor. Maples trimmed so the branches dangled like willows or cypress. Big columns out front, an old-fashioned lantern hanging way above the front door and lighting it the way curators lit Renaissance art in museums.

Being in charge of ten thousand social and moral rejects had its upside. You couldn't feel pity for a guy who had to work behind bars all day long if he got to come home to this.

Pulling up at the curb, Dane tuned the radio into a fifties station and sat back. It was his father's music, which rooted him to his blood. His own life might be adrift, but still he was connected to the foundation of his forebears, going back in a line through the years. You had to take what you could get, even if it was only a dead man's stability.

Propping his fist under his chin, Dane stared at the windshield and remembered what it was like to become one with the glass, and the pain. Advancing through one and into the depths of the other. His scars pulsed. The metal plates warmed.

Music filled the car and swelled within him, pressing

out everything else. His thoughts began to slowly pour away as he settled further into the seat.

It took a while, but eventually the voices on the radio acquired a different tone and began speaking in languages Dane didn't understand. The music faded until it became nothing but static intermittently broken by distant cries and appeals. Mournful, occasionally frantic.

Dane shut it off and turned to look through the passenger window, knowing what he would see.

The warden—Robinson Howards III—naked in the hot-burning light high above his doorstep, coming straight for the car. Skin glistening pale and mottled pink. His gait awkward, like he couldn't get his arms and legs moving together, head lolling. He got in the backseat, reached to close the door but it was already shut. Dane snapped on the interior light and leaned over so the warden could see his face.

"John Danetello," Howards said, accepting the situation without question. Then his features contorted, the confusion setting in. "What are you doing here? How did you find my home?"

"Everybody knows where you live, warden."

"What?"

It was true. The leader of the Aryan Brotherhood had hired a sleazy private eye a year or so ago to track Howards and a few of the guards. Insinuating that the brotherhood was going to knock off a few bulls and the warden himself in a cutthroat show of power. It didn't matter, because the Nazi Lowriders punked out and never did make a move. They spread the home addresses around, hoping the Mexican Mafia or the Black Guerrilla Family would do the deed and they could still take credit for it.

Dane knew the area pretty well. Some of the Monti as-

sociates lived nearby. Years ago, Vinny used to take him
out there for big family parties. Vinny would go off to a
cabana and screw around with some mob accountant's
daughter while Dane sat poolside, wearing sunglasses,
maids bringing him pink drinks with lots of fruit in
them. He'd watch a hundred people he didn't know
swimming, playing croquet in the four-acre backyards,
and talking tax shelters.

Afterward, Vinny would come out with the girl looking a little rattled, and he'd give Dane a wink and grab
the foofy drink out of his hand and go, "The fuck is this?
Melon balls with tequila? Hey, you're gonna get burned
without any sunscreen on, man. You want her to rub you
down?" The girl smiling but a touch scared, Vinny's
glass-eyed gaze pinning her to a lawn chair. Her sweaty,
mussed hair sticking to the side of her face.

Howards looked down at himself in the back of the
Buick, noticing his shriveled pecker but not feeling the
cold. "Why am I here?" he asked.

"I wanted to talk with you," Dane said, and pulled
away from the curb. He drove slowly along the roads
closest to the water.

"Make an appointment. Have I been hypnotized?"

"No."

"Drugged?"

"No, warden. We're on a night ride together."

"What does that mean?"

"Relax and find out."

Dane couldn't get into it too quickly because the warden never allowed anybody else to speak. He'd have to
blather on for a while and, after he wore down a little,
he'd act like he'd been giving the other guy a chance to
talk the whole time, and say, "Well?"

Stroking his slight trace of beard stubble, Howards

stared out at the fog undulating across the Sound, swarming around the car. "It's dark. And I find myself sitting in the back of a GM with you. And I'm most certainly naked. This is quite literally the stuff of nightmares." It struck him as funny and he let go with a confused smile. "I'm occasionally plagued by dreams of being gang-raped by prisoners."

"Put your mind at rest about that," Dane said.

"Are you going to kill me, Mr. Danetello?"

"No."

It was the "Mister" that always got to Dane. The guy saying it more like he was a high school principal trying to shake up a kid caught in the hall without a pass. Dane hated and enjoyed it at the same time, in about equal parts, but he wasn't sure why.

"You're not really here, warden."

"I'm not?"

"No. You're still at home in your bed."

"How ridiculous. Your psychiatric examination results showed you were a borderline schizophrenic, but I never saw any evidence of that until now."

It actually annoyed Dane, hearing that sort of shit about the psych tests. The cons who talked to the doctors usually fooled them into an early parole, saying how they were cured, they just wanted to give something positive back to society. Then on the morning of their release they went and took out a whole family with a meat cleaver. They go right back into the can and the doctors start flipping through their files trying to figure out where they went wrong.

"Do you remember getting into the car?" Dane asked.

"Yes."

"How'd you do it?"

"What a foolish question."

"Then answer it."

"I—" Howards said, and fear reared up in his eyes. The warden did a good job at keeping control and not losing his cool. Dane had found him hard but fair. A bit too stuffy for his own good but not often judgmental. He was a little street ignorant and so he was more honest than other men in similar positions of power. Because he didn't have quite so much on the ball, he was somehow easier to deal with.

"How?" Dane repeated.

"I never opened the door, did I? I simply . . . entered." Still reasoning his way through it, voice calm but lifeless. "I feel rather disconnected, which is not an altogether unpleasant experience."

If he didn't feel that way, he'd be screaming his ass off, halfway out of his head, knowing his soul was separated from his sleeping body. "Glad you're enjoying yourself."

"I didn't say that. Is this what the New Age metaphysicians would call my astral self?"

"Call it what you like," Dane told him.

"What do you call it?"

"I don't put a name to it."

"You often avoid questions put directly to you. The prison psychiatrists noted that in your files as well."

Dane tried not to sigh and failed.

Sort of funny, the way the warden started staring at his hand, like he thought it might become transparent. Bringing it up to his eye, looking at the palm and inspecting the other side, touching his fingers together. What would those fuckin' doctors tell him now?

Howards bent forward and said, "How odd and unique, to be born with this gift."

"It's not unique and I wasn't born with it. At least I don't think I was." He still wasn't sure. Maybe the burden was always there, like with his grandmother, and the crash just made it heavier, stronger. Who knew, maybe Vinny was right, and they'd both been dead since the accident.

"Someone else has it?"

Dane found himself measuring his words. "Similar anyway."

"Who?"

"Vinny Monticelli."

"Ah, I see. I've heard strange stories about him. How he believes he has visions and the gift of prophecy. So it's true, then? My God, how awful that'd be."

"He doesn't seem to mind."

"And you?"

"I get along," Dane said.

"How did you both acquire such facilities?"

"We went through a windshield together," Dane told him.

Looping over to the parkway, heading down to the beach. When he was a kid his parents used to take him out there to go swimming, the waters a lot cleaner than the sludge over at Coney. They'd build sand castles and his father would make sounds like the seagulls, his voice echoing among the dunes.

Almost nervous now, thinking about it all a little more, the warden asked, "What happens if I wake up?"

"I don't know."

"Might I die?"

"I suppose it's a possibility."

"Oh, this is terrible. You don't understand what Edna's snoring is like. I must wake up twenty times a night. I suggest you get me back soon."

"In a minute. I need answers first. What have you heard about the Monticellis' action lately?"

"What makes you think I'll tell you the truth?"

"You don't have any choice."

"Oh my."

Howards thought about it and appeared to consider his options at the moment. Deciding whether he should say anything more to an ex-con released only this very morning. Sitting in the backseat of a Buick trying to stare through his hand. Scared that his wife's nasal drip might inadvertently kill him. But Dane meant what he said. Nobody on the night ride could lie to him.

"Almost nothing," the warden said, wagging his unwieldy head, looking out both windows, hoping they were on their way back to his house. "You must know that their business operations are almost completely legitimate at this point."

"More or less. But our problems aren't business, they're personal. And they still had some reach into your prison. They put a hit on me this morning while a couple of your boys looked the other way."

It rattled Howards and got him refocused. "The incident with Mako and Kremitz? In the showers?"

"Yeah."

"They said they'd attacked each other because of pilfered cigarettes."

"They're trying to save their skins. The Monticellis still have enough muscle to cause trouble. I'm just not sure why they'd bother going about it like that."

"Give me the names of the offending officers and I'll look into the matter."

Dane told him, just to nettle the bulls a little. The charges would never stick, but maybe it would shake them up. Word would get back to the family.

"If what you say is true, Mr. Danetello, then I'll make sure these men are properly dealt with."

"Okay. Anything else you know that might help me?"

"The FBI did inquire about you. There was some discussion on whether you'd be willing to wear a wire for them."

"What? If the family is so legit now, then why would the feds care enough to wire somebody? What are they after?"

"Almost completely legitimate, I said. I assumed they wanted information about past activities, unsolved murders, that sort of thing."

"When was this?"

"After the fire in your cell."

"So why didn't they approach me?"

"I only dealt with a single agent. A man by the name of Cogan. He read through your case file and seemed to feel that contacting you was either unnecessary or could wait indefinitely."

That sounded like a fed all right. Plays it close to his vest, even in front of Howards. Makes some kind of a show about getting Dane to wire up, then just lets it drop. Something was stirring in the Monti camp.

Dane drew up in front of the warden's mansion again. He checked the rearview and nodded to Howards. "Thanks for your help."

"Am I going to remember any of this? On a conscious level?"

"No, you'll pass most of it off as a dream."

"I highly doubt that."

"We'll see."

The warden began to make his way back up the walkway, outside of the car without opening the door, gait unnatural and his ass cheeks clenched. Scared that his neighbors might be watching.

Dane let out a chuckle and Howards's shoulders tensed.

Like he might turn around and say something else, but he vanished before hitting the pool of light surrounding front door.

Mostly a wasted trip, but he had nothing better to do. Dane started to pull away from the curb when a blur of motion caught his eye.

Coming straight for him, running across the lawn, was Aaron Fielding, the dead grocer.

The old man appeared as despondent as when he'd shown up in Dane's cell. Holding his arms out and waving them, his mouth moving but no sound coming out.

"Ah, shit."

Like Dane didn't have enough troubles already. Now he had to get into the middle of this, whatever it was.

Fielding had almost reached him when the guy started to dissipate, becoming dim and ashen, evaporating step by step until, only a few feet away, he dissolved into the fog.

"Okay," Dane said. "I get it. There's something important you want help with. I'm sorry I didn't listen before. Come back and tell me."

Dane waited there another five minutes, hoping Angie or Fielding would return. Or anybody else who wanted to come and talk with him. But no one did.

All this, and some prick named Cogan skirting around in the shadows too.

EIGHT

Staring down at his grandmother's list, written in her crimped script, Dane walked into the La Famiglia Bakery and asked the girl behind the counter for ten anisette-almond *biscotti,* a half pound of *pignoli* cookies, three *sfogliatelle,* and six *cannoli.* The girl let out a small chirp of anguish, turned pale as pork belly, and stared at him, her bottom lip trembling so badly it looked like it might flap away.

He didn't want to do it, but he did it anyway. He spun and checked out the scene behind him. It was bad. He rubbed at his forehead, and went, "Uyh."

A three-man crew had made a move against JoJo Tormino. Two were dead, and the third held his quivering hands over his shredded belly, spurting blood and other colorful fluids between his fingers. The hitter whimpered, "Jesus Christ, get me to a doctor . . . I'll pay you anything, give you whatever you want. *Please.*"

Dane turned away. JoJo had troubles of his own. He'd

been shot four times: the left elbow, the left thigh, a graze along his jaw, and the one that really counted taking him high in his upper chest. Small caliber, maybe .22s, so the gunfire didn't bother anybody out on the street. Anything bigger than that and he'd already be dead.

Still, JoJo was dying fast although he appeared to be calm, sitting at a little table with a folded newspaper in front of him, holding tightly to an empty cup of coffee with one hand, his .32 in the other.

"I know you?" JoJo asked.

Dane nodded. "I'm from the neighborhood. My father was a cop. Sergeant Johnny Danetello."

"Lucia's grandson."

That stopped him. You didn't expect your grandma's first name to fall out of the mouth of a dying mobster. "You know my family? My grandmother?"

"You're the one who had all the troubles over Angelina."

"Yeah."

"Johnny. Used to pal with Vinny Monticelli when you were teenagers, right? You're the soldier boy, uh?" Blood seeped around the edges of JoJo's mouth. "Been in the army?"

Dane was starting to get interested. "That's right."

"And in the joint."

"I just got out."

"Sit with me for a while."

In twenty-five years, Dane might've said five words in passing to JoJo, who was a low-level lieutenant in the Ventimiglia family. They looked into each other's eyes and it seemed to hit them both at the same time. Their lives had meant nothing to each other so far, but this moment took the structure of a great and fateful sharing.

You couldn't get away from it. Sometimes people entered your sphere only by the force of their own deaths.

The sucking wound in JoJo's chest gurgled faintly, but didn't affect his voice much. Strings of blood trailed down his chin and dribbled over the fresh carnation in his lapel. Fat beads of sweat stood out on his forehead and clung to his brow, his skin now a sickly, bright yellow. The bullet graze along his jaw had cauterized the flesh in a fiery, jagged pattern.

"Please—God, please—"

The bakery girl remained frozen in place, so completely still that Dane wondered if she'd fainted on her feet and just hadn't fallen down yet. Apparently no one had called 911. Dozens of people strolled past the store window, everybody so wrapped in their own worries they didn't even glance to one side or the other. Fifty bullets flying around and not one crack in the plate glass.

"You need help," Dane said.

"Too late for that. Were you over there in the Middle East?"

"No, I spent most of my time in the stockade."

"For what? Brawling? You look like a brawler."

"Apathy, mostly," Dane admitted.

He thought, Hell, if only Grandma hadn't gotten a sudden jones for sugar, I wouldn't have stepped into this mess. She's probably climbing the walls by now, waiting for her *biscotti*. The thought alarmed him nearly as much as all this shit.

The hitter squirmed on the floor, his dripping hand stretching for Dane's ankle. Touching him lightly there the way Mako had done in the showers.

The stink grew worse, but there was also a pleasant aroma of fresh *struffoli* and *sfogliatelle* wafting in from the back room. Dane eyed the scarred knuckles, wavering, praying the guy would just die already. *"Please—please...am...ambulance—"*

"Don't let that piece of shit bother you," JoJo told him. "Listen, I need you to do something for me."

The gun barrel eased into an angle, leveled directly at Dane's guts. Dane said, "Threatening me isn't going to help you much at this point."

The .32 steered away and pointed toward the far wall again. "Sorry about that. Bad habit." JoJo grinned, his teeth smeared with bile. "I suppose all my vices have about run out to the end."

"Jesus, you gotta help—" The hand wrapped itself weakly around Dane's cuff, those ragged, dirty fingernails clawing. Dane tugged his foot away.

"I need you to give a message to Maria Monticelli for me," JoJo said. "You know her?"

"Yeah."

Dane had been in love with Maria since he was about seven. Every guy his age had been and maybe still was. A soft tragedy welled inside him at just the mention of her name. And Angelina had looked so much like her.

JoJo was fading fast, but he tightened his face against the pain. He reached his blood-smeared fingertips into his jacket pocket and came out with a satin box.

"I'll pay you ten grand to tell her I love her. That I've always loved her. You give her this."

"A ring?"

"An engagement ring. I planned on asking her to marry me."

"I don't mean to bring you farther down, JoJo...but why's it matter now?"

That made the dying man chuckle until his lips were flecked with bubbling red froth. He strained to keep his voice under control. "I've been carrying this engagement ring around for six months but I never managed to get up the nerve to give it to her. I've meant to propose . . . seriously, you know, doing the whole down on one knee bit . . . three or four times, but something always threw me off track. Some deal that had to be done or another enterprise. But I always loved her. I don't want to kick without her knowing . . . for certain."

"Isn't that the kind of thing she'd already know?"

"Probably, but it always went unsaid. I finally want to say it to her."

Dane let it go by that JoJo wasn't going to be able to tell her anything much in another five minutes.

"We all got one thing in the world that we love more . . . than anything else, Danetello. That makes us do . . . what we do . . . makes us who we are. You understand that?"

"Yeah."

"I've got the money on me. A hundred c-note bills. A deadbeat sold his house and finally paid off the vig from three weeks ago. You give me your word of honor you'll tell her for me, and it's yours."

Dane looked over at the killer, who was still on the floor plying his guts, pulling out pieces and moaning in torment. "Isn't Don Monticelli the one who sent him?"

"Nah, not the Don. Probably Roberto. That bastard never liked me. It's all so stupid. Not even about business."

"Because of Maria?"

JoJo's eyes opened wide and he shook his head as if he still couldn't quite believe what had brought him to this. "Yeah. He wants her to marry a dentist. Or a podiatrist like her sister Carmella did. I worked a lot of good deals between them and the Ventimiglias. For ten years I've been making money for them, good enough to hand over . . . green bundles that could choke a cow. But because I walk in his father's footsteps . . . I'm not good enough for his sister. The hypocritical *stugots.*"

It was like a scene out of *Romeo and Juliet.* Dane had never read the play but he knew it didn't end well.

JoJo gave an agonized leer. "You're smart, and you're a little *pazzo.* I'm glad. You'll get the job done."

"It might take me a while. I got some other pressing matters. What makes you think she'll talk to me?"

"The rest of us, we know you were only trying to help Angelina. Maria . . . she'll listen."

That sent a buzz through Dane's chest, his heart rate picking up speed at the sound of her name. "You think so?" It came out almost joyful, hoping that Maria was the one person in the family who didn't hate Dane's guts anymore.

"Sure—"

"What can you tell me about what's been going on in the Monti family since I went away? The feds have been sniffing around."

JoJo let out a dry laugh. Wheezing harshly, at least one lung collapsing. "Heard you nearly got clipped your . . . last day in the joint."

"Something's been stirring them up. What is it?"

"Dunno, but your friend Vinny . . . he thinks he's the new Bugsy Siegel."

"What do you mean? He wants to start up in Vegas?"

A clot of ruby dark blood poured over JoJo's bottom lip. "You . . . haven't given me your word. I want . . . it . . . your oath . . ."

"I'll tell her," Dane said.

JoJo reached inside the folded newspaper and pulled out an envelope stuffed with cash. He started to rise, like he wanted to die on his feet, then fell over backwards. He hit the floor hard with a crack and his death rattle lurched loose. Dane looked over at the Monti hitter on the floor and noticed he was dead too.

The baker's girl stood there gasping with tears tracking her cheeks. When Dane said, "Go get the cops," she finally broke into motion and ran out onto the street.

Dane took the money and the diamond ring, thinking of Maria's exquisite face, and the sorrow of his life.

NINE

His myths were quiet ones without heroes, where the storms broke wide and heavy across the lawns of churches, and neighbors hid in their homes full of small tragedies.

Dane had always been too observant for his own good. He could clock the passing of time by the divorces down the block. The swelling bellies of his schoolmates. Those who went missing, one by one, down through the yearbooks. Who drowned off Fire Island, and which one died in a car crash over on the Major Deegan. And how *she* died on this surgeon's table, and *she* died on that one, and *she* was the first girl he ever felt up, who died a year ago from ovarian cancer.

Dane hadn't hung around the bakery waiting for the cops. He expected them to find him by the end of the day, but they never came to see him. It made him wonder, were they just sloppy, or had the baker girl been too out of it to identify him? Or were the feds on to this too, and already had him under surveillance? Bugged?

Now that he was back in Brooklyn, he didn't want to leave. It stirred too much inside him, kept his head alive with memories that made him bark laughter for no reason. It wasn't so much the going away as it was the constant coming back.

When he was a kid, every Friday afternoon Grandma Lucia would send him down to Fielding's market for the same order. First time he did it, he was about eight. He clenched the cash tightly in his fist, walked the four blocks to the store. She'd made him recite the order about ten times before he left, and he'd let Mr. Fielding have it word for word. "Gimme two portions of shrimp, two of potatoes, three fillets and don't burn them."

But Mr. Fielding screwed him up and asked, "How about fish cakes?"

"What?"

"Your Grandma Lucia want some fresh fish cakes? I bet she does. She loves my fish cakes!"

Dane frowned and repeated the order like he'd been drilled, feeling the squeamishness of terror filling his stomach.

"Is she sick?"

"No."

"She always orders the fish cakes, every week the past thirty years. What's this? You don't look after your poor grandmother? She's so sick she doesn't order fish cakes and you're just standing there?"

Dane panicked, nearly let out a scream, and tore out of the store. He rushed home like he was running for his life. He told her what had happened, asking if she was all right. He thought this test had been a sign that she was on the long march to her death bed.

She stuck her fists on her hips and her face hardened into granite. "You tell that Aaron Fielding down there that I only order the fish cakes when your Aunt Concetta is here for a visit. Me, I can't stand his fish cakes anyhow. You make sure you let him know, and he better not burn the fillets."

Eight years old, standing there in the foyer trembling, staring up at her, and sensing that something wasn't the way it should be. He'd wandered into somebody else's circus.

Grandma Lucia took him by the shoulder and yanked him back down the street. When they got to the store she stomped in and started describing the awful taste of Fielding's fish cakes to the other customers, top of her lungs.

Fielding finally threw her order on the counter and told her to take her fish and get the hell out. She tossed her money at him, grabbed the oily package, and slammed the bag into Dane's chest like she was handing off a football. He was this close to crying.

When they got home and unwrapped the package they found three fish cakes and a note written on a napkin sitting on top of the shrimp, potatoes, and fillet. *You always order the fish cakes. I never burn the fillet. Aaron.*

So driving out to the Hamptons kind of got depressing after a couple of days.

The long ride down the Belt to the Southern State Parkway, over to Sunrise Highway, and out to where the Island started to change over to the real ritziness that dominated the east. Seeing where the celebrities lived and relaxed on the beaches. Boatyards, tennis courts, and golf courses all over the place for miles.

He could feel himself starting to pick up speed when he hit Westhampton every day. His foot easing down on the gas pedal and a low-level anxiety working itself between his shoulders. He'd tense up and start really moving through traffic, crossing double yellows and passing on the wrong side.

Needing to move faster, to push himself and the machine. He'd tuned the limousine himself until it hummed and whispered entreaties. His passengers would sometimes let out squeaks of annoyance but nobody ever said anything to him, and they still tipped well.

He'd drop off the fare, drive to the Point and pay the ridiculous parking fees, then walk around by the lighthouse and head down to the shore for a few minutes.

The ocean swelled against the stone buttresses, boulders slick with foam. He'd think about his parents on the beach. Sitting on a giant towel but the two of them squashed together on one small corner of it. His father rubbing lotion on Ma's shoulders.

Some folks got married up there at the top of the lighthouse, staring down at the riches of the world. Looking out at the sea and knowing there were centuries of shipwrecks right offshore, still there under ninety feet of water. It made Dane feel almost lonely, and he'd hightail it back to the limo and tear out of there. Cruising past the quaint fishing villages and down into the East End tourist hot spots. The domains of the new emperors of chic.

Now, quarter to eight in the morning, Dane walked into Olympic, and Fran told him, "You got somebody special today." She said it with a mean air. Smiling but really putting something nasty into it. She seemed just as much on the edge as the first time Dane met her. For a while there, he thought that Pepe might've been kidding about the stress management courses, but now he was hoping it wasn't just talk.

"The hell's that mean?" Dane asked.

"Just what I said."

"You didn't say anything."

"A *personality.* A celebrity."

"Who?"

"Oh, you're gonna love her." Slapping the twining curls out of her eyes again, like trying to swat a bee. He didn't know why she just didn't get a haircut.

Pepe stepped out from the office, looking excited, and said, "That actress who's in that movie about the guy who's a government assassin and he's got to stop World War III. The blonde."

Off the top of his head Dane could think of about twenty movies with the same plot. He started going through actresses, trying to remember which ones were blonde. He named a couple.

Screwing up his lips, Pepe tried to puzzle it out. "No, the one who got married to that director. He took a fall about four, five months ago, turned out he was a drug kingpin, selling mostly heroin and ecstasy. Laundered the money through his company. Something called Six-Guns Productions."

"You remember all of that but not her name?"

"I got some kinda block." It was a matter of ego now. Pepe refused to look down on the sheet. His lips moved while he tried out different titles. "Above...above... wait... *Under Heaven?* No, that's not it. I saw it a few times on late-night cable, one of those after-midnight movies 'cause she's mostly topless in it. Her and the assassin working together, she dances for the terrorists to try to distract them." Pepe let out a slow smile that was a little spooky. "She's got these serious titties and knows how to work the room, going from guy to guy"—like he'd seen her at a bachelor party instead of TV—"swinging around on the pole. I'm telling you, she must've been an exotic dancer before she got to Hollywood."

It took him a minute but Dane finally remembered. *Under Heaven's Canopy*. Stupid title for an action flick. He'd never seen it. He thought it had come out a week or two before he went in the joint. "Glory Bishop?"

"Yeah, that's her! Anyway, you're due there before nine-thirty so get rolling. She's over on East 61st." Finally, Pepe grabbed the paperwork and fumbled it over. Jesus, she must've really worked the pole. It made Dane want to stop in at a movie rental place, see if any of them were open this early.

"Any other instructions?"

"Try not to be smirky with her, eh? And brush your hair, you're an ambassador for the company here."

Pepe grabbed Dane by the elbow, led him into the bathroom so he could watch him actually comb his hair, like he was prepping Dane for a blind date. Fran just stood there, smug and venomous, so sure that something bad was about to come down on Dane, and liking it.

These two were both starting to give him the creeps.

Dane grabbed the keys, headed for the garage, found his limo, and slid in behind the wheel. The engine growled with some real muscle.

The morning rush was on, so Dane stayed off the main highways and slipped through Queens to hook over to the 59th Street Bridge. Taxis kept blaring, mufflers off half the cars on the road, everything so loud it set his back teeth shaking. There was roadwork going on, of course, and one lane of the bottom level was closed off, but he managed to make pretty good time. He drew up to the address and spotted her in front of the building.

Glory Bishop.

She stood with the doorman, looking bored and a

touch stifled, or maybe just burdened by renown. The doorman blew his whistle and motioned Dane to the curb, like he wouldn't have parked there anyway.

Designer sunglasses on but they weren't very dark. She had the slightly alarmed look of a beautiful woman who'd recently slipped out of her prime and was doing everything she could to get it back. She couldn't have been more than twenty-five, but there it was anyway. Something like fear in her eyes, but—no, he decided after a second, not really. More like an oppressed wariness and hip distaste.

The doorman danced around to the driver's window and knocked on the glass. Dane opened it and the guy leaned down with his full weight on the door. "Hey, listen up, buddy. You take good care of our Miss Bishop here. You drive careful and you don't stop off to run any of your own errands. She don't like smoke, so you don't smoke in the limo while she's in back. She likes old music, you know? From the seventies, so you put that on for her and nothing else. No news stations, she's got enough problems without having to listen to that. And don't blast the heat. You got that?"

"Get the fuck away from me," Dane told him, and put up the window.

She got in back of the limo without a word, not even a nod of acknowledgment. Her titties were indeed serious. He tried to imagine her working the pole but couldn't do it. The doorman glared, his hands open and out like a cat getting ready to claw something. Dane gunned it, letting the tires squeal for a second, the way his father used to do in his cruiser.

Sometimes passengers liked to talk, sometimes they slept. Glory Bishop stared straight ahead through those shades that didn't really conceal her eyes. He could feel her disquiet starting to affect him.

Most of what he'd learned in the army and in the can about staying cool under pressure didn't seem to be working for him on the outside.

He couldn't get the image of Pepe's slow, scary smile out of his mind. Every time Dane caught a glimpse of his combed hair in the rearview it bothered him.

Down on the sheet Fran had written an address in Montauk. A one-way drop-off. Glory Bishop remained silent for over an hour, until they were on Sunrise Highway and heading past an endless array of strip malls. By then, his head was so loud with Angelina, Phil Guerra, and JoJo Tormino's dying confession of love that when Glory Bishop spoke, he nearly rocked in his seat.

"Are you a cop?" she asked.

He left it out there for a few seconds, then said, "That's your icebreaker?"

"You want to answer?"

The question didn't really surprise him. Pepe said her husband had taken a big drug fall a few months ago. The feds had probably been all over her. But why'd she wait so long to ask? "No."

"No, you don't want to answer, or no, you're not a cop."

"No, I'm not a cop."

"A federal agent?"

"Wouldn't that qualify as a cop?" They were at the last light before the Brookhaven barrens, miles of tress still black and gnarled from a wildfire a few years back. Traffic was scarce out here this early in the morning, especially heading east off-season. "I mean, if you're asking because you think you're under surveillance?"

"I don't know, maybe." Not taking it too seriously. Like she had nothing else to talk about, so why not this. "Anyway, are you either?"

"No."

"How did you know I'd be thinking that?" She sat up a little straighter. "That perhaps I was under surveillance and asking for that reason?"

"My boss mentioned your situation. He's a fan."

"What you're saying is he likes my tits."

So it was going to be like that.

"He did mention your rack," Dane told her. "In passing."

Her chin firmed up and she waited a while before saying anything more. "I don't know if I'm paranoid or not paranoid enough. I've got to ask that of everybody I meet for the first time, that I have any contact with. If they're cops. What a way to start every conversation. The police have been tailing me for months."

"I thought they already put your husband away."

It made her half close her eyes, the ridges of her eyebrows coming down. "They think I was in it with him, like I'm one of those Colombian drug czar's wives that take over the empire when their husbands get shot."

"But you're not?"

"No, I was stupid, I thought he was a good director. He was moving up to more lavish mansions even though, I found out later, his last three movies lost money. We were only married eight months when he was arrested. The lawyers start showing me this paperwork, all his tax shelters, his write-offs, the production company receipts. On paper he was in debt up to his eyes, but he's buying me four-carat chandelier necklaces and sable coats."

"You can't be too mad at him then."

"I was stupid."

Dane didn't know why, but he believed her. She probably wasn't quite as unaware as she made out, but diamonds and cash had a way of fouling your vision. He said, "How long's it been?"

"Since they got him? Almost five months. They weren't satisfied just bringing him down and about twenty of his associates, from Beverly Hills to Bolivia. They think he was connected over here on the East Coast and they want to shake up the New York movie industry the way they did LA. They don't realize there's hardly any connection at all, it's two totally different worlds. Now they've got my apartment bugged." She was getting more nervous, keeping her eyes on his in the rearview mirror. He could feel how urgently she wanted him to believe her. "They were a couple of fun years, and eight good months of marriage, but all in all I would've been better off if I'd never gone to Hollywood."

"And kept on dancing?" The words were out of his mouth before he realized it. He really hadn't learned much about keeping his damn mouth shut when it counted.

"How do you know about that?"

"My boss again. He said you've got a dance scene in one of your movies that you couldn't have faked."

"He's got a good eye for talent, that guy."

"He knows what he likes."

"You see the film? *Under Heaven's Canopy.* I do the dance because I have to keep the terrorists amused while this supersoldier killer saves the planet from nuclear war."

"I swear," Dane said, "I'm gonna rent it tonight."

"You said your boss was a fan, but not you?"

"I haven't had much opportunity for watching movies, the last couple of years."

She picked up on what he was saying. "Oh, I see."

"But back to the feds," he said. "You're giving them too much credit. They must've built a solid case against your husband in order to take him down, ferret out the laundering fronts. It's been months, you say, so if they haven't brought you into it by now, why do you think they'd keep coming after you?"

"Because I'm an actress. They think it's fun, rubbing elbows with movie people while they're trying to crack some international drug cartel. They want to bust me because it ties the film industry in with importing. Like they never realized before that where there's money, there's drugs."

"They realize it. They just have to pretend they don't, or they'd have no jobs."

"So that's why they're clinging to me."

Dane didn't buy it, but she seemed committed to her reasoning. "If they've already got your man, I don't see why they'd keep after you, even if it is fun for them. Rousting producers and all that. Feds walking into Silver Cup Studios and getting sitcom stars' autographs. Even that would get old quick. They would've either busted you with your husband or right afterward."

"That's not what my lawyers say."

"They're stringing you on so you keep paying them."

"Everybody who's supposed to help clear up the situation just keeps perpetuating it so they get paid?"

"Exactly."

She thought about it for a minute, doing the math, counting up all the cost for unnecessary hours. "You might be right. But what if you're not?"

"I don't think asking every person you meet if he's a

cop is going to do you much good in the world. Be patient. Stay out of the action for a while, go back to LA
and make your movies. *Under Heaven's Canopy Part 2.*
Kick the shit out of a few more terrorists on screen. Get
in a few snappy one-liners."

"I don't fight them. I just dance for them, you know,
seduce and sort of beguile them. Except for at the end, I
get to shoot a rocket launcher into the main bad guy,
blow him off a bridge."

"Yeah?"

"Uh-huh. My cool action hero line is, 'I'm gonna rock
your world, baby!' Then I blast him."

"You do a commentary track on this movie?"

"A special extended edition is due out next year, but
with my husband in the joint, I don't think they'll be
asking me to participate for a while. Too much bad pub-
licity right now. Later, who knows?"

She'd taken off her shades and Dane could see a mischievous glint in her gaze, maybe because he was talking
to her without judgment. Maybe something else they'd
eventually get around to. She seemed pleased with herself, playing up to him.

The tabloids and newspapers must be putting her
through the wringer, printing her nude pictures with
little black x's over the nipples, showing how degenerate
she was. "If it's not cost-effective for them, the feds will
have to pack up their shit and go on to the next case. If
they're even watching you at all."

"Feds never give up," she said, like she knew it for a
fact. "I've learned that much. All they've got is time. I
saw that when they kept coming after my husband, going through every piece of scrap paper, reel of film, inter-
viewing hundreds of members on his film crews."

"If you're really clean, they'll eventually veer off."

"I'm not that clean," she said.

It almost made him laugh. "No one is. You've just got to be less dirty than the guy next to you."

"I was, but they're still on me."

"Maybe."

All that talk and she'd never once mentioned her husband's name.

Dane settled back and she did the same, and the mood grew comfortable, kind of friendly. He double-checked his map and the address on the sheet as he pulled into the village, then drove around the traffic circle and up to Montauk Manor.

A ritzy old-fashioned hotel built a century ago, where some investors owned suites and rented them out like time-shares. Middle of October, with the hint of winter rolling in off the ocean, the place looked pretty empty. He wondered who she was meeting and felt an unexpected pang of jealousy.

He got out and opened the limo door for her. She fumbled for her purse and he said, "It's already taken care of."

"You deserve a tip."

They'd shared a little too much and he couldn't take her money, not like a chauffeur, which is really only what he was. Hour to hour, Dane kept forgetting.

Glory Bishop took a few steps toward the fancy front doors of the hotel, then turned and gestured for him to walk closer. He came around the car and she said, "I've got a friend's premiere to go to Saturday night. You want to come?"

"I thought movie premieres were in Hollywood. Where they talk about your dress the next day, say who looked like shit on the red carpet."

"No, this is an independent feature done mostly in the city."

He looked at her, trying to decide if she was asking him on a date or whether she was being nice and just wanted to hand out free tickets. Maybe so he could bring Pepe, her number one fan, and she could watch him squirm when she made eyes at him.

It took her a second to let out an authentic smile, not the shining artificial kind celebrities gave the media. Dane liked it, but still said nothing.

She told him, "You'll like the movie. It's got a lesbian scene in it. Two hot chicks making out in a hot tub."

"Are you one of them?" he asked. There went his mouth again.

Tongue flicking over her top lip, trying to see how easy it might be to get him agitated and start him down the road to infatuation. "Come watch the movie and find out."

TEN

Back from a weekend pass, with the moonlight flowing over him and pooling, silver and bone white, into his cupped hands, Dane would lie in his bunk with the rest of the squad smelling like beer and the cheap perfume of town whores. He'd shut his eyes tightly against the thrust of his own memories.

They weren't particularly bad ones. Not like he was always thinking of his father with his head laid open like an oyster, or the couple of times he'd seen violent shit in the street when he was a kid. Black guys clubbed to death for walking into the neighborhood. A bag lady frozen in an empty lot one winter, after the dogs had gotten at her.

He'd had warmth and occasional laughter, but somehow the past became the province of wreckage and remains. He had no control over it. Start fantasizing about Maria Monticelli's hair pouring over his chest, and the next thing he's thinking about his mother choking in the back room, or the girl who didn't dance with him in the ninth grade, the rage as harsh and alive inside him as it had been the day she turned him down.

He drank too much but never managed to get drunk. It made him a little stupid, and he wound up doing things like stealing jeeps and driving over to the target range. He'd wait out there until they'd start shooting. Rifles, grenade launchers, or 20mm chainguns. While he waited under the jeep, on his belly in the dirt while the explosions heaved fire around him, he'd think to himself, I'm not suicidal. I'm not really sure what this is all about.

Now he was sitting on his grandmother's couch, those same webs of memory tugging too much into his head at one time. He sort of just awoke from time to time, staring at the television and drinking 151 rum, hating the taste but still hoping it might quell his noisy mind.

Grandma walked in, smiling, her pocketbook swinging on her arm, jingling a plastic container full of pennies. It was bingo night and she must've hit on one of the round-robins, the way she was grinning.

Her fingertips were stained red from the dye she used to blot numbers. She'd been playing for maybe fifty years, and still, every time, she got her hands covered like she'd found some guy in an alley with his throat cut and tried to staunch his arterial spray.

See, like that. You think about your grandmother playing bingo and now JoJo Tormino is dying in front of you again, and the boy with the sick brain whose skull sutures are tearing apart. You feel the hot wind of another memory coming in fast. Ma in the kitchen putting icing on your birthday cake. Six years old, you got the little pointy hat on, the rubber band holding it tight to your head and cutting into your chin. Ma using a rubber spatula to finish covering up a chocolate angel food cake. The phone rings and she turns to answer it, the smile seared onto her face, the fear always there that the caller will tell her Dad is dead. That same hideous smile every time the fucking phone rang.

He threw back his drink and let the ice rest against his teeth for a second. Since he'd gotten back to the neighborhood he'd been moving fast without any focus. He had to work on that too.

Grandma Lucia spent ten minutes washing her hands but couldn't get them entirely clean. She sat beside him, sniffed, made a face, and said, "*Che puzz!* Rum. It'll make you sick."

"I'm okay."

"You drunk? If you get sick, don't throw up on my nice rugs."

The rugs might be nice, but they were mostly covered by plastic runners. He didn't think he could hit the carpet if he tried. "I'm just trying to wind down."

"There's licorice in the candy dish. Have some. It's good for you."

"All right."

"You're like your grandfather, you should stick to wine. You drink wine and maybe you chuckle every now and again, remembering something funny. Maybe sing some opera. You drink anything else, and you start thinking too much about your troubles. Just like your grandpa, he'd sit around the house with a bottle of amaretto and mope and fume. He'd shine his shoes until they shone so bright they'd blind him. Liquor doesn't do for you what it does for everybody else. It closes you up even more inside."

"That's what I'm hoping for."

"It shouldn't be. You can never get so closed up that

you don't hear your own thoughts. What's'a'matter for you? Try more wine. You might laugh a little."

The two of them stared at the shelves of photographs hanging over the television. Different kinds, going back to the late 1800s. Old Italians who had been dead for Christ knew how long, with names he couldn't pronounce. Black-and-whites of his parents in the sixties, his father looking hep cat cool, hair greased into a DA when it was already out of style. Dad had held on to something long gone, the same way Dane now did. It gave them more common ground.

Looking at the pictures used to calm him, even get him mellow sometimes. But if he kept at it too long, the assault of the past shoving at him too hard, it made him even more edgy. He turned and saw the muscles in Grandma's jaws clenched tightly and thought maybe the same thing happened to her.

"I've been dreaming about that JoJo Tormino," she told him, organizing her pocketbook, taking out her bingo chips, the blotters, the used-up sheets and boards. "Always dressed so nice, with a fresh flower in his lapel. Never went by without saying hello. You didn't tell me you were there when he got clipped."

Why hadn't he said anything about that? He'd walked into the house and she'd yelled about the *biscotti,* and he'd turned around and walked out and gone to another bakery to get them, the *pignoli* cookies, *sfogliatelle,* and *cannoli.* He came back and they had dinner and he never mentioned talking to JoJo while the man died in front of him.

"He's still got a heavy heart that won't let him rest," Grandma said, patting his wrist, telling him something more in her touch. That Dane shouldn't go out the same way, or he'd just hover around the neighborhood forever, like so many of them. If he could lighten his load any before the curtain, he would.

"He had some unfinished business," Dane said.

"That JoJo," she said. "I always liked him. He didn't go out alone, did he?"

"No."

"How many did he take down?"

"All three shooters."

"Dio!" Grandma giving a smile, showing her admiration for that. Dying with a gun in your hand, a bloody carnation on your chest.

Dane figured he'd keep the rest of the story to himself, about the ring and swearing an oath to tell Maria Monticelli that JoJo had always loved her. If Grandma dreamed about it, then fine, but he didn't have to let her know every goddamn thing.

She said, "The .38, it's still under your pillow. I think you should start carrying it. Now that you're walking in on hits, it'll be safer for you. And I shouldn't have to say these things to you. You should know them already, if you want to stay alive."

"You're right. I will."

"I told you already, have some of the licorice. Your breath."

Grandma picked up his empty glass, started for the kitchen, and stopped short. She looked at the video box on top of the television, turned it over in her hands.

She hit the play button on the machine and the movie started from where he'd left off twenty minutes ago, right at the end of the pole-dancing scene. Glory Bishop panting, her hair a wild wet tangle, jugs dripping sweat.

"Madonna!" Grandma Lucia shouted, throwing a hand over her eyes. "What's this you got? A porno movie?"

"It's an action flick with a racy scene in it. I drove her out to Long Island, that actress, yesterday."

"This *putana*? This is the clientele you're picking up now? Escorts? You're gonna get arrested again."

"She's a real actress."

"Yeah, I'm sure the Academy Award committee is gonna shortlist her." Walking out of the room, crossing herself, and talking over her shoulder. "You think she'll do that dance at the Oscars?"

He stared at Glory Bishop on the screen, watched her doing her thing again, and thought, Oh, Holy Jesus Christ. It got him going, imagining her in a hot tub with another woman. He rewound the scene and watched it again, and once more.

An intensifying ache expanded within him, trying to free itself with such influence that Dane had to hug his guts in while he shrugged back a grunt of despair. Abruptly, Angelina was sitting beside him.

"You should visit me," she said. "It'll make you feel better. You don't have anything better to do most days anyway."

Chewing his tongue and tasting blood, he tried to say her name but couldn't do it. There were a great many words of power in life—common ones, familiar ones somehow too hard for him to speak. He wondered how you did it, died with style, drinking coffee and a sucking wound in your chest.

"You need to go, Angie," he said, urging her on, trying to shove her through the veil. "You're not doing either of us any good. I don't want you here anymore."

"Of course you do."

"No, really."

"What do you think, I'm gonna play the harp, Johnny?

You think that's what it's like over here? You want me to tell you how it is?"

"No."

"I didn't think so."

Angelina enjoyed taunting him the way the last person to leave a party cherishes the power of staying too long. She slid up against him, put her head on his shoulder, her hair covering him the way he dreamed of Maria's hair draping over him, even though he couldn't feel it. They sat there watching Glory Bishop distract the terrorists with her tits, the government assassin in the back of the room screwing around with his high-tech laser scopes and shit.

"It's okay," she told him. "I can make it all right, if you'd only let me help. We're gonna get through this."

"I'm not so sure most of the time," Dane said, quietly, hoping his grandmother didn't have her ear against the wall.

His regrets seemed to have sinuous limbs that reached into places where the living couldn't fit. The girl here, always around him. "They're going to come for you soon."

"Your brothers and the Monti crew?"

"Berto thinks you've been out long enough now. They've been spreading the word around the neighborhood. People are waiting to see what happens."

"I still don't know why they haven't made their move yet."

"They're weak," Angie said with a cute giggle. "And JoJo single-handedly killing three hitters who ambushed him has sort of set them back. They're scared of you. They think you might've learned all kinds of assassin stuff in the army."

"They watch too many movies," he said, with the

government assassin movie playing out on the television, Glory working her way to her one big action hero line. "What's he got planned for my spectacular exit?"

"I don't know."

"Vinny isn't saying?"

"Vinny doesn't say anything."

That didn't sound right. "What do you mean?" Dane asked, but Angie just stared affectionately at him, like she was watching a dog trying to perform a difficult trick.

Berto didn't have much of an imagination, so he'd leave it to Joey Fresco or Big Tommy Bartone. Those guys knew how to whack somebody and make the rest of the town grimace.

"Your mother," Angie said. "She wants me to tell you something."

Stopping there, staring at him with sad but loving eyes, waiting to see how it affected him. How important it might be to speak to his mom again.

What the hell did it say about you when the dead looked at you like they wanted to cry?

He knew some guys who walked out the door at sixteen and never looked back. Others, in the joint, who'd whacked their parents for insurance or in a lunatic rage. One huge Nazi Lowrider by the name of Buford, telling his story in the cafeteria one afternoon. Explaining how he'd never gotten over the fact that his mother had thrown all his comic books away. He's thirty-five and firing machine guns with all the other white supremacists up in Michigan. They have a bonfire afterward, where they bring their children out and everybody dances around to kill-the-Jew songs with German lyrics. One of the kids is about eight, wearing a swastika on his sweatshirt and a baseball cap with the Batman symbol on it.

Buford left the rally, drove back down to Indiana,

walked into his mom's place, and put nine rounds into her face.

There were insignificant microtraumas that could eventually turn your conscience to dust.

Dane still couldn't get beyond his mother's death and never would, he realized. There was an unmined anguish there that he needed for some reason. Maybe it made him more human when he needed to be that, and more inhuman when he had to become something else.

"What does she want?" Dane whispered. "Why doesn't she visit?"

"She can't. Because you need her too much."

He watched Angie, wondering if he really could keep her sane in hell, or if she'd gone over the edge. Or if it was just him. "Of course I need her."

"Too much. If she came back, it would ruin you. Who you are and what you've got left to do. You're always this close to death."

"Hey, Angie, you think you're telling me something new?"

He could see his ma, languishing day by day, for years. Withering in darkness, tormented by her own body. It made him want to drive a fist inside her and squeeze out whatever was doing this to her. His mother, torn in half, peeling away from the inside out. Dad unable to bear witness, working longer and longer hours.

You can give yourself blood poison by tearing open your scabs. You dig into a scar long enough, it'll crawl forward on its own, cover you up until your mouth, nose, and even your eyes are sealed.

"You should go," he told the dead girl he'd sort of killed.

"She wants you to know—"

"I don't want to hear."

"But you do, Johnny, you really do."

He glared at her, a girl who'd spoken her last words to him, and kept right on speaking them.

"I don't give a shit, Angie. That's enough."

Glory blowing the guy off the bridge with the rocket. *"I'm gonna rock your world, baby!"*

"You ever gonna go back to Bed-Stuy and settle the score for me?" Angelina asked.

"Yeah."

"When? When are you gonna do it, Johnny? Please tell me. Tell me!"

The current of the past took him again and rolled him along. Drawing him one way and then hurling him another. It brought him back to the last time he'd seen her alive. A red awning over the door. Flower boxes filled with petunias. The cop with his hand up.

ELEVEN

He hadn't been a very good cab driver either, because he didn't gun it up and down the streets driving like a maniac, rushing all day long trying to make a buck. You'd think it would've played into his strengths, his instincts, being a driver and always digging the speed, but it just didn't work like that.

Fatigued most of the time for no reason but his own inertia. Bodies at rest tend to stay at rest. It was either a Newtonian law or somebody in a mortuary talking about the plastic-faced cadavers laid out on gurneys.

The Olympic Cab & Limousine Company would've fired him after the first week, except the guy in charge at the time knew Dane had a tenuous connection to the Monticelli clan and didn't want to kick him free. Not until he had a clearer idea of how much trouble he could expect from it later on.

If a fare brought Dane back over the bridge to Brooklyn, he'd take his time returning to Manhattan. He'd cruise around Headstone City for a while, take a long lunch break, and wander the neighborhood. Head over to the Grand Outlook Hall, walk the galleries, and consider his options.

There weren't many left. He thought he might join the force. Or maybe take up Vinny's offer to become a Monti lieutenant. It was mostly for show anyway, he wouldn't even need to wear a piece if he didn't want to. Just carry Vinny's coat for him, hold the doors open.

Neither choice appealed to him much, but then nothing really did.

His own apathy weighed on him like a sack tied to his back. He could sometimes see the shadow of the bitter old man he was going to be someday. The old prick wishing he could go back and kick his younger self in the ass. Get him moving in the right direction and avert more tragedy.

Dane had just gotten back into his cab and started to pull away from the Hall when Angelina Monticelli threw open the door and got in back.

"You need one of those pine-fresh deodorizers in here," she told him. "Doesn't this atrocious smell give you a headache?"

"I kind of like it."

"That's because it gets you high. So little oxygen getting to your brain. Death by sinus attack."

Fifteen years old and seething with hip attitude. She hardly ever smiled but there was always a glint of superiority in her gray eyes. He knew she could verbally outmaneuver him with ease. It scared him a touch but also made him admire her.

She'd dressed down today, wearing an oversized black sweater and midnight-blue jeans, no makeup, her dark hair falling straight back over her ears, showing the slightest curl of bangs up front.

He heaved a sigh out like throwing a rock. "Angie, what're you doing?"

"What do you think I'm doing? I need a cab. You're a cab driver. You know simple economics, yes? The law of supply and demand?"

"Shouldn't you be in school?"

"Just drive."

"I'm on break."

"You're always on break, Johnny, you sit around here for hours. How do you make a buck?"

"I don't need much," he admitted.

"That means you're gonna live with your grandmother forever? Don't you know what they say about you, a grown man living with his grandma? Even if she does make the best *ziti*. She brought some to the St. Mary's book sale last month. Bishop Dilorenzo couldn't tear himself away, the cheese hanging off his face. He was a pig, it was disgusting to see, but kinda fun too. Why don't you get married?"

It was the kind of conversation he was easily led into and had to consciously avoid. "Don't you have school?" he repeated. "How do you learn things like the law of supply and demand if you don't go to class?"

"It's almost four. Don't you own a watch?"

"Yeah. It's at home in a box with my tie clips and cuff links. Where are you headed?"

"I'll tell you when we get there, soldier boy."

"I need to call it in to the dispatcher."

"This one is off the books. Come on, what do you care? I can see how much you fret about following the rules and bringing in as much money to Olympic as you can. Besides, you don't need to worry, it's not like they'll

fire you." Saying it with an edge, like she had something
to do with the boss not firing him, by way of her being
part of the family. He checked the rearview and she fluttered her eyes at him.

One of those girls that, when she's little, she's cute,
bright, and funny, and makes you wish she's your own
younger sister. But then, when she hit thirteen or so, you
grew acutely aware of her sex appeal. The angle of the
jaw, the shape of those legs, and suddenly your whole
cerebral cortex got rewired.

You found yourself vying for her time, grinning a lot,
then smacking yourself in the forehead going, What the
fuck are you thinking?

"Come on," she said. "It's important and I'm running
late. Cut through the plaza, make a left."

"You don't want to give me the address?"

"I don't know it, but I've been there before." Taking
out a compact and checking herself in it, making kissy
faces until she was sure her lipstick was okay.

He'd known her all her life but just started seeing her
in that new light two years ago. As her transformation
into adulthood continued he knew he had to watch himself, stop sweating so much around her. It wasn't totally
his fault. It was chemical. She was becoming what he de-
sired, just as her sister Maria had before her.

The shape of her nose, the pouty lips, and the brash
knowledge in her gaze that made him want to ask her,
Hey, what are you thinking? Angie had the right curves,
and they were getting better every month.

Ignoring him just enough to get him irritated. He
supposed that made it worse because he liked to be cut
down. His own streak of masochism going pretty deep.
The army psychiatrist used to ask him if Mom or Dad
used to smack him around as a kid. If his mother would

hit him upside the head and then yank him to her bosom. If she used to take bubble baths while he was sitting on the toilet. All kinds of shit, that shrink had a goddamn dirty mind. No matter how many times Dane told him no, the doc would just nod and ask the question again in a different way.

Knowing his flaws didn't help him most of the time. The indifference could lead him to do stupid things.

He wanted to ask Angie about her sister, see how Maria was doing. If she was still going out to the clubs every weekend, if she had anybody serious in her life.

Angelina reached forward and touched the back of his neck, fingering his scars. "These the ones you got when you and my brother went through the windshield?"

"Yeah."

"Jesus Christ, there's metal!" She knocked twice on the plate. "I didn't know you could actually feel it, with it sticking right out like that. Man, that's freaky! I thought safety glass was supposed to keep people from getting cut this bad."

"It wasn't so much that as rolling thirty feet down the street."

It made her smile for a second, seeing the humor of two guys bouncing down the road after doing something as foolish as trying to ram a roadblock. But then the image must've cleared up for her, seeing the blood and their bodies skittering into the gutter, and she looked away.

"How'd it happen?" she asked. "I mean, I know some of it, but I never heard the whole thing."

"Why would you want to hear about any of that? It happened while you were still in the crib."

"I'm curious."

Dane told her almost everything, leaving out the part about the girls in the sand, but without really knowing why. Like she'd think less of him because of that? And did he really care?

Sometimes it seemed like nothing mattered at all, then a minute later it was like everything did. Every moment of your past, every inch of your body.

"You going to tell me where we're going?"

She gave him a few more directions, leading him along Fulton Street through Bedford-Stuyvesant.

"Almost there, make the next left, pull over to the right, middle of the block."

Playing with his hair, she traced the scars down the back of his neck, probing as far as she could go beneath his collar. It started to excite him, the way she did it, as if she had a perfect right.

"What is this?" he asked her.

"Don't you know?"

"You out of your mind? Quit it. I'm practically an older brother to you—"

"Is that what you tell yourself?" Flicking her nails now, digging in too hard, trying to make him howl. "Why is it you never break the rules, soldier boy?"

It took Dane back some. You could say a lot of shit about him, but he never got the impression that he followed anybody's rules. If he did, he wouldn't be a third-rate hack driver living with his grandma.

He found the place she wanted halfway up the block. A four-story apartment building with a red awning over the door and flower boxes filled with petunias hanging from the bars on the windows of the first floor. The front door, stairs, and railings had all been recently painted. A sign read *Welcome to Our Block Association. Please Help Us Keep It Clean, Quiet, and Safe.* Next door was a vacant lot with an abandoned car in the corner where some kids were playing house, the hood up and no engine inside.

She hopped out and said, "I'll be back in a minute."

"What are you doing?"

"Seeing a friend."

"You want me to go with you?"

"No. Don't get all overprotective now, big brother. I wouldn't want you to strain yourself trying to climb out of the fuckin' cab. Since you don't have a watch, just count by Mississippis. If I'm not back by the time you get to five thousand, you might consider looking for me."

"Which friend is it?"

"No one you know."

"Let me come with you."

"Hang tight, soldier boy."

She ran up the front stairs, hitting each one hard and fast like a little kid, bop bop bop bop, and walking in without pushing the buzzer.

Dane sat there thinking about his options again. Grandma Lucia had told him there was an opening at the bingo parlor, calling out the numbers on the Ping-Pong balls. It about tied with being a cop or a Monti goon.

The radio screeched. The dispatcher wanted to know where the hell Dane was. Pepe tried to buffer the boss, yelling at Dane in Spanish that was supposed to sound like Italian. Lightening up the moment with some of the other drivers pitching in, laughing and being wiseasses. Dane shut it off. Maybe he should go back in the army, argue with the shrinks some more.

After five minutes he realized why he'd been dumb enough to let her go inside alone. It was the petunias. They'd thrown him off. Even more than the fresh paint and the sign. Here they were in Bed-Stuy, poverty-stricken, segregated. Abandoned buildings right around the block, the whole place fallen to shit, and he'd just let her walk in.

Dane threw open the door and moved around the back end of the cab. He started for the building and then he saw Angie walk out onto the stoop. Sort of smiling like she was happy to see him, but stumbling down the steps.

Her face crumpled then as she tried to hold back tears and failed. A dapple of blood smeared her chin. He launched himself and caught her in his arms as she pitched forward.

"I screwed up," she whimpered.

"I knew I should've gone with you," he hissed. "Fucking hell. What is it?"

Eyelids fluttering, she coughed violently, bringing up black phlegm. Her breathing went ragged and her chest heaved violently. She grinned at him, and her teeth were red.

"Bad stuff."

"Ah, goddamn it, Angie." Those goddamn petunias. "What stuff? What did you take?"

He felt immensely stupid, trapped where he stood, uncertain whether he should head back inside the house and call an ambulance, or throw her in the cab. He wanted to kill someone.

Bed-Stuy, he didn't think an ambulance would even come out this way, no matter how many coffee shops you put up the road.

Hauling her to the cab, he was surprised at how light she was. All those muscles and curves, and she didn't break ninety. She really was only a kid.

Before putting her in the backseat he hugged her tightly. He slammed the door, jumped in, gunned it, and held his fist on the horn so the noise tore up the block. So everybody inside that building would know he was screaming through his machine and he'd be back. Someone would pay.

"Angelina, don't fall asleep. Sit up." Weird that he could shriek through the cab horn, but his voice was almost lethargic. "Tell me what you took."

". . . fake . . ."

"What?" He turned his ear to her lips. "Angie, what was that?"

"Flake."

All his life on the street but he'd never so much as smoked a joint. Just something he never got into. Here she's saying flake and all he can think of are breakfast cereals.

"The fuck's that? Why are you doing that kind of shit? Hold on."

"Doesn't hurt. I'm swimming." Letting out a giggle that made the back of his neck tingle worse than when her nails were brushing against him. "It's too . . . late."

"Like hell."

She slid down so he couldn't see her in the rearview anymore. "It's nice."

"Talk to me, Angie."

"You love me?"

That got him stomping the pedal even harder, swinging through traffic as it thickened around them. "Yeah, of course."

"I mean . . . me."

"You."

"Not just 'cause I . . . look like Maria."

"You, Angie."

"She thinks you're . . . funny . . . but not tough enough—"

He grimaced and clenched his jaws until it felt like his fillings were about to buckle. "I knew I should've gone inside with you."

Smiling, the foam smearing her face. "You love me."

He'd been working the lights pretty good, catching them as they turned green, but Brooklyn always had to do what it could to make you go insane. As he wheeled to the top of a rise, an ocean of brake lights in front of him, all the signals as far as he could see all went red at once. The cars piled up while he tried to make it out of this shithole neighborhood, still unsure of where he was going.

He spotted a traffic cop getting up from a bus stop bench on the corner and stepping into the middle of the street, grimacing at drivers that passed too close to him. The light changed and he held his hand up, stopping everybody dead.

Dane let go with a grunt, wheeled around the Honda Civic in front of him, and drove out to look the cop in his eye.

The cop ignored Dane out there in the intersection, two inches away. Horns blared. He just put his hand out, blowing his whistle, and started gesturing for the cross traffic to proceed.

"I need a hospital," Dane said, knowing he should wail to get the guy's attention. But he couldn't let it out.

"What? You got a pregnant lady in there with you?"

"A girl who's sick."

"All you hacks, every one of you's got pregnant women in back during rush hour. Today alone there musta been twenty of 'em. I couldn't spit across the street without hitting a lady who was preggers."

Dane reached out, took hold of the cop's tie. "You prick, point me to the hospital."

"Hey, you want me to run you in? You accosting a police officer? You know what you could get for that?"

Like he was a cat burglar. Like this was a bank heist,

instead of a guy trying to save a young girl's life. But this fucking *stugots* traffic cop has to puff out his chest.

The cop was about thirty, with a sour face and the pale outline of a mustache he'd recently shaved off. Full of impatience and annoyance, not one of those guys you see dancing and singing the traffic along, blowing their whistles to some funny tune. This one must have been recently busted down for doing something serious. They put him out in the middle of the street so they could see where he was all the time.

"Back this up and get out of the intersection, buddy! Now!"

Yeah, he was new all right, and trying to change the course of the world because he was pissed off at his commanding officer. As if anybody ever backed up in New York, for any reason.

"Tell me," Dane said. "Which way?"

"Three blocks up, two right. If you don't know Bedford-Stuyvesant, the hell are you doing driving through here? Are you from the Heights?" Stepping out in front of the cab, shaking his head. "You people from the Heights act like you own the whole goddamn city. Hold on a second."

Dane gunned it. The cop actually pulled a face and stepped forward, sticking his hand out again. One of those types who think the badge somehow makes them invincible. He still looked cranky and in control up until the instant he was lying up on the hood of the cab, spread over the windshield.

Dane drove two blocks like that and the cop finally fell off at the entrance to the hospital parking lot. A couple of attendants came running down the sidewalk to help him.

Engine shrieking, Dane drove up to the emergency

room and almost plowed into the electric doors, his fist on the horn.

He glanced back at Angie and saw she was blue, foam coursing down her chin, her throat three sizes larger than normal. Blood leaking out of her nose.

The cops nabbed him for vehicular assault. The traffic cop had a broken collarbone and a fractured pelvis. During the trial he still wore a sour expression of impatience, pointing at Dane with his shoulder in a cast, screaming in a high, girlish voice.

Angie lasted almost a day and a half after going into anaphylactic shock from a speedball mix of heroin and flake cocaine. It had been slightly diluted with lactose and enhanced with amphetamine, ephedrine, and caffeine. Sort of a delicacy on the street, Dane found out, but she'd been fatally allergic to the ephedrine.

Twelve hours later, while he was still in lockup, his best friend Vinny Monticelli put a contract out on him.

TWELVE

On the night Ma died, the boy with the sick brain told him how much *he* loved Dane's mother, how wonderful she was, how beautiful she was there in the bed, her skin yellow, the machines forcing air into her lungs. Heaving her against the pillows like a careless lover.

The kid had sutures all across his head, bone showing through on one side. Jagged raw red scars cross hatching his frontal lobe. Pieces of his skull had been removed and replaced with plastic and steel. He walked like he had five angry people inside grappling for control. Dane followed him around the room where his mom was dying and he was walking the same way.

Dane was seventeen and didn't know his mother well at all. She'd been ill for years and had spent most of her time in the back room, waiting to die. Their conversations consisted of lists and catalogues of delirium.

What did you do today? Today I went to math class, gym, went down to the pier with Maria, stole another car, and played stickball in Venucci's parking lot. What did you do today? Today I dreamed an angel with golden wings as shiny as coins sat with me on the end of the bed. In its hand was a burning sword. I watched the television for a while, but it wasn't on. I bled in the toilet. Go out and play.

He came home from a weekend in Atlantic City, where he'd stayed with Vinny in one of the Don's hotels, and found her on the bathroom floor. Eyes shadowed and skin turning a delicate shade of blue. Dad in his grave only a few months, Grandma at bingo. Dane drove her over to the hospital, stunned by how quickly they set her up in ICU.

They allowed him to stay with her while the symphony of mechanical discord spiked his skull. Red lights snapped on and glowed like eyes of furious judgment. You could go crazy in this room waiting for your mother to die.

He learned more about his mom from the ill kid, who spoke as if he'd known her all his life. He'd spent much of his youth in the hospital, where they tore at his skull and pulled out pieces and jammed transistors in. Other people lived between his ears. He understood how to read the medical charts. What each machine's purpose was. The kid had strange eyes, one staring straight ahead, the other never quite settled, always jumping.

The room flashed with wild hands. The kid kept reaching over and running fingers over Dane's scalp. His own jagged stitch marks hadn't completely healed yet. The wounds were still a bright pink, his hair coming in choppy and discolored in those areas. The boy with the sick brain giggled and did a little rumba around the room, excited to see somebody else with a fucked-up head.

Dane kept rubbing his mother's hand with his thumb. He couldn't stop, the rhythm of his motion timed to the beeping machines. He looked down at the floor, searching for the pool of blackness that shuddered beneath his feet. Sometimes he had a shadow, and sometimes his shadow had him.

The kid spoke with a beautiful voice, in English and other languages. Occasionally hissing his words, with a deep meaning and an awful emotion. He told Dane that Ma had spent so much time crying that she couldn't stop, not even now, in her coma. Her sleep would never be pure. She'd always struggle, restless and weeping, for the remainder of her hours in the hospital bed, and afterward into purgatory.

Thumb moving back and forth on your mother's yellow, bloated flesh. The machines speaking in ancient rhymes you can almost comprehend.

The boy touched your scars, matching them against his own. You're glad that he keeps talking.

"*Was wünschen Sie von mir?*"

"I don't want anything from you. What the hell do you want from me? Why are you even here?"

"*É bonita. Eu quero-a. Você não merece uma mulher tão maravilhosa. É minha. Mãe. Mãe.*"

"She's not your mother. She's mine."

"*Mère. Mère.*"

"She's my ma, damn it."

"*Mia madre. La mia madre!*"

"No matter how many times you say it, she's not yours, she's my mom."

Thinking about how easy it would be to snap the

boy's neck, Dane waited for somebody to come save him. His grandmother, with her red fingers. Uncle Philly, who would be off shift in a half hour. The nurses out in the hall gossiped loudly about possible pay cuts and breast enhancement.

A doctor who looked maybe twenty-five peeked his head into the room and flashed a brilliant smile at Dane, showing off his caps. His hair had some kind of wet-look mousse in it, sculpted into small curved thorns rearing in every direction.

In Jersey, when Dane and Vinny were laid up in the emergency room, there had been a doctor with the same kind of haircut who'd wandered around smirking. Did the hospitals hire these guys just to roam the halls like maître d's?

Dane wanted to pace. He stood and tried to move, but it was like he was fused to the spot. It took him a minute to realize he couldn't stop rubbing his mother's hand, not even if he wanted to. He had to keep this contact, no matter how long he had to stay here.

A voice came from under the bed.

Dane couldn't understand it. He lifted the hanging sheets and saw the kid crouched under there, arguing with the floor, pausing between incomprehensible sentences as if the floor was talking back. Maybe it was. Dane tried to listen, but the cruel grating of his mother's respirator kept dragging his attention back to her frail chest.

The kid's head was coming farther apart, sutures and staples pulling away. He crawled out from beneath the bed and stared at Ma's body, then turned away, beaming, needy but appearing innocent.

Dane knew what the boy wanted.

The rage and grief grew inside him until he was

grunting and groaning in his seat like a pig. He tightened his free hand around the arm of the chair. He wanted to smash the kid with one of the machines and scatter the shards of his skull across the wall.

"Go on, damn you," Dane whispered. "Do it, if you have to."

The boy with the twisted head crept into bed with Dane's mother.

He held her tightly and began to weep, whining and mewling. In time his sobs became a single word, repeated over and over but never growing any louder. "Mama, mama." His tears rolled off her bony chest each time the machines drove her to take in another breath. "Mama." He cried for almost an hour until finally, exhausted, he slept.

Dane sat there watching as her body functions grew even slower, and though it felt as if they would never stop, eventually they did. It really hadn't taken that long, he realized, checking his watch. His hand was free to move again.

The respirator still forced her lungs to heave, although Dane knew she was dead. The boy with the sick brain grinned in his sleep. His eyelids fluttered as he dreamed. The flaps of his head barely held together, the meat of his mind throbbing, flesh trying to pull open.

For an instant, Dane saw a black, indistinct shape in there waiting to be born into existence. Perhaps it was the boy's soul. Or Mom's. Or his own.

Scar tissue could be more alive than the rest of your skin. Itching, dead, but full of answers. Cut it open and it reproduces. Not alive, but giving birth.

He left before he was certain. There were some questions that should never be answered.

That leering doctor met him in the doorway again and bared his teeth. Dane looked at him and said, "I ought to kill you, you crazy grinning fuck." The guy still didn't drop his smile, but he vanished quickly down the hall.

As Dane drove home from the hospital, it felt as if the neighborhood were slowly growing aware of the death of his mother. As if the streets were learning of it mile by mile, as he made his way to the house.

Dane stared down and saw his hands were scuffed and bleeding, the knees of his pants dirty. He must've fallen a couple of times in the hospital parking lot, but he couldn't remember. His scars were singing.

Grandma Lucia's house, which for years had suffered the presence of the dying woman, now expressed relief. The place looked like it was waiting for loud Italian music, parties. The wide hardwood floors where his parents had danced Christmas mornings when he was a child appeared freshly polished.

The photos on the shelves above the TV shifted at the edge of his vision. Those faces darkening with intent. The names he couldn't pronounce had a power over him, already inside his veins. The face of his mother, once out in front, now hid behind other angry women. Blurred and growing more clouded even as he watched.

Dane went to his room, and when he looked up, his dead father was walking across the floor. He sat on the bed.

There were times you wanted to talk to ghosts and times you didn't. Dane wasn't sure what he wanted now. He waited for his dad to speak. Maybe the death of Dane's mother had somehow called the man up, brought him home.

A cold knot of tension throbbed in Dane's belly. Part anxiety but mostly expectation, thinking that perhaps it was finally time to learn the lessons of his father. Answers might be revealed, if his old man could be handled properly. His father might set him on a course he could understand.

A dying breeze clawed at the window over the desk. Leaves clung to the battered screen and skittered across the broken bricks outside. Odd to feel himself tugged in this fashion, knowing his father was buried even while the man sat on the mattress behind him.

You could survive almost any injury so long as you left one version of yourself behind and allowed a different one to continue.

Dane started a slow turning he would never completely finish.

His father had been dead for a little less than six months. Dane had found him down the block, parked in front of the Gothic gates at the mouth of the cemetery with his brains blown out, the gun still in his hand.

The papers gave ambiguous hints about corruption, making it seem like he had to go on the take to cover rising health-care costs for his terminally ill wife. Once he'd been caught, he'd killed himself out of shame. It sounded believable and almost romantic. Tragic without any of the usual saccharine.

The man's photo was on the news every night, not looking tough at all. Sort of soft actually, smiling a bit self-consciously.

Anywhere else in the country it might've been true, but not in Brooklyn. This was the town that had perfected *the Bounce.* Five cops bringing in sixty keys of heroin, a squad room of police officers surrounding the evidence, and somehow it disappears in front of everybody's eyes. Nobody worried about exposure in Brooklyn. Graft went with the territory. Phil Guerra had once been caught with an underage hooker, the two of them trading a crack pipe, and all the brass did was throw him into rehab for three months and make him go to Sex Addicts Anonymous.

Brooklyn cops never ate their pistols over something like possible corruption. It would be like a bus driver drowning himself because he didn't like making left turns.

As Dane shifted in his seat he saw his old man still seated in the center of the bed, waiting for something no one with a heartbeat could name. Dane couldn't see the gunshot wound in the man's temple from this angle, but it would be there. It had to be. It was as sharp in his imagination as if he'd been shot in the head himself.

"Is she there yet?" Dane asked. "Where are you? Is that purgatory? Is there anything I can do to help?"

For some reason, it felt as if it would take time for his mother and father to find each other. Both of them so gloomy and always staring at walls.

Dad didn't answer.

"Who did it to you?"

An enduring silence broken only by the breeze skirting past outside, the soft scrabbling clatter of pigeons on the roof.

Angling his chin, Dane was unable to meet the man's eyes, which were passionate and alive. His father appeared to be searching for something to say. He opened his mouth and closed it again. He held his hands up in a helpless gesture, like a baby trying to reach for an object beyond his grasp.

His father gave a sickly grin and lay back on the bed. It had been the bed he'd slept in as a boy.

"At least try to talk, Dad. Make an effort. Can't you even do that?"

The window frame vibrated in the staccato breeze. It felt like a ploy to get Dane to turn away from his father for an instant, giving the dead enough time to slip away unseen. He wouldn't fall for it. He touched the back of his head and his scars writhed, the metal plates hot to the touch. When he pulled his hand away his fingers were covered with blood.

He stared at his father lying there, the man looking up at the ceiling as if remembering what it had once been like to be alive in this room, not so different from Dane himself.

Sweat dripped through his hair and soaked into his shirt collar. Surrounded by death and connected to the dead, but not quite there yet. Feeling the weight of murder in the dirt and concrete of the neighborhood. Embarrassed by his own excitement, at this moment, of being alive.

"Find Mom, if you can. And next time, try harder to talk to me."

Dane allowed himself to look away, and when he glanced back, Dad was gone.

There were important words waiting for him. Solutions that his father was unable or unwilling to give to him. Maybe only for the time being or maybe forever.

Dane was certain he would find his father's murderer eventually, in the angry years laid out before him like the rutted paths that threaded through Headstone City. There was time.

Grandma Lucia walked in, her pocketbook chiming, a plastic container full of pennies rattling, and said, "*Madonna mia,* what the hell's that smell? You buy a bad salami? Something die in here?"

THIRTEEN

Glory Bishop didn't tell him the movie was premiering in Bridgehampton, or that she expected him to drive the limo. He walked into Olympic ready to ask for the day off, and there it was on the sheet. Her address.

Fran's voice held a sharpness that he'd never even heard in the can. "She says you can wear that same suit again, but you need a better tie." Really letting her disdain rule her face, but throwing her whole body into it. Hips thrusting, her chin right in his face. She seemed to have more muscles in her top lip than anybody he'd ever met before. No matter how much a guy hated you, he couldn't let you know about it as well as a woman could. "She picked one out for you. She thinks burgundy is your color."

You did what you could to hide what you were thinking, but sometimes it still slipped out. "Shit."

"So, Miss Super Titties has got herself a new pet to play with. If you're lucky, maybe she'll pick you out a nice diamond-studded collar. I guess the stink of prison on you must remind her of her husband."

"Maybe she just likes my eyes."

"Yeah? But not enough so she lets you ride in back with her though, eh?"

Dane killed a few hours driving his patterns around Brooklyn, down Rockaway Parkway and around the circle to a broad cobblestone pier sticking into Jamaica Bay. The cold wind came off the water and made him think of Maria Monticelli when they were teenagers, and how he'd come down here with a couple of six-packs and pine for her. She'd talk about how she wanted to act on the New York stage and eventually make it to Hollywood. He'd listen and imagine her on the screen, that face sixty feet high and looming over him, a smile so much larger than himself he could waft away on her lips.

Your thoughts could break off one of your own ribs and jam it into your heart. He went home, changed into his suit, but didn't bother with a tie.

Dane took the 59th Street Bridge into Manhattan again, but drove a little faster than usual, like he might actually be on a date. If he thought about it too much, the slow surging anxiety would start tightening his belly, so he let it go.

This time he pulled up in front of her building and parked in front. The doorman mashed his lips but must've sensed the score. Maybe because Dane wasn't wearing a tie. He walked up and the little fireplug of a guy squared his shoulders and said, "Miss Bishop will be right down." He held his hand up in front of Dane's chest.

Someone else who thought you could stop the world by putting your palm up.

Dane got back in the limo, lit a cigarette, and turned

on the radio. A blue spark leaped from his fingers and a sudden squawk of voices started berating him. It snapped him up in his seat because he thought, for a second there, that he could hear his father and JoJo Tormino among them. Upset but not angry. He could feel their frustration. Static rose up and drowned the agitated muttering, then regular music faded in. He switched the radio off and finished his cigarette.

Glory Bishop stepped out the front door and now she looked more like she did in *Under Heaven's Canopy*. Beautiful and with the sensual aura turned all the way up. Twenty-five feet away and he still felt the pressure of it. Whoo baby.

The doorman held the rear door open for her and she slid in with the supple movement she'd shown on the dance pole. It put a hitch in his breath but he said nothing. He gave her one look over his shoulder and she knew what was on his mind.

"Look," she said as they pulled away. "We're going together, this is just so the media doesn't blitz us too early on. You get to be the 'mystery man' when they do their write-ups tonight."

"Couldn't I be a mystery man in the backseat with some other mook driving?"

"This is more mysterious. Besides, I thought you liked to drive?"

"I do when I'm not getting paid for it."

"That doesn't make any sense whatsoever."

He went, "Uyh," and tried to play it off. Not take it so seriously, but he had a bug up his ass about it. "Listen, if they see me driving the limo, all they have to do is call Olympic and get my name."

"They're not that smart," Glory told him. "But they'll

follow us around and take plenty of photos, so try not to look too unhappy or punch anybody out, all right?"

"I'll do my best, but you're asking me to go against my grain."

"I get the feeling that going against the grain *is* going with your grain."

"That makes no sense whatsoever," he said, and let out a chuckle. He felt a nice flush of victory at the rimshot.

"And don't be mad if I'm unresponsive," she said. "We'll talk when we get inside the theater."

"I thought that's when we watch the movie."

"Nobody's really going to watch it. We've all heard it's a piece of shit."

"Even the lesbian scenes?"

It got her laughing, and the three-hour ride out to the Hamptons went by fast. She talked about how she went from modeling in her teens to bit parts in bad horror films where guys wearing rubber suits with tentacles chased her around sorority houses wearing only her nightie or a towel. She'd had her throat cut in three flicks and been stabbed in three others. She thought screen-writers were mostly mama's boys with a few screws loose who only got their rocks off by chopping women to pieces on paper.

She met the husband during auditions for a movie he produced but didn't direct. She thought he was a real artist, showing up on set like that to keep an eye on everything. A control freak but not heavy-handed about it. "I was the worst kind of stupid," she said. "Because I thought I'd been through more than everybody else."

Dane thought, yeah, that was kind of stupid. No matter how slick you thought you were, there was always somebody else on the corner who had you figured out.

The husband still had no name, even while she told his story. Glory leaned forward, funneling her words right into Dane's ear. How they'd dated for a few weeks but it was nothing too serious. He did some coke but not a lot, and she never guessed he was involved with distributing the product. Then he asked her to move in and it still didn't seem very serious. He'd already started pre-production on *Under Heaven's Canopy* when—

Dane cut in. "Listen, I want to ask you—"

"What the title means, right? It drives everybody crazy. There's all these weird theories running around on the Internet, geeks who find all kinds of bizarre symbolism and make these freaky connections to the Bible."

He nodded. "I watched it twice the other night and it still makes no sense to me."

"The original title was *The Mouth of Hell.* Think about that one for a minute, see if it makes any more sense to you."

He remembered that the caves deep in the mountains where the terrorists hid the missiles were called that. "Okay, see, now that's a cool action title. And it ties in with the story."

"Sure."

"But why heaven? And where's the canopy?"

"Everything is dependent on test screenings," she explained. "They show the movie to a couple hundred people and have them fill out forms on what they don't like about the film. It allows them to feel powerful. You turn two hundred fans into film critics and they start tearing the whole movie to shreds. So a bunch of them said they didn't like the title."

"Why not?"

"They said it didn't resonate enough. That's one of the

boxes they could check. If the title resonated with them."

"And *Under Heaven's Canopy* resonates?"

"They thought it sounded more like a date movie. And the producers were already hung up on the hell part, you know? It was in their heads. They couldn't clear their minds of it, so they just turned it around, turned the hell into heaven. If the viewers in the screenings didn't like hell, then they've just got to love heaven, right?"

"These producers, they make a lot of money?"

"Christ, yes."

Dane was starting to think maybe he should move to the West Coast, where it seemed like any shithead could make a bundle. Dane tried to picture *Under Heaven's Canopy* as a date flick. A couple of teenagers out on a Friday night, feeding each other popcorn, and then Glory Bishop comes out onto the stage and goes buck wild. It might make a few watchdog groups unhappy, but maybe that was really the whole point.

As they drove down to the south shore and started getting closer to the Hamptons, Dane felt her personality begin to shift. Getting into movie star mode, putting up a front that was attractive but still a wall.

The theater was much smaller than he'd anticipated and he nearly drove past it. On the main drag, about a hundred yards from the beach. With a bait & tackle shop on one corner and a boatyard across the street.

"Good, we're right on time," Glory said. "A few cheesecake photos up front as we enter. We watch the damn movie, and we're out of here."

"It starts this early? It's barely even dark."

"This is the indie circuit. Personal projects. It's for the

fans and the new directorial geniuses just making their
mark."

"Which are you?"

"I'm only going as a favor to a friend."

"To make the movie look more important?"

"Yes."

"So you're not in the hot tub with another chick?"

Home to dozens of the wealthiest, most notable
celebrities of the day, Bridgehampton stood out as one of
the swankiest areas in New York, but that didn't mean
they knew how to throw a party.

The premiere was held at a regular, small movie theater, was small with an old-fashioned ticket booth and
velvet-rope barricades out front. Dane kept waiting for
stewards to come around with caviar and champagne,
but everyone who showed up looked fresh from a frat
house. He recognized two movie stars dressed down in
jeans and wearing stocking caps, their clothes so wrin-
kled it looked like they'd just gotten off a bus.

There were maybe a dozen members of the press and a
couple of reporters from the local station. About a hundred fans lined up, folks taking pictures and waiting for
autographs. Dane knew he was going to feel out of place,
but he never thought it would be because he was over-
dressed.

Salty mist blew heavily over the building, and sand
wove along the sidewalk. Memories of Atlantic City
heaved again but Dane fought them back, trying hard to
hold on to his good mood.

He caught on quickly. He wasn't really allowed to
talk. Just grin noncommittally at people, wave like he
knew them. Every time he asked Glory Bishop a question, she nodded and let out a little laugh. No matter

what it was, he got the nod and the laugh for the benefit of the cameras. So he shut the hell up.

She kept finagling him to walk in front of her. He realized he was supposed to look like a bodyguard more than anything else. He decided to pose as much as possible. He imagined one of the Monti mooks handing Vinny a supermarket tabloid with Dane's face on the cover. At a premiere with a movie star only a week after getting out of the can, and with a Monticelli death warrant hanging over his head. Not too shabby.

None of the celebrities talked to each other. They went out of their way to ignore everyone but the paparazzi and entertainment reporters. Glory answered a few questions and Dane stood in the background, glancing left and right, playing his part. When she peeled from the press, Dane kept a step in front of her and walked into the well-lit theater.

"How'd I do?" he asked.

"You smiled too much. All bright-eyed and happy. Fame and wealth are supposed to make you sullen."

"I'll start mauling photographers next time."

The director of the film jumped up onto the stage and gave an introduction to his movie. It was an artistic vision he'd had since he was in high school. It had cost 1.2 million to make and was already up for a Spirit Award. Dane didn't know what a Spirit Award was, but the crowd was impressed, so he applauded with them. He asked Glory how the flick could already be up for awards when this was the premiere and she explained that it had already done the festival circuit. This was just the general release. It would be shown on about twenty screens in three cities and then go straight to DVD and do well on cable.

"That'll get them their one point two back?"

"Hell yes."

"All that cash in movies and your husband went in for trafficking? What'd he do wrong?"

"He's a dumb, greedy shit. The risk was part of his juice. And the coke habit made it that much worse."

The film opened with a panning shot of the East Side IRT City Hall subway station. There were no gorgeous chicks in a hot tub. After a half hour he realized there were hardly any women in the movie at all. As near as Dane could tell, the film was about three homeless guys who lived in the subway riding trains all day and night long. Shaving in their seats, eating whatever the other passengers left behind, reading lost books. For a while Dane thought it was a comedy. He laughed out loud a couple of times and got shushed by a woman in back. Glory Bishop giggled beside him.

Afterward, the director and some of the actors stood in front of the screen and answered questions from the audience. The director said the film was a metaphor for limbo. The way station between heaven and hell as represented by Manhattan social strata. Folks applauded politely.

Dane leaned over and asked, "Is it going to be the same on the way out? You might have to give me a crash course in how the wealthy look sullen. I've been told poor people like me appear too bright-eyed."

"Don't worry about it, we've done our part."

"You mean you don't want to hang around and schmooze with your buddies?"

"They're not my friends. The guy I'm doing the favor for isn't even here."

He figured she'd want to eat at one of the fancy seafood restaurants in town. He drove slowly, checking out the

establishments that might meet her criteria, but Glory
Bishop asked him, "You afraid of speeding tickets?"

"No," he said.

"Shouldn't you be?"

"Yes," he told her. "Why? You in a hurry?"

"I thought we could have dinner at my place."

"You should probably let your driver know about an
invitation like that, he'll definitely get you home faster."

"Kick it, Jeeves."

It got his mind turning. Maybe he was charming,
smirky eyes and all. He kept a lookout for cops and made
it back to the Long Island Expressway in ten minutes.
Traffic moved along well and he managed to keep it between seventy and seventy-five most of the way back. He
felt proud of the work he'd done on the engine.

"Where do you live?" she asked.

"Headstone City."

"Where the hell is that?"

"In Brooklyn."

"Well, yeah, I figured, since that's where the limo
company is, but where? A nice part?"

"Do you know Brooklyn?"

"No."

He wanted to ask her what the difference was, then,
but he held back. "Used to be called Meadow Slope. A
lot of silent era movie stars lived in the area near Outlook
Park."

"Tell me about it."

"About silent movies?"

"Don't be an asshole. Tell me about the place. The
longer I'm in New York the more I want to learn about
it. You could live in LA for ten years and never figure out
all the satellite towns and the suburbs and the lines of

demarcation. Here, you've got your five boroughs, no confusion. So tell me."

"I'm not sure I can. And even five boroughs can get pretty messy."

He made the effort, a little annoyed by the sound of his own voice.

Living in Headstone City meant walking out of the house past two bakeries, three meat markets, four bars, the candy store, the ice cream shop, two bridal shops, a couple of jewelers, and the hardware store. The mob guys acting slick on the corner, but dressed like shit. The firehouse and the police precinct right around the corner from each other, their back parking lots touching. When Dane was a kid he spent a lot of time with the firemen and the cops. He'd sometimes bring his father his lunch in a big Tupperware bowl, *ziti* and meatballs, coffee in a Thermos. His father would eat at his desk, poring over papers or on the phone the entire time. Dane would sit beside him staring at the perps handcuffed to chairs and making statements.

Afterward, his dad would send him home with the empty Tupperware and Thermos, and Dane would cut through the parking lot and wander into the firehouse. On slow days the fire chief would take him around and show him the gear and equipment. Occasionally he saw the ladder crews covered in soot and sweat after fighting a four-alarmer. It gave Dane another kind of pride, thinking there were men who risked their lives every day to protect the neighborhoods.

He checked the rearview and noticed she had a faraway look in her eyes. "You all right back there?"

"You make it sound kind of sweet."

"Jesus, do I?"

"You're surprised?"

"Well, yeah."

Even though he could separate the stories, he couldn't discern his feelings. He couldn't talk about his parents' lives without thinking of their deaths. You talk about Tupperware but you still see the ladder company weeping for one of their own dead. You still see your dad's head opened up like a shucked oyster shell.

"What'd you do time for?" she asked.

"I ran over a cop."

That got her. Wide-eyed but still smiling, thinking that even if it wasn't a joke, it was still sort of funny, she said, "Come on, you can't be serious. Wouldn't something like that get you life? Hey, you serious?"

"Yeah."

"Were you just not paying attention or what?"

He told her the basic facts about Angie overdosing in the backseat of his cab. "But I already had a record for stealing cars. That put the kibosh on me."

"I'm so sorry. You speak of her like she was your little sister."

He said nothing, and though the miles passed quickly as they cruised into Manhattan, the mood stiffened.

Glory Bishop leaned forward again, her hand on the partition like she wanted to reach through and touch him. "I know that name. Monticelli."

"Most folks around here do."

"I'm not from New York. I just moved here to get away from the craziness of Los Angeles for a while. That's where I heard the name, out on the West Coast. My husband used to do business with them."

Dane's pulse started picking up speed. "What kind?"

"Those people, they invested in his movies."

He remembered what JoJo had said about Vinny getting more like Bugsy Siegel. Was that what he meant? Vinny wanted to make movies? Was that why fate had nudged him off in a new direction?

"You mean they did drug deals together?"

"I don't know."

This time, he pulled up down the block from her building. Glory didn't wait for him to open her door. She stepped out and came around the limo to meet him. She moved in close, hugged him about the waist, and leaned into his arms, kissing him lightly. He made an effort to shake his tension and go with it, holding her gently but with need. He wondered what the hell was going on but knew well the lesson of the gift horse.

They walked arm in arm toward the building's entrance and the doorman frowned, his upper lip curling to reveal an incisor. Dane stared at him without anger, but making it clear he wasn't going to take shit off this guy pulling faces anymore. He thought he might very much enjoy breaking this prick's neck. The doorman let his lip drop and scampered away.

Glory tugged him into the elevator. He expected her to hit a high number, the thirty-fifth or fortieth floor, where she could look out over the city and see the action of Park Avenue below to the west, and beyond that the great lawn of Central Park. It surprised him when she hit four.

She handed him the key to her apartment. For a second he thought she was telling him to keep it, stop over whenever he liked. Then he realized this was a throwback to more courteous times. When a man escorted a lady to her house, opened the door for her, ushered her inside. Is that how her drug dealer husband had gotten her? Lighting her cigarette for her, handing her a towel after she got done dancing the pole?

The apartment's design was totally retro. Jesus. What they would've called mod thirty years ago, right down to the shag rugs and the sunken living room. Silver shiny furniture and geometric shapes on the walls. Dane started flashing on his childhood, seeing his dad with a big mustache, flared collars.

Glory said, "I bought it furnished, so don't blame me if the place makes you want to put on lemon-striped bell bottoms and grow muttonchops."

"It certainly takes me back."

"Whenever I walk in, it's like somebody's got AM radio on. I start humming 'Billy Don't Be a Hero.' Or 'Seasons in the Sun.'"

"'The Night Chicago Died.'"

"Yeah, that one too."

He said, "No wonder your doorman thinks you only like seventies music. Aren't you a little young to have caught these hits the first time around?"

"I used to play my mother's old forty-fives. With the little plastic thing in the middle so they'd fit on the record player. You want something to drink?"

"A beer if you have it."

"There's a fridge full of imported stuff, but I don't drink it. Mexican okay?"

"Sure."

He checked around the place, the record in his brain stuck on the fuckin' *Nananas* from "The Night Chicago Died." Goddamn song.

Over in the corner of the living room there was this weird device, sort of like a swing. All these rubber cords and this freaky leather seat. He looked at her and she said, "It's a love swing."

He tried not to miss a beat but had already paused for too long. Nodding, he just said, "Oh."

He'd heard of things like this but had never seen one before. Not even in a bedroom, much less right out in somebody's living room. He pushed at it and the love swing jangled and clanked. He wasn't sure who was supposed to sit in it or how the deed was to be done. But it seemed if you used the thing wrong, you could hurt yourself pretty bad.

It would be worth it though, as he imagined her climbing in there and hitting him with her action hero line. *I'm gonna rock your world, baby!*

He tried to figure out what the swing there in the open was telling men who came into her place. That she was wild and knew how to please? Or be pleased? Or that she didn't give a damn what anybody thought of her sexual habits? Or was it part of the furnishings left behind? Fuck, gross.

He let himself imagine what Maria Monticelli's living room looked like, and if she'd ever been in one of those devices. Strapped, tied, swaying by chains. After about three seconds his brain started to hurt.

"Is something wrong?" she asked.

"No."

"You look a little sick."

"Do I?"

Dane's scars began to heat. He tried to keep his hands at his sides but couldn't. He rubbed at the back of his head. Sweat coursed down the side of his face, and a sudden wave of nausea passed through him.

He looked toward the doorway and saw a flickering image of Vinny standing there with his mouth moving. Staring at Dane but talking to himself. Wearing a gray Armani suit but no bulge beneath the jacket, so he hadn't come packed.

Dane took a step toward him as Vinny faded in and out, solidifying for a second, then dissolving from the scene. Finally, he was gone.

Glory Bishop came over and handed Dane a beer. "Jesus, don't worry, I'm not going to make you get in the swing. Not if you hate it that much."

"Thanks."

Dane thought he knew what had happened. This situation was one of the three tracks that Vinny had been able to step into, wander around in for a few minutes before returning to where he started. Vinny had stepped into it for a few seconds—meeting with Dane here in Glory Bishop's apartment—then rejected the reality. The same as he'd done in Chooch's that day. Facing Dane down but then vanishing, moving into some different track.

So, Dane thought, he'd waited long enough to actually make Vinny impatient. Look at that.

Enough with this shadow dancing around each other. Tomorrow he was going to have to visit his old buddy and get the ball rolling.

But right now, as he sipped the Mexican beer and Glory Bishop came into his arms again, licking at his neck, he looked up at the ceiling to see what kind of supports that weird swing had. Maybe he'd try it out after all.

FOURTEEN

There was a new Monticelli crew member Dane didn't know standing at the door of Chooch's. Big kid, maybe twenty-one, with a flinty glare he practiced on everyone who passed him in the street. He probably gave it to his parish priest, trying to get the Jesuit altar boys to tremble during Mass.

He had to start things off right. He stepped inside the place, noting the few goombas who were already drunk at the bar. Three in the afternoon and these guys could barely keep their faces out of the ashtrays.

The mob was a young man's organization. The old dons and their original crews, if they'd survived into their sixties, usually wound up hitting the skids and living worse than folks on social security. They lived large while they could, but over the years they slowly shrank inside their ratty sweaters until they disappeared.

The kid pressed his meaty hand to Dane's chest. There

it was again, the hand, like that would be enough to stop anybody who wanted to get past.

This thug barely moved his lips when he spoke, hissing so he'd sound tougher. He said, "Listen, bud, we don't open to the public till eight tonight, so——" and Dane punched him in the gut. Even if a guy had six-pack abs, he'd still fold if he hadn't tightened up. The kid doubled over and Dane brought his elbow around and cracked him in the chin.

It felt better than when he'd fought in the showers, somehow more natural to do this sort of shit in Brooklyn.

Dane drew his .38, pressed it into the kid's nostril, and told him, "You've probably heard about me. My name's Johnny Danetello."

The thug coughed blood and said, "Who?"

Now that just pissed Dane off. He turned the gun around and smacked the kid between the eyes with the butt, let him drop, and walked farther inside.

He spotted Vinny in the back at the VIP table, drinking with most of the main players left in the Monticelli clan: Georgie Delmare, *the consiglier*; Joe Fresco, the hitter; and Big Tommy Bartone, the last of the real capos.

Vinny hadn't bothered to look up yet, letting the moment drag out a touch longer. That was okay. Everybody needed a little drama in their lives, hoping to milk every drop of cool out of the scene that they could.

Georgie Delmare was pure poise. The Don's former right-hand man had been inherited by Vinny. An attorney who managed to make everything look legal when the feds and the IRS came knocking. Sharp in business and always clearheaded. Pint-sized and soft, with bland eyes and a rugged complexion like he'd taken a lot of knocks when he was a kid.

Delmare said, "John, was that show of force really necessary?"

"Ask a skinhead named Sig about being excessive, Georgie. He charbroiled himself in my cell but he still didn't get the job done."

Delmare had heard the story. His face crumpled and he slid back uncomfortably. Even he knew the Montis were going off track.

Joey Fresco's hands were under the table and Dane knew he'd be holding a gun in one and the butterfly knife in the other. He was a real edgy bastard who used to boost cars around the Heights. Drive them down to Atlantic City for the weekend, then bring them back and leave them right where he'd stolen them, in people's driveways with a full tank of gas. He liked to consider himself a gentleman bandit, eccentric but also personable. Except sometimes the cars would have a body locked in the trunk, some charred corpse with its face blowtorched off or a bullet in each eye. That sort of thing tended to ruin his cavalier image.

Big Tommy used to be Don Pietro's number one capo, in charge of all the dirty work. He ran the legbreakers and the shooters, and clearly enjoyed his work. Tommy had a smug smile and overconfident eyes that danced with a kind of mischievous light. He was stocky and his jacket bulged with hardware. His leather holsters creaked and rasped when he moved. His ferret face was drawn into a perpetual sneer. Dane was still a little surprised that nobody had put a hit on Tommy just for the way he looked. Always grinning and arrogant as hell, ready to toss his wine on someone's shirt.

"You're brash as hell, Johnny," Big Tommy said. "I could've used you back in the day. But right now, you should probably move out of here before something happens and we gotta do a lot of cleanup. Drag you in back and spend all night at the sausage grinder. So back away now."

"Sure, Big, in just a minute."

Dane still had his .38 out but kept it low against his leg, not pointing it at anybody. He stared at Vinny and waited, wondering what it was that Vinny had been saying to him last night in Glory Bishop's apartment.

"I think you should stop this thing now," Dane told him. "Before it goes any further."

"That right?" Vinny's fake eye looked like it might be giving Dane the *malocchio,* the evil gaze, but with emerald hints of chagrin mixed in. "It's only got a little ways left to go."

"You sure about that?"

"Yeah," Vinny said. "You will be too, soon. Don't you feel any different than you did a few weeks back? I knew all we had to do was wait and you'd step up. You're looking healthier. Happier."

Big Tommy had been inching his left hand under his jacket, where he kept his knife upside down in a holster. You had to give it to a few of these crews, they had some style left.

Dane put the barrel of his .38 in the wiseguy's ear and said, "How about if we just remain respected adversaries, eh, Big?"

Tommy's hand strayed another half inch under his arm. Dane sighed, still not too bothered by it, but wishing he and Vinny could just go and slug this out someplace alone.

"You listening, Big?"

"Sure, Johnny."

Vinny wiped his lips with the cloth napkin and finally

glanced straight into Dane's face. You always got the feeling the fake eye knew a little more about you than it should.

He nodded to the crew, the slightest tilt of his chin. They moved off from the table, settling in close by, Joey with his gun out, the barrel angled toward Dane's belly. If it was going to happen, they wanted to keep him alive and make it last for a good long while.

Dane reached across the table, took Vinny's glass of wine, and drank the remainder of it. He asked, "Hollywood, huh? You want to produce, direct, or star?"

"You had to come back. You had to show up here. I understand. We'll get through it all eventually. Enjoy your happiness, don't feel embarrassed by it."

"What?"

"Really, you need to stop hurting yourself." The words coming out of him as if rehearsed for months. "What is it that pushes you down onto the blade, eh? All this inner conflict? You even got an answer?"

Dane stared at him, trying to find something to say.

"Don't worry about it."

It was good to know that Vinny, for all the rest of their troubles, could still read Dane well. When you needed a friend, you went back to the guy who knew you best, even if he wanted to kill you.

"You know what happened to Angie wasn't my fault."

Vinny's voice took on a different tone, like he had fallen into a deep well and couldn't climb out. "She was fifteen. You take her to Bed-Stuy and sit outside with your thumb up your ass, and you're surprised by my reaction?"

"Not really," Dane admitted.

"Then we know where we stand. I know if you ever

gave a shit about anybody or anything, maybe even your-self, she wouldn't have died in the back of your cab. You couldn't have saved her, but it wouldn't be on your shoulders."

"You're as complacent as I am," Dane said. "Or you would've done it by now. You send half-assed cons after me for two years, then you let me walk around for weeks after I get out of the stir?"

"I told you, don't worry. I've got something special planned for you."

"You've had plenty of time to make it happen if that's what you wanted."

It seemed they were both discouraged about what was going to happen. Dane felt a sudden and intense sorrow, missing his friend desperately for an instant. Then it was gone, replaced by his own anger.

One of them was going to die because Dane had been a lousy taxi driver, too lazy to go out and hunt fares, too weak to say no to a teenager with a fast rap.

It made him sigh. "Which trail do you see now, Vinny? You see me thrashing around and pissing myself? You got robbed by fate, seeing only three possibilities. Let me guess what they are. One where I pop you, one where you pop me, and one where we just walk away from each other."

"Something like that," Vinny told him, letting his grin out, like this had all simply been part of the warm-up act. "But not quite. At least we'll go through them together."

"Okay."

The kid from the front door had managed to get to his feet and stumbled through the bar, his arm extended, gripping a Baretta. His hand was wavering because he couldn't see straight. If he missed, he'd take out Vinny on the other side of the table. The crew perked up over there, shaking their heads.

Might be fun to see what happened, but he didn't want the kid to get killed over nothing. Joey Fresco had already raised his pistol above the table, getting ready to fire.

"You bastard, you broke my nose!"

Dane shot the kid through the upper leg, same spot where he'd stabbed Mako and Kremitz, where it would hurt like hell but hardly do any damage.

"Settle down, junior."

"You bastard, I'll get you for this!"

"You have no idea who you work for." Maybe he'd saved the asshole's life, or maybe they'd already decided to bury him for being so stupid.

Dane turned to go. But he knew Vinny would have to yell something after him before he left. He waited for it.

"Hey," Vinny called. "That swing I saw in her place. It looks like it'd crack your nuts wide open. You get into that freaky thing last night or what?"

FIFTEEN

Back at La Famiglia Bakery, with another list written out by his grandmother. It felt like he was always at a bakery, grabbing almond *biscotti, cannoli, tiramisu,* and *napoleons.* Jesus, how the hell did a seventy-eight-year-old lady eat sugar like this and not wind up with diabetes? He'd known crack addicts who didn't need a fix as bad as Grandma Lucia needed her dessert.

It had only taken two days to clean away the blood and bodies, for the crime-scene tape to go up and come down again, and then business was back to normal. There was a different girl behind the counter and she was fulfilling orders with swift efficiency. Dane glanced across the shop, hoping he wouldn't see JoJo Tormino sitting in the chair where he'd died.

JoJo wasn't there but somebody else hung back in the seat, staring at Dane. Straw-yellow hair chopped at the sides and a little too long in front. A hee-haw smile full of thick square teeth. Wearing a jacket with specially made creases so that the hardware underneath wouldn't show. Sunglasses carefully folded and lying on the little table.

Immediately Dane figured this had to be the fed who'd been nosing around. Cogan. Keeping Dane under surveillance until he'd determined his routine. Then jumping ahead and just sitting back to wait for Dane to stroll in with his grandmother's list.

It was pretty sad when the feds didn't even have to chase you around the block because you were in such a rut they knew where you'd be all the time. Buying Grandma some fuckin' cookies. It made him want to sulk.

Somebody's leftover paper stood open on the table, and Cogan sipped a cup of coffee. It wasn't his paper, no newsprint ink on his fingers. It was just a prop he used. Dane stepped over. The smile got wider.

"You got some real brass, John, stepping into an outfit-owned place like Chooch's when there's a hit on you." He pronounced it *Choochie's* with a slightly Southern twang. Sounded like Tennessee or Kentucky.

"I grew up with just about everybody in there," Dane said. "It doesn't take much backbone to go see them again."

"It does if they want you dead, don't you think?" Talking in a normal voice, not whispering or worried about anybody overhearing. No one at the counter even looked over.

Dane took the chair across from Cogan and slipped the list into his pocket. This was embarrassing enough. "The contract's more symbolic than anything. Only one of them really wants me dead."

"Two, including his brother Roberto." Saying it like *Robert-oh.*

"Okay, you got me there. Two."

"Maybe even one more, depending on where the old Don stands, right? Yep, and the sons do run the rest of that there crew now, am I right? They control all the button pushers and muscle?"

That cheerful smile was starting to get Dane down. "You already know that."

"Tha's right."

Cogan thought he was doing pretty good, right in there with the hip guy chatter. On the inside track to getting Dane cracked open and talking.

Like Dane might actually give a damn at this stage. All these mooks trying to polish their dialogue, make it sound natural without being real.

"I've got to tell you, I like Brooklyn," Cogan said, glancing out the window at the busy street traffic. "I've been in DC most of my career, but this place, with these people . . . I could really get used to this. There's something special about this city. The atmosphere, I don't know, the mood, it makes me excited, makes my belly tingle. One heck of a sight different from Hazardsville, Kentucky, let me tell you that, son." The broad, authentic grin reaching his eyes. "Here you can talk about mob hits and nobody even looks twice at you. It's all so natural to them, they're not even interested."

Sure, you look around and your neighbors are flowing in and out, some catching your eye but most just going about their business. That's how it had to be in Headstone City. The same way Dane had to be when he walked in here the last time and found corpses all over the floor.

He tried to bear up under the weight of his promise to JoJo Tormino, the ring still in his pocket. Struggling not to think of Maria Monticelli right now even though he had no control over it.

Imagining her turning her head with her hair flipping back, revealing the side of her neck as she drew forward.

"Lordy, my pa would skin my back if he saw me acting with such poor manners," Cogan said, reaching to shake Dane's hand, clasping it firmly. "I'm Special Agent Daniel Ezekiel Cogan."

"Let me ask you," Dane said. "I've always wondered about something. The regular agents, do they get jealous of you special types?"

More of Cogan's teeth came out for show, but his eyes hardened the slightest bit. "I think you can help me, Johnny."

"How so?"

"Don't you want to know what's in it for you first?"

"No," Dane said.

Cogan gave Dane a long look without altering his expression, deciding what his next move should be. At the end of it he pursed his lips and said, "Hellfire, son, I just want some information."

"Yeah, I figured that much out. The fact that the 'I' part in FBI means investigation sort of pointed me in that direction, you know? So what are you after?"

"Anything."

Dane said, "I've got to ask, does this tactic work for you often? Sitting across from guys saying, 'Hey, tell me about whatever'? It just doesn't seem too practical to me."

"I want help with the Monticellis."

Still playing it close to the vest, not wanting to give away any information. Use Dane, give him as few details as possible, then when it—whatever it was—went down, drop him in a world of shit and let him sink.

Dane tried to focus, but he couldn't stop seeing Maria. Seeing her beauty in his head always gave him a rush of giddy schoolboy joy, and who didn't need more of that in their day? "You sound like you've got a grudge."

Was that it? Had the feds gone after the Don and somehow missed him? Were careers on the line?

"Naw, nothing like that. Your friend Vincenzo's just been investing money outside his usual orbits. That sort of thing makes us special agents perk up some." Cogan kept staring over Dane's shoulder at the counter. He finally couldn't take it anymore and said, "I think I got to have me one of them napoleons. They good here?"

"Yes," Dane said. "My grandmother says they're the very best, and believe me, that woman knows pastry. I'll get us a couple. You want more coffee?"

"I'd appreciate that, son."

The new girl at the counter took his order without expression. He got Grandma Lucia's desserts in a pink box tied with string, a napoleon and a cup of coffee on a tray. Cogan took one bite of the pastry and groaned with delight.

Dane waited, wondering if this was the type of unbalanced fed they stuck in the field when everything else failed. Hoping he'd get results no matter how he did it, then retire him early.

"Anyway, about Don Pietro," Cogan said. "The old man's still pretty sharp but he doesn't get his hands dirty anymore. He leaves all that to his sons, and that Roberto, he mainly just wants to shoot craps and get laid."

"Yeah?"

"All that money and he spends most of his time prowling around down by the river for whores. The real kinky jobs usually. Those there trannies. Latinos mostly.

Ugly ones too, the ones that ain't gotten the whole pro-
cedure done yet, still got their danglin' willies."

That got Dane's attention. He tried picturing Berto
down by the Brooklyn Bridge, paying fifty bucks for
half'n'half from a chick with a dick. "If you're in close
enough to see that, what do you need me or anybody else
for?"

"Like most of the families, they're smart about business but dumb as a bag'a hammers about almost everything else."

Dane said, "Still sounds like you've got them in your
sights."

Carefully wiping his fingers with his napkin, now un-
folding his sunglasses and putting them back on, Cogan
grinned, some sugar clinging to his lips. Getting serious, covering his eyes. "I want you to help me bust it
down."

"It's already busted down. They're legit now."

"Just 'cause everybody says it don't make it true.
There's still plenty of juice in the Monticelli family."

"Maybe. What new orbits is Vinny laboring in?"

"You already know, don't you?"

Still unwilling to say anything. Hoping Dane would
roll over out of fear. Yeah, this Cogan had a grudge all
right, and was probably flying without much official say-
so. He was off the radar.

"Now, I don't suppose you know who did JoJo
Tormino in here?" Cogan asked.

"Three Monti shooters, probably new guys trying
to make their bones. JoJo said Roberto Monti was behind it."

That took Cogan back some. He really hadn't been expecting an answer. "That right? Why you think?"

"He was mad because JoJo was in love with his sister Maria."

Cogan appeared thoughtful. "You folks with that there Mediterranean blood sure do get your drawers twisted easy."

"Not like you Hatfields and McCoys, eh?"

That got a laugh out of the fed, who tipped himself back in his chair, turning his face aside while he pondered what he'd toss at Dane next. "Oh, by the way—"

"Yeah?"

"Those two who came after you in the joint? Who told the guards they were really fighting each other?"

"Uh-huh." Cogan was definitely plugged in if he knew about that. He had some reach. "Kremitz and Mako."

"Tha's right, those are them. Well, they got themselves into even more of a jam. See, they were recuperating okay from their knife wounds they, ah, allegedly inflicted upon each other—"

Christ, everybody had to work on their sense of subtlety. "Yeah? And what happened to them?"

"Last night they were force-fed poisoned cocaine in the infirmary. Well, we don't really know if they were forced to do it, you see? Maybe they were just tryin' to get high and somebody made sure they got a bad batch."

Saying nothing more than that, waiting for Dane to ask the question.

"Either of them make it?"

"Both, but they're on life support, in comas. Doctors ain't sure if they'll pull through or be brain-damaged or what all yet."

When you got right down to it, the Monticelli clan hired some real shitheads to do their dirty work for them. They were sloppy and spent more time cleaning up after their own mistakes than getting the job done.

Cogan finished his coffee, reached into his wallet, and pulled out a business card. Dane was surprised that there wasn't only a phone number but a city address. A ritzy hotel around the corner from Glory Bishop.

"You come by some night and we'll chat. Anytime. I'm easy to get hold of."

Dane took the card and said, "I might just do that."

They stood, shook hands, and walked out of the bakery together, Dane carrying the pink box. Cogan made a left down the block and Dane went right, turned the corner, and watched with mild surprise as the boy with the sick brain stepped up.

He was just suddenly standing there, leering so wide that the corners of his mouth had split and leaked a little blood. He still had on his hospital jammies and slippers.

"If you've got something to say to me," Dane told him, "let's hear it. In English."

The kid cocked his head at that, and the smirk eased up enough that his lips managed to cover his teeth.

He took a step forward and his knees nearly buckled. Dane moved to catch the boy and felt a sense of loving, encompassing warmth, but no weight.

The boy followed him home and in through the front door without ever saying a word. Dane lay on the couch and stared at his grandmother eating her dessert while she watched soap operas and got ready for bingo.

She finished her *cannoli,* got her coat and kerchief on, and stood in the doorway. She looked at Dane with concern. "What's'a matter for you?"

"Nothing."

"Don't tell me that, you've been on pins all evening. What? That dead girl bothering you again? She's got nothing better to do, that one. Always with the sassy mouth, I hear her sometimes."

"No, Grandma."

"The mess at Chooch's? With the gun and the shooting the *strunzo* in the leg? You only did what had to be done. You should be proud, not taking shit off one of those strong arms. They watch a few cable television shows, a couple Scorsese movies, and suddenly they're mobsters?"

"I know. It's not that."

"Don't mope, it's not healthy," she said, and shut the door.

Dane sat back and stared into the boy's eyes, looking deeply, hunting for intelligence and answers.

"Is there anything going on in there?" he asked.

"Yes," the boy with the twisted head answered.

Then he pressed the side of his face against Grandma's afghan and appeared to go to a comforting, but not yet eternal, sleep.

SIXTEEN

Glory Bishop, on her stomach naked in bed, read through a pile of scripts with one leg tapping the air while Dane ran his hand over her thigh.

She'd wanted another go in the funky swing, but he thought maybe he was just too old-fashioned at heart. He couldn't get over the nagging fear that if they got too wild, they might go out the window.

Now he listened to her tinkling the ice cubes of her White Russian, talking about the shitty screenplays that her agent kept sending on.

"This one here," she said. "I should fire the bastard for even wasting my time with it. Another horror movie. Naked bimbo in the woods running with her tits out while a serial killer stalks her. She's screaming her ass off, swims through an icy river—"

Dane pictured it and thought it might be something he'd like to watch. Glory Bishop in the water. Every dumbass flick should have one scene like that, so if you

caught it on cable late at night, you'd sit there waiting
for it to come around. Her agent wasn't so stupid.

"—she makes it to the other shore and the killer slips
out from behind a tree and uses a wrench on her. Go
through all that because the male audience wants hard
nipples. No mention of this wrench up until now. No
mention of how in the hell the bad guy managed to get
to the other side of the river and still be in dry clothes.
This bimbo role, it has exactly thirty-two lines, half of
them are screams."

She leaned over and showed him the page. Dane read
the dialogue. *Augh. Yeee. No, please, I'll do anything you
want. Wah.*

He asked, "These writers, they make a lot of money
too?"

"Yeah, and this one is also directing." She started
working her thigh against his hand, eyes shut and face
softening for a second. "He figures he doesn't need characterization if he's stylish enough, with the angles and
music. Lots of rainy shots at night and quick edits. He
wants to play the role of the killer too."

"Sounds like he just wants a cheap feel but still say he
was acting. While he wrenches you to death."

She reached over the side of the bed and brought up
three more scripts. "This one, they're trying to pitch it as
science fiction. Called *Zypho: Creature from Beyond the
Edge of Space.* Monster with these penislike tentacles tries
to impregnate the all-female crew as they fly around the
galaxy."

"In shiny latex outfits?"

"And high heels."

More lesbian scenes, Dane thought, shifting onto his
side so he could stare at the curve of her jaw, where the
light showed the soft blond hairs just beneath her ears. It

couldn't be hard to make a profit in Hollywood just so long as you knew a few strippers.

He reached for her drink, took a sip, and nearly gagged. Jesus, Kaluha, the hell did anybody ever drink it? "You got only regrets about doing *Under Heaven's Canopy?*"

"It sorts of annoys me that all anyone remembers is the pole scene. But I wouldn't call that a regret exactly." A crease appeared between her eyes. "Not yet anyway. Feels like it could become one."

He looked around the bedroom, stared through the open door at the living room beyond, thinking how this place probably ran about 2 million.

She picked up on it and told him, "It's not drug money that's paying the bills here. My husband really did make a lot of cash through his films, before he fucked it all up. Property, stocks, a couple of good productions. The lawyers say more of his assets will be frozen soon. I need to start getting back into the game."

Dane wondered why, then, if she needed to play it so straight, was she bringing him along to premieres instead of some hot director or producer or actor? "You want to break into serious roles?"

"I'm not interested in doing Lady Macbeth, if that's what you mean. But I'd like a film with some real dialogue, a fleshed-out character behind it. Maybe keep my nipples under wraps."

"What kind of movies did the Monticelli clan want to invest in?" It was the second time he'd asked. The first was right after playing around with the swing the other night, after Vinny had stepped in, then stepped back out of that particular existence. He didn't get an answer then, as they got frisky in the funky seat.

"I'm not sure, but it had something to do with the daughter."

Dane's chest tightened. "How's that?"

"The old mobster's daughter. She wants to be in pictures. She wanted him to set her up with the beginning of a career. Like it's easy to do, buy your way into a production company, tell the investors your daughter's going to be the star, even though she's never even been in a high school play."

"You sure about this?"

"I'm sure of what I heard, but I don't know how true it is. People love to sling shit, especially at anyone who might be trying to steal their credit."

"Who'd you hear this from?"

"Just gossip between a couple of my husband's cohorts. Nothing serious, just a bunch of talk."

She stared at him with a real curiosity, like she was waiting to see what this information might do to him. He kept getting the feeling that she knew more than she was telling him, but he couldn't see how that would fit in with anything else. He stared back at her the same way and she let out a giggle like he was just being goofy in bed.

So Vinny wasn't getting into the film industry to make money, he was doing it for Maria. Vinny used to talk a lot about the history of the neighborhood, pointing out the buildings where the silent era movie stars once lived. If Maria wanted to be in film, Dane figured it was because of that. Growing up in Headstone City, on the hill that still held on to the respect and history of Meadow Slope.

"You know her, don't you? The daughter, the one I was just talking about."

"Yes," Dane told her, and could hear the ache in his

own voice and the hint of puzzlement. Still not sure why he cared so much about Maria, but glad to have anything in the world that made him feel this way.

"That voice you used just then," Glory said, "the way you just spoke . . . you care a lot about her, don't you?"

"I hardly know her anymore. Haven't seen her in years. We grew up together and for a while I thought maybe—"

"You've had a thing for her since you were a kid."

"Yeah. All the guys from the neighborhood do."

"You want me to help her out? Introduce this mafia princess to a few people? I could make a couple calls. Get the ball rolling for the Don. Maybe he'll make a movie where I could keep my shirt on all the way through. Or at least until the third act. You want me to try?"

Dane sat up in bed, looking at her. He grabbed and lit a cigarette, trying to decide if Glory was making the offer in that jealous woman trying-to-rise-above-it sort of way. Or if she was acting buddy-buddy with him, like they were only pals now, because their relationship had just hit the wall.

He said, "No, Glory, don't do that."

"Why not?"

"If her family has any strings to pull, let them pull 'em. You don't want to get involved with any of that again. Look where it got your husband. Besides, the Brooklyn mob should stay the hell out of Tinseltown. That place sounds too crazy even for them."

She dug through the bundle of their clothes on the floor, searching for her panties. She found his jacket, and an uneasy grin flooded over her face.

Now a slow, dramatic turn of the head, like she was staring into a camera, preparing to speak her lines. *Yeee.*

No, please, I'll do anything you want. Wah. There was a reason why the only scene anybody remembered was the pole dance.

He sat there smoking, waiting for it.

Glory Bishop yanked out the .38 and held it away from her like a plate of bad fish. "You got something you want to tell me?" she asked.

"Ah—"

You couldn't even lie in bed with your girl for an hour without your past catching up to you, even here between the silk sheets. If she went into his other pocket, she'd come out with JoJo Tormino's wedding ring for Maria Monticelli. The dead followed you down to the mattress.

"I'd like an answer, Johnny. The hell are you doing with this?"

Some questions you didn't bother to answer. He furrowed his brow, wondering if he should get into the whole story now. She waited for an answer, which kind of bothered him. All this time and he still didn't know her husband's name, and she wants Dane to explain himself.

"So you're packing heat."

"Heat?" He smiled at her. "If you're going to say that, you might as well go really old school and call it a 'roscoe.'"

"What's the Brooklyn argot, then?"

"I don't know. I just say 'carrying my gun.'"

It got her working the muscles in her jaw, head tilted back a little so she could look down on him like Sister Bernadette squaring off on him in the fourth grade. "You want to tell me why? Explain how dangerous the world of limo driving can be? I could've gotten up in the dark to get a drink of water and blasted my foot off, for Christ's sake. You bring a gun into my home and don't even mention it to me? Why?"

"I've got some issues with an old friend."

"Pretty serious issues, I'd say."

"Yeah, but we'll work it out."

The tip of her tongue jutted and wet her top lip. "Without one of you dying?"

"Well, no, probably not," he said.

"Oh for the love of baby Jesus."

Dane was beginning to think he should call it a night. He checked his watch. Still pretty early, not yet midnight, but he'd ruined the mood here and Glory was panicked and probably angry.

He said, "I should go."

"You don't have to. I didn't mean to pry."

"You haven't. I really do need to leave. I'm sorry I didn't fill you in. It wasn't a matter of trust, if that's what you're thinking. There's just a few things I need to handle on my own, and you're better off not knowing what they are."

"At least tell me what's going on."

"Like I just said, it's better if you aren't in on it."

"I still have a little money. Maybe I can help. Get you out of the city. It'll be safer for you in LA, so long as there are no earthquakes or mudslides."

"Or the wildfires and riots. And you were complaining about the possibility of shooting your little toe off? How long'd you live in that town? Staying there sounds like a death sentence."

He turned and she started tugging at his wrist, like a little kid who wants what she wants and refuses to let go. It was the first time she'd been like this. He looked down at her hand on him and said, "What?"

She repeated herself, with a firmer voice. "Let me help you. Discuss the circumstances with me. Tell me what's going on and we can work through it. I know we can.

My lawyers might be shysters, but hey, they're the best shysters around."

"Glory, give it a rest."

And there it was, the first edgy moment between them. Where neither of them knew what to say next. He knew he'd fucked up in a big way but wasn't sure exactly when. With the gun? Talking about Maria?

He had to leave anyway. The timing was bad. It would look like he was either pissed or scared, neither true. He searched for some way to lighten the moment as she drew her underwear on, but there wasn't anything for him to do. He got dressed too.

She straightened the bed while he poured himself a double Chivas with a splash of water. His father's drink. It went down smooth, and he waited for the fire in his chest to move along and burn into his thoughts.

Glory watched and said, "I thought you didn't touch the hard stuff."

"I don't really. It's what my father used to have every night, to unwind. Doesn't have anything to do with the drinking."

"After what we just did in there, you feel the need to unwind?"

"No, I just feel the need to be close to my old man."

She sensed his honesty and it relieved some of the tension. She came up into his arms again. "Is there anything I can do to help?"

Still pushing it, like a cop nudging. "Nah."

"I was serious about the attorneys. They might be able to help you get out from under whatever you're in."

"You still paying them?"

"Yeah."

"And how much time is your husband doing?"

"He's hoping to plea-bargain it down to eighteen years."

"I think I'll take my chances alone, thanks."

He started to pull away and she held on for another second. She had real muscle. He drew her chin up, pecked her bottom lip, and said, "Don't worry about it, okay? I'll be fine."

"Exactly what my husband said. If you don't get killed, maybe the two of you can share a cell."

Dane laughed, and that made her smile. They kissed again, long and with more meaning, as they tried to get back to where they'd been before.

The Chivas was just giving Dane that relaxed feeling by the time he hit the street. He got into the Buick and drove it around the corner. He parked in front of the hotel where Special Agent Daniel Ezekiel Cogan was staying.

Dane snapped on the radio and had another cigarette, thinking about Maria. Every guy had a woman in his life who meant more to him than she should. You couldn't call it love, or even an obsession. It had a greater complexity than that. It dealt more with the man you wanted to be than with the man you were.

He had always been tied to her, just like JoJo Tormino had been, and Dane figured he'd wind up just as dead, and probably for the same reason.

He leaned his chin down on his fist and focused, feeling a little resistance at the back of his skull, where the metal doors hadn't quite opened. Cogan was in bed, fading but not yet asleep. Dane could feel him in there, starting to slip into the comfort of darkness.

It took half an hour before the music began to change, the voices shifting and growing harsher, like people starting to argue. The drumbeat got steadily stronger, more primal. The music dissipated until it became only static disturbed by faraway, forlorn cries. Dane leaned in, put his ear to the speaker, concentrated on trying to make sense of what they were saying, but he couldn't make any of it out.

For a second there though, he thought he heard his mother moaning, the way she did in the back room while she was dying, seeing angels with golden wings as shiny as coins.

Carefully, he snapped the radio off, hoping to avoid sparks. He settled back into the seat and waited, feeling Cogan up there coming closer.

Step by step, nearly here.

Dane looked over through the passenger window and saw Special Agent Daniel Ezekiel Cogan standing naked on the sidewalk.

SEVENTEEN

The straw-yellow hair was a wild mess. It looked like Cogan was one of those types who didn't sleep well, thrashing around for a while before he got into REM. Dane clicked on the interior light. That hee-haw smile broke out on Cogan's face when he spotted Dane in the car. He fumbled his way to the curb, arms and legs moving clumsily. He sat in the backseat and said, "Well, ain't this somethin' special."

"You said I should come by some night."

"Tha's right, I surely did."

"This is what happens when I come by at night," Dane told him.

"My word, son. Some folks do have themselves special consideration under the Lord!"

"That what you call it?"

"My blessed granny would say so," Cogan said.

"Mine calls it a burden. In Sicily they burned her with sulfur for having visions."

"Even those graced by the angels got their hardships and trials."

Dane took off, enjoying the ease of the empty streets, the rhythm of the traffic lights allowing him complete access. He was a touch surprised that Cogan was taking the situation so well. He looked happy back there, at perfect ease with the situation. Just enjoying the night ride.

"You spend a lot of time doing this thing right here? Moseying on along with all kinds of passengers in the dark? You can do this to anyone?"

"No. Hardly anyone at all."

"Then how is it you know who all to pick up?"

"I simply know." It sounded stupid, but just about everything did when you were driving around with somebody's soul in your backseat. "No real way to explain it, except that I feel a nudge inside my head."

"The angels tapping at your brain. So what exactly is the purpose of all this, son?"

"I have some questions and I think you can help me," Dane said. "You said Vinny was investing money. Did you mean movies?"

"Yes, that's a new orbit for the family."

"Any idea why?"

"It's good for laundering. A lot of these wiseguys, they like the idea of being entertainment stars. Puzo, Coppola, Tarantino, HBO, they all make it look like it's downright fun to be in the mob."

"My grandmother says the same thing."

"And except for James Caan, almost all the real interesting folks live, at least to the end of the movie. The ones who turn up in the bay, well, those there are the squealers, the ones who ain't clever enough to make it with the rest of them. You got yer little kids growing up thinking, 'Hey, I can be witty and fire me off a few one-liners while I'm beanin' some old boy on the head.'"

"I think it's because his sister, Maria, wants to be in the movies. Vinny was losing money on drugs so Maria could be in film."

"That girl's pretty enough to be a box office bomb-shell without the mob backin' her up."

"You're right."

"You sound sorta sweet on her, and I can't say I blame you 'bout that right there. Maybe you can help her out some."

"What do you mean by that?"

Cogan grinned. "I'm just sayin'."

Look at this. You're trying to get information from the astral self of the Kentucky cornpone fed who's messing around in your life, and now you've got to switch the subject.

"You staking out Glory Bishop?" Dane asked. "She says she's got cops and feds all over her."

"Naw, nothin' like that," Cogan said, sort of bouncing around on the seat like a kid on a family trip. "My boss at the Bureau wants me to keep an eye on her, see if she's connected to everything her husband and his buddies was into, but it hasn't happened yet."

"What do you mean 'yet'?"

"She hasn't made the move so far, but I think she will. That's why she's using you."

Dane glared into the rearview. "What was that?"

"Hellfire, son, you really think you're lucky enough to land a beautiful sex kitten like her on your own? With-out even working for it?"

Dane scowled, feeling vaguely insulted. "She likes me. Who the hell are you to comment on it anyway?"

"She don't like anybody too much, that there girl. I think she's only using you to get an upper hand on the Monticelli family."

"I haven't even talked to her about Vinny and the crew, not even once, so what could she use me for?"

"I reckon she has her reasons. Maybe to take over where her husband left off. Wait for it. She'll hit you up eventually, when she's got them hooks in deep enough. She ain't been askin' a lot of questions?"

"Yeah, she has lately."

"There it is, son."

Dane didn't like how this was going, everything being thrown back at him. It felt as if Cogan was somehow still able to deceive. But that was impossible on the night ride. What was the point of stealing someone's soul if it could still lie to you? Dane studied Cogan's smirk in the rearview and couldn't really be sure what was going on with the guy. Maybe he'd gone through a windshield too. Or was more capable at carrying his burden.

"You said you weren't staking out Glory's apartment," Dane asked. "Now I get the feeling you have her place wired."

"Naw, that ain't it. I've followed you lovebirds around here and there, but so far you ain't done much to whet my interest. Weird coincidence though, ain't it? You hooking up with her, and her under surveillance because of some things leading back to the Monticelli crew? And you and Vincenzo with all the history?"

"Yeah," Dane said.

"My blessed granny, she'd call that a curious happenstance of fate."

"Mine would say somebody's thrown the *malocchio* whammy on me."

"Maybe so."

Dane glanced into the rearview and saw Cogan back there with an expression of knowing amusement. "Did you check on the JoJo Tormino hit?"

"That there Roberto Monticelli, he covers his tracks pretty good. Like you said, the boys that did the deed were brand-new to the crew, so there's not much connecting them to the family. And he got hisself an alibi."

"Playing poker with five other guys?"

"Exactly right. And none of them Brooklyn folks had anything at all to say about the matter. Not even the girl working the counter at the time." Cogan sat up straight and started hopping around on the seat. "Hey, hey, there's that bakery again. Pull over I want me some more of them napoleons."

They were already in Headstone City. He'd been driving without thinking, cruising with a fluidity of force and motion, and his instinct had brought him right home. "The place is closed right now."

"Goddamn."

"Besides, you're not in any position to eat anything at the moment."

"Oh, tha's right, 'cause I'm not really here in the flesh. This is my soul, and you've gathered me up like an angel of death, in your fiery chariot. My mama used to have walkin' dreams like this, she told us, 'fore they locked her away."

"Why'd they do that?"

"The good churchgoing folks of Hazardsville don't put up with craziness like this. The Right Reverend Matthew Colepepper had my father commit her when I was just a boy."

"You ever have words with the reverend about that later on?"

"No, he died a long time ago. But I did kick the hell out of my daddy when I turned seventeen, the drunken, deceitful bastard. And I ain't been back to Hazardsville since."

So much for Cogan's daddy skinning his back for poor manners.

"We anywhere near Coney Island?" he asked.

"Not really."

"Hellfire, I was hoping to see that, I heard so much about it. The roller coaster, and that dang hot dog place. And the freak shows, though I suspect some folks in Hazardsville might give those fellas a run for their money. I seen my share of pumpkin-heads and flipper babies. Where are we?"

Dane had never taken a night ride with someone who enjoyed it so much, and he didn't know what to think of it. "The Heights."

This was the neighborhood of choice, glowing across the East River from lower Manhattan. The most famous view of the Brooklyn Bridge came from these aristocratic brownstones.

Cogan had his hands splayed on the window, staring at the ironwork patterns on heavy wooden doors. You could look inside the arched windows and make out the ceiling molding and chandeliers in those homes.

"What's that right there?" Cogan asked, pointing at a massive building. "I've never seen the like."

"The Bossert. You've got to be a Jehovah's Witness to live there. They have their headquarters in the area, and own about a third of the Heights."

"Lordy. You think they go door to door and hand out them *Watchtowers* around these parts? Or do they figure, hell, all our neighbors, they're already saved, we won't bother. I mean, where's the line of demarcation?"

"They use midnight-blue vans to transport their members all around, including to the printing plants where they print up their pamphlets."

"That must be a sight."

"Yeah."

"You don't do much besides drive, do you?" Cogan asked.

"No," Dane admitted.

"I had a cousin like you, name'a Cooter. He used to run moonshine across three counties. But then the shine makers, they decided to call it quits on account'a the law, and he had no one to haul for anymore. So ole Cooter just drove around the back hills every night, without a reason, never stopping."

"It relaxes me."

"Sounds like you've spent too much of your time bein' relaxed. Man like you is nice and calm until the day he snaps. I seen some like you go to pieces more than once. Everybody says, 'My, he was so nice, that considerate child, we never expected something like this of him. Rampage through the Thanksgiving Day parade, shooting old ladies in the head. It sure is a damn shame.' You might want to apply yourself to something more socially redeeming."

"Thanks," Dane said. "I'll take it under consideration."

They headed across the Brooklyn Bridge and the moonlight laid across the car hood like a woman in white linen. He took the FDR up the east side of Manhattan and waited to see if these events were merely a curious happenstance of fate or if he was just being set up.

"Hey, who are these old boys?" Cogan asked.

Dane looked and saw the slumped figures of Mako

and Kremitz surrounding Cogan in the backseat. It threw him for a second and he veered into the wrong lane. The swerving of the car threw Mako's and Kremitz's comatose forms against Cogan.

"It's the two who were force-fed poisoned coke in the infirmary," Dane said.

"They finally dead?"

"No."

"Then what in the hell they doin' here?"

"I'm not sure. I suppose they came along for the ride."

Cogan clucked. "You got yourself some hefty weight to carry on your shoulders, son."

"Don't I know it. What do you know about a dirty ex-cop named Phil Guerra?"

"That your father's partner?"

"Yeah."

"He's dirty?"

"He killed my old man."

Cogan leaned forward and spoke with some real sadness in his voice. "Your daddy killed hisself. Don't go off on no crazy tangents now."

They were quiet the rest of the way back. Dane pulled up to the hotel around the corner from Glory Bishop's apartment and Cogan sat there smiling with all those thick, square teeth.

Dane stared at him and said, "You won't remember any of this."

"The hell you say, son! I'm not likely to forget a night like this, that's for damn sure. I'll see you again real soon."

Special Agent Daniel Ezekiel Cogan stepped onto the sidewalk and up to the front door of the hotel. His movements were less awkward now, maybe even graceful, as if he was comfortable being parted from his sleeping body.

Dane gritted his back teeth, wondering what it meant. Grinning, Cogan turned and gave a little wave before evaporating away. Mako and Kremitz hung in there for a while longer as Dane sat smoking. Their heads lolled, mouths hanging open as if they might begin speaking ancient, majestic secrets at any moment, but never did.

EIGHTEEN

Dane was in the limo driving aimlessly, stuck at a red light on MacDonough Street in Bed-Stuy, when Big Tommy Bartone pulled up beside him and started shooting.

You had to laugh. All these men, all this firepower, and the Monti family sends its top guy to come after Dane like a carjacker. No style anymore, no finesse, and no need for real balls.

It was a good thing that Tommy hadn't popped anybody personally in about ten years. And when he did do it he'd go for the sweet spot behind the ear. Or use his knife. Him and Joey Fresco, these guys had a thing about knives like they were black ops or Green Berets.

Tommy had chosen a .32 and he didn't know how to aim from any distance. The limo passenger window had been enough to deflect the bullet, giving Dane time to duck low beneath the dashboard. Tommy didn't get out of his car. He sat there and fired three more times, hitting the top of the driver's seat and sending wads of foam flying.

Dane stomped the gas pedal and drilled through the red light. He rear-ended a tan Datsun making a left turn ahead of him, spun the wheel hard, and floored it. Tommy followed along behind.

Dane had just finished dropping off four teenagers who'd rented a suite at the Montauk Manor for off-season rates. Two nervous, young couples who spoke in whispers broken by excited giggling. He envied them their first foray into an adult world. On their own for a few days playing house together.

The girls kept blushing. The boys did their best to look unimpressed with themselves but couldn't quite pull it off. They overtipped Dane without looking him in the eye, and the kids headed up the stone walkway of the resort hotel like they were strutting out of frame at the end of a black-and-white movie.

It got him thinking about what life might've been like without the Monticelli family in his past. Vinny and his violin, the Don and Berto always staring everybody down. Maria in her silk skirts and perfumes imported from Sicily. Angie talking circles around him while he sat there being lazy and dense.

No matter how he imagined it, he figured he would've been just as full of shit madness no matter where or how he'd lived. You're drawn to the things you need, no matter how lethal they might be.

Tommy was driving a '69 cherry-red Boss 429 Mustang, with 375 horsepower and 450 lb-ft. Sounded like it needed a tune-up and a muffler job. He hadn't spent much time waxing the body either. The paint was dull with a couple of rust spots on the hood. Dane's father would've bitten his knuckles thinking of a classic like the

'69 'Stang going to waste on a capo who didn't give a damn about the car.

Traffic grew heavier and Dane drifted a little higher on the adrenaline than he wanted to go. A hazy white light invaded the borders of his peripheral vision, cutting left and right while Tommy came on behind him. He let loose a slightly crazed chuckle. He eased in and out of lanes with perfect efficiency, the limo cutting a big enough swath for Tommy to easily follow. This was going to get bad.

So what the hell. Dane cut left and gunned it, shimmying the steering wheel a touch so the limo zagged. It was enough to make Tommy overreact and pull too far to the right, raking against a parked car and tearing off the side mirror. The brutal scrape of metal on metal made Dane grin.

He couldn't figure it out. Why the hell would Big Tommy Bartone keep coming at him, playing out a car chase, of all things? You didn't send a button man after a driver.

They roared through intersections together, and Tommy began to batter at the limo's rear bumper. He was an amateur behind a wheel but aggressive. The jolting crashes made Dane's back teeth hurt and he must've bitten his tongue because his mouth was full of blood. He let his intuitions guide him through the streets, knowing what was going on around him, where he was heading, but distanced from the moment.

So far, they'd been lucky, catching only green lights. Dane maneuvered easily from lane to lane. Making fast but careful turns as Tommy moved in tight behind him, sticking close and following Dane's lead. Even driving the limo, Dane knew he could shake Big Tommy if he really gave it a go; but he held back, sensing some clarifying appointment up ahead.

No cops yet. He still felt relatively safe. Believing he could get away without the added trouble of trying to explain the situation to the police.

Horns blared and a few shouts went up as they gunned past blocks of dilapidated buildings; Tommy chipping away at the limo's rear. It was stupid. The 'Stang's front end would buckle long before it did any real damage to the limo, but Tommy seemed a little crazed. He held the gun in his left hand and fired a couple times out the driver's window, but both shots went wild. A group of gangbangers selling drugs on the corner scattered, drawing their own weapons. Dane saw two Tec-9 submachine guns pointed his way and he stomped the gas.

Brooklyn wasn't always home after all.

Doing sixty down a side street, they passed a four-story apartment building with a red awning over the door. The flower boxes hanging from the bars of the windows on the first floor were empty. The abandoned car in the corner of the lot next door was gone.

Your conscience knew where to take you. Dane sped through the intersection where he'd run over the traffic cop.

Big Tommy hung in with him pretty good until Dane made a wide swinging right that was nearly a U-turn. Tommy's front end locked with the rear bumper of the limo for a second, and when they detached Tommy skidded into an empty bus stop bench. He dropped back and two hubcaps rolled out ahead of the 'Stang.

Dane slowed, drew into the parking lot of the hospital where Angelina Monticelli had died, and pulled up to the emergency room.

He reached into the glove compartment and grabbed his .38 from beside the envelope with the ten grand JoJo had given him. He got out, stuck the pistol in his belt, buttoned his suit jacket over it, and calmly walked in through the automatic sliding glass doors.

He waited inside for a second until he saw Big Tommy Bartone come screeching to a stop behind the limo. Tommy got out, holding his gun pressed down against his leg, looking more upset than pissed, and came jogging up the sidewalk.

So, it was going to be like that.

Dane shook his head, turned, and wandered down the corridor leading deeper into the hospital.

Nobody ever looked twice at someone else in a hospital hall. Patients could wander around the place for an hour without a nurse coming up to offer any help. He checked down the corridor and saw that the administrative station was empty.

Two Asian doctors walked out of an office. Whispering and staring down at their feet, they stepped into another room and closed the door. Dane kept moving casually, knowing Tommy would come bumbling along any second.

He looked at a sign on the wall: Pediatric Oncology Ward. The only people you were likely to find here were dying children and their parents huddled around wellmade beds. The pillowcases always fresh, even when their flesh was rotting.

The corridor lights were too dim. One end of the hallway looked like it was being remodeled. Wires hung in a colorful knot from the ceiling, and below stood a wooden ladder, stained cans and tools placed on every other step. He hadn't seen a wooden ladder in years and it reminded him of his father, the man's thick hairy arms speckled with paint. Yellow caution tape had been strung across the width of the passage.

A whisper to his left. He turned and listened as a child's muted voice called, "Hallo?"

The greeting barely recognizable. Taking the vague form of a word shoved through a pinhole cut through layers of scar tissue.

Dane looked down to see a girl, maybe twelve years old, touching his wrist. Tufts of coarse gray hair stuck out in odd cusps and notches across her pink scabbed head. Bandages swathed her throat and forehead, and there was hardly anything left of her face.

He couldn't tell if she'd been in a fire or if this was some kind of cancer, chewing her away an inch at a time while the doctors tore more away with their scalpels and radiation. She looked at him with one perfect eye, beautiful in its depth and full of understanding, perhaps even forgiving. The dark angles of her ruined features drew together to form an inexplicable shadow.

She used what remained of her lips to ask, "Are you real?"

It gave Dane some pause. "I'm not so sure anymore. I have my bad days. How about you?"

Something like a tongue prodded forward. She grunted a sound that could've been either yes or no and tried to give him a grin.

However frail life might be, the appearance of it was even more fragile. No matter how closely you looked, you still couldn't tell who was alive and who was dead.

He patted her head and felt the softness of bone beneath all the gauze, the thickness of the scar tissue so much like his own.

They both turned away from each other in the same instant, the girl drifting back to her room as Dane headed farther into the hospital. He came across a visitors' lounge filled with a few chairs, a worn couch, a soda machine, and a pay phone. At the end they tell you to go call any family members who might want to visit one last time. Like you ring them up while they're watching one of their yuppie sitcoms, sitting around in sweatpants, a one-year-old napping in the bassinet, and they'll come charging into the night.

Pounding footsteps resonated up the hall. Dane drew his gun and faded around the corner into the alcove, his back to the wall.

Tommy's leather holsters creaked loudly as he stormed down the corridor, too wired to play it with any tact. They were all losing their cool so easily nowadays. What the hell had happened to everybody?

Dane could feel Big's attitude approaching first, an oppressive aura of anxiety. In the army, Dane's drill instructor used to talk about how some people went out of their way to make their presence known. Without saying a word, without even an odor. But you could pick up on it if you made the effort.

With his .32 still pressed down against his leg, sort of tiptoeing like a little kid does when playing hide-and-seek, Big Tommy Bartone wandered past facing the wrong way.

Dane stuck the barrel of his gun in Tommy's ear and said, "Hey, Big, you really think this was a good idea?"

Tommy's bulk stiffened but the muscles of his face went slack, glad the game was over. Maybe everyone was just getting too old. "Ah, no."

"You want to tell me what's up with all this Steve McQueen car chase shit? Coming after me out in the middle of the goddamn street?"

"I'm sorry about that, Johnny."

"I just bet you are, Big. It's a nice car, you should take better care of it. You know how many people we could've hurt? I thought you wiseguys like to keep things quiet, up close and personal."

"I do."

"Then, really, man, following me around a hospital? You want we should shoot up a few leukemia patients? Turn the ICU into a fire zone? Come on, what the fuck?"

Tommy held the gun out, a moderate offering. He must've had three other pistols in holsters all over his body, plus the knife. "I got no clue, Johnny."

"What's that mean? And don't move for your upside-down blade, Big. That shit might look cool but you won't clear it in time."

"I won't go for it." None of the smugness there anymore, all of it washed away in a kind of juvenile humiliation. "Listen, everybody, even the Don, knows what happened with Angie was an accident. We know you ain't responsible. But we got no choice, see? An order is an order."

"Put the pistol away, Big, and keep your hands clear of the other hardware." Tommy did it carefully, afraid to move his arms. "Now, use your head. You guys really want to be part of a crew run by somebody like that?"

"Not much we can do about it. We signed up for the long haul. We betray the Montis, and nobody else will have us anyway."

"The Don isn't dead yet. He's old but he's not senile. Why isn't he putting his foot down about stupid moves like this one?"

"He's sick and in a lot of pain. It makes him a little loopy sometimes. He lets Berto run the show any way he likes."

Dane hadn't expected Roberto's name to come up at

all. He figured everybody was really following Vinny's orders. "And Vinny?"

"He spends a lot of time alone. He's playing the violin again, I hear it in the house every once in a while. But on all of this, he don't say much."

Angelina had told Dane the same thing. Vinny doesn't say anything. The hell was going on? Vinny was taking a backseat while Berto ran the show? Dane couldn't see it.

"And what about Delmare? Even the old school *consigliere* goes along with this sort of crap? He's supposed to be the one with the brains. He tells the family when they're acting *pazzo*. What's going on over there?"

"His brains will be all over his breakfast plate if he doesn't go along with Berto."

But no, that wasn't a good enough answer. It was the goomba in him talking, a natural tough guy response. "You're scared of him, Big?"

It skinned his ego, being asked a question like that. "I'm not scared of anybody."

"Then why not put your foot down?"

"I got three kids in college."

Dane snorted. "You wiseguys, everything you do is for your kids' education. You squeeze a guy's nuts with vise grips, and it's because Tommy Jr.'s gotta take a class on French Renaissance poetry."

"You're from the neighborhood, Johnny, you know how it is."

True enough, and maybe that explained everything, and maybe it didn't and never actually would. Dane stared into Big Tommy Bartone's face and remembered how, when he was a kid, he used to see this man strutting down the sidewalk in front of Chooch's with a beautiful woman on his arm, heading for a Lincoln Continental, and think how much he wanted to be like him.

"Where is everybody?" Tommy asked, his eyes weaving left and right. "We been here for fifteen minutes and I ain't seen anybody."

"Not even the sick kids?" Dane asked.

"Who?"

"Forget it. They're busy. Now, tell me about Vinny's movie plans."

Tommy wet his lips. "I don't know much about that."

Dane pressed the barrel harder into Tommy's nose, really working it into his nostril. "Does it always have to be the hard way, Big? Tell me what you do know so we can both go home."

"Vinny wanted to get back into the drug business, cutting deals with some shithead out in Hollywood."

"Yeah. Glory Bishop's husband. You know the dink's name?"

"No."

It was starting to get to Dane, not knowing the guy's name. "And you all just went along with it? After working so long to get out of the drug trade, get everything legit so the feds would get the fuck off your backs?"

"It was a way to get all the way out."

Dane repeated the line out loud and it still made no sense. "Explain that, would you?"

"If we had to pick up the drug trade a little so we could have the cash flow to invest in some production companies in Hollywood, it seemed like the wise choice. Delmare agreed. We don't need to score all that much coke for these California types, and the cash is easily laundered. It was an okay business proposition. Do a little of the old business so we could invest in a new legitimate one. After a while, we drop the drugs and we're totally set up on the West Coast with new friends, new opportunities."

"Except the guy, Glory's husband, was already being watched by the feds."

"They were all over him. I ain't never seen anything like it before, the way they were on him. The idiot was bringing the stuff up from Central America on his own, and the people he was working with were paying off by transporting guns. Down there, they have revolutions like we have garbage strikes. I don't think the feds even cared about the stuff, it was about the weapon shipments in and out of the country."

Dane's scars began to heat.

The nausea rolled up through his belly and almost made him gag, but he swallowed the sickness down. Icy sweat slithered across his scalp, and his skull started to burn. He tightened the muscles in his legs to control the trembling. He jammed the gun harder into Tommy's face so he'd turn away.

Behind them in the alcove, Dane saw the flickering image of Vinny standing there pulling a cigarette from the pack. He held it out in Dane's direction like he wanted a light. Vinny looked only half-formed, like a child's inaccurate drawing. He moved his mouth carefully so Dane could read his lips. *You're real, all right.*

Dane frowned, hoping Vinny would step forward into this particular reality, but he only stood there dissipating, strand by strand, one line after another erased until he was gone.

Games, always with the games. Dane's head cleared. He waved Tommy off with the .38 and said, "I gotta worry about you and a fuckin' drive-by now? Like the *mulignan* gangbangers? That what the Monti crew is down to?"

"No. That's not what I want."

"Good. Now go back home and tell them you missed, but it's no problem. Johnny Danetello will be visiting soon."

"I can't tell them that."

"Say whatever you want, Big, but if you come at me again, I'm going to have to kill you, okay? We clear on that one point, you and me?"

Big Tommy Bartone, who used to be Don Pietro's number one capo, the heaviest hitter, in charge of the dirty work and the shooters, with eyes that used to dance with a kind of insanely happy light whenever blood was spilled, looked at Dane with a thousand-yard stare and nodded.

It made Dane a little sad, seeing that nod, wondering where all the old-time good guys and bad guys had gone.

Tommy started off down the hall, stopped, and turned back. "There's something else."

"What's that?" Dane asked.

"I don't think Vinny's really mad at you at all. I just think he's out of his fuckin' mind."

NINETEEN

The pink hair like neon fire.

With little grace but full of commitment, Grandma Lucia plodded along, those powerful arms swinging at her sides, the pocketbook really jumping. As if she were heading off to face the village elders who'd forced her to deny the Virgin Mary. How it must still bother her even after seventy years, those wide hands balled into fists. You knew where you stood in the mortal chain when you saw that old woman walking toward the cemetery where your parents were buried. Seeing her like that, you realized how weak you really were down where it counted most.

The brisk wind heaved through town, seeking your broken bones, cooling the metal in your head, the fractures in your skull that would never heal, where your thoughts would always seep.

Grandma stood framed in the front gate of Wisewood, waiting like she was going to catch a bus. Dane pulled up, rolled the window down, and she told him, "Go park the car at the house, we're going to visit your parents."

"Grandma—"

"Come on, let's go."

"Why walk?" he asked.

"It's important."

Maybe it was, he couldn't tell anymore. Besides, he wasn't sure he could drive through the cemetery, and try to buck his pattern around town. "Why?"

"There are things that have to be done."

"Oh Christ," he said. He drove down the block and parked the GN in the driveway and jogged back to her. He was tired as hell from working all morning on the limo's dented back bumper.

She stood set like marble. When he got close enough her hand flashed out and grabbed his arm, as if she feared he might run away.

You could forget you were in a cemetery when you walked through Wisewood. The park landscaping made it seem like a retreat where you'd come to read poetry, make chicks, dream about the faces of your children. You became a part of history there, connected to the past of Outlook Park, Meadow Slope, and Headstone City. You became one with the dead, and through you they met the world you helped create.

They walked the rutted paths they knew so well, no different than going to the bakery or the butcher shop. Instead of passing your neighbors on the street, you wandered by the weathered, eroded faces of granite seraphim and martyrs.

Dane felt himself drifting back to his childhood, the pull always there. Grandma Lucia had to pull him closer so he didn't run into the peaked headstones and jagged tree trunks. They stepped together over a gnarled clutch of wildflowers growing defiantly along the curb.

Johnny Danetello, he's waiting for his death to find him.

The swords of the archangels were painted fiery red in your catechism books, but it didn't burn like that pink hair.

"That dead one, she still bothering you?" his grandmother asked.

"Not so much lately. You still dreaming of her?"

"No," she said, shaking her head, the pocketbook swinging, catching Dane painfully in the ribs. "The other one."

"JoJo?"

"I only wish."

"So which, then?"

"The one who's buried nearby her . . . what's his name, the Jewish fishmonger?"

"Aaron Fielding."

"So pushy, how he fights his way in."

"Do you know why?"

"Not yet. I don't like him doing that. Where's it say I have to put up with that? I refuse to listen. He wants my attention, he can go about it by showing some manners. This is how it's done? They want you to notice, so they just bully right in?"

Next time, Dane thought, I'll make sure I make the time for him. These dead, they'll take you right down with them if you turn a deaf ear.

The smooth thrum of a finely tuned engine made them both look to the narrow roadway. Grandma swung her chin and let out a prim grunt of dissatisfaction.

Phil Guerra's '59 sky-blue Caddy drew up beside them. The Magic-Mirror acrylic lacquer finish blazed in

the sunlight and almost managed to snap Dane's attention from his grandmother's hair.

"It looks like a rocketship with those *pazzo* fins on it,"
Grandma said.

"It's supposed to."

"You men, every one of you likes this thing, but I say
it's ugly. You ever decide to boost cars again, you should
start with that one."

"I think I just might," Dane told her.

"Ah, *Jesu*, when's he going to get rid of that rug?
Like something you keep at the front door to wipe your
feet on."

Phil parked up ahead, near Dane's parents' graves, and
waited while Dane and Grandma walked the rest of the
way down the path. Phil opened the door and got out,
wearing aviator glasses, his caps too white in the middle
of that artificially tanned face. He acted like he was leaning back against the car, but Dane noticed he wasn't
really touching it. Looking cool but afraid to mar the
shine.

"This one's wife," Grandma whispered. "She always
smells like gin and she cheats at bingo."

When Dane was a kid he used to go to the bingo parlor with her all the time. The biggest payout was something like $25. "How the hell do you cheat at bingo?"

"She tries her best. Yells out 'Bingo!' and half the time
the numbers don't check out. She disrupts the game. She's
always talking, gossiping, bothering the other players.
Butting into everyone's business, looking at their boards.
It's a mental assault, what that woman does. A psychological tactic."

Jesus, Dane thought, these old ladies take their shit
very seriously.

He stood close to her, feeling the stolid weight of

seventy-eight years of firmness and consistency. She took his hand and squeezed it. The fact that her father, husband, and son had all died in the line of duty seemed a fact of duration. As if her endurance drew murderers to try their hand against her blood. The death of cops hovered around her, the way it did around Phil Guerra, the man who'd killed Dane's dad.

Under her breath she said, "When you start moving you don't stop until it's finished. You can do it. Understand me?"

"What?"

Look at how much you're still a little boy. Walking and holding your grandmother's hand, feeling small in the eyes of Uncle Philly.

Dane had a moment where he thought maybe he'd missed out on the anniversary of one of his parents' deaths. Or maybe forgotten a birthday. Was visiting their graves so important today? Dane looked at his grandma and she was smiling with a false geniality. She said, "Nice to see you, Phil."

"I stop by when I can, Lucia. It's good to remember."

"Yes, it is."

"My own mama taught me that."

"A kind and decent woman," Grandma said.

"I visit her and my dad when I can. Some of the rest of the family." He sniffed. "Cold today."

"It'll be a bad winter."

"That's why me and Mabel are going to Florida. I'm getting out. We've been here too long."

Dane looked into his grandmother's face, wondering if this was why she'd brought him here. To listen to this one little fact about Phil leaving. Telling him in her way that the clock was ticking. You have to take him out soon if you're going to do it. Before he finally escapes.

You'd think you'd have fewer questions the older you got, but it only seemed like you wound up with more. One leading into another.

They stood there and prayed in front of his parents' graves, his grandmother muttering in Italian. While Dane had his eyes closed, Phil put his arms around him. Drew him in close, pressed his cheek to Dane's the way the Mafiosi in the fifties would kiss somebody right before they punched his ticket.

"I miss them," Phil whispered.

A wedge of hate snapped loose inside Dane's body and lodged in the back of his head. He thought of how easy it might be to reach over and grab your partner's gun, hold it up to his temple, and pull the trigger. No brawling, no real force necessary. One swift motion and all the brains go out the other side, you don't even get any blood on your slacks.

You stared at the graves and the graves stared back.

"I'll drive you both home," Phil said, showing those teeth.

Dane thought his grandmother would shrug off the offer, but she said, "*Grazie, va bene.* This wind, my arthritis is acting up."

So now Dane had to watch his grandmother clambering into a '59 Caddy, squeezing herself into the back because she'd never sit in the death seat. Whenever Dane drove her someplace, she'd perch directly behind him, talking in his ear the entire time.

But this was different. She relaxed and stared out the window while Phil Guerra drove up through Wisewood and out the gates, making a wide left for the Danetello house without slowing down or looking both ways. They cut off an oncoming Miata and the blaring horn made Phil giggle.

Halfway up the block, he pulled to the curb in front of the house and put his hand on Dane's leg, gripping pretty hard. Dane got the point and didn't get out of the car. Grandma must've seen the move. She shoved the seat forward and crushed Dane against the dash while she climbed out. He grunted, staring into the dust that had gathered there and thinking, Christ, it's never easy.

"I'm going to talk to Johnny a little longer," Phil said.

"You sure you don't want to come in for coffee and *biscotti*?"

"I wish I could, Lucia, but I need to get home soon."

"Say hello to the wife for me."

"I'll do that."

"Always nice to see her at bingo!"

Phil drew away from the curb without checking his mirror and nearly took out a Chinese delivery kid on a bicycle. The kid screamed and almost flopped off the bike but managed to keep from going down.

Phil looked over and stared through the yellow lenses of the aviator glasses. The hell kind of statement was he trying to make wearing those things? "It true that you and Big Tommy Bartone had a shoot-out in a hospital in Bed-Stuy?"

"No," Dane said.

Phil was connected and had the story down. Big Tommy wouldn't have lied about the specifics, not even to save his ass. He'd play it up that Dane had spent time in the army, knew all kinds of Special Forces moves. He had a reputation firm enough to bear up under the brunt of that, and it would make the rest of the crew that much more reluctant to deal with Dane.

"It's not true? That's all anybody's been talking about in Headstone City the last couple days. You're saying it's a bunch of lies?"

"It wasn't a shoot-out. I got the drop on him and let him go."

"That was stupid! He'll just come at you twice as hard next time."

"I think we reached a general understanding."

"Which was?"

Dane still didn't know where Phil fit into it all. Sometimes you had to make yourself extremely clear so nobody misunderstood your position on a particular issue. "That I'd kill him if he took another run at me."

Phil cut loose with a jolly laugh, genuinely tickled. It almost made Dane smile. He hadn't heard the man's honest laughter in years. Phil touched him on the knee. "You think that'll scare him off?"

"It doesn't matter. If he tries again, I'll clip him."

"And anybody else who makes a run at you?"

"Yeah, and anybody else."

"You've got a dangerous view of the world, Johnny. I don't know how you've survived this long. Acting like everything is a joke. A silly game."

He probably did, Dane knew, but it was the only way to make it through the day.

They circled the area, and Phil drove past his own house, like he might be checking to see if his wife was on the front step making a nasty face. Waiting for him, expecting him home to clean out the garage. He circled Wisewood and drove under the highway, jamming the brakes to avoid hitting other cars, cruising through intersections just as the lights turned red. Talk about dangerous.

"You shouldn't be hanging around this part of the neighborhood, Johnny."

"You already told me that."

"It's not the safest place for you."

"You said that too."

"Did I?"

"Yeah. Relax yourself about it. Nobody's going to get the drop on me." Dane thought that maybe Phil had fallen back into his cop role, reading his script to the punks on the street. He seemed a little lost, unsure of where he was supposed to be now. No longer a cop, no longer a real player. Sitting comfortably in the pocket of the Don, but only because he was a neighborhood boy and was content to play fetch.

Phil took the next turn so sharply they wound up bumping over the curb. Dane reached into the glove compartment and pulled out Phil's thick glasses. "How about you take off those aviators and put these on now."

"I see fine."

"Really, you might at least consider it. You don't have to wear them all the time. Maybe just now and again, you know? On cloudy days. At night."

"I don't need them."

Dane put the glasses back, waiting for whatever was going to happen next.

Phil started to screw around some more. He honked the horn and waved at people on the street. They stared at him in terror. Dane tried hard not to fidget but all he wanted to do was grab hold of the wheel, show him how to really groove with a '59 Caddy.

"I've got some money I could give you," Phil said. "It might help you to make a fresh start. So you can get away from here."

"Where'd you get the money?"

"I earned it on the job. It's not much. Maybe five grand. But enough for you to have a stake and move to a new city. Somewhere warm."

Dane still couldn't come to a decision on where Phil

stood. The man was actually much more perplexing than he should be. Was Phil trying to get rid of him because he realized Dane knew what had really happened to his father? Or because he had orders from the Montis to make a show of friendship?

"Just think about it," Phil told him, and pulled up in front of Grandma's house again.

Dane looked at him and asked, "Where were you that night, Phil? When my mother died."

Phil scowled, his lips tugged back in a near pout. "What do you mean?"

Some guys could play dumb with a real tact and delicacy, and then others, they just looked at you, frowning, trying to make it seem like your question made no sense.

"I phoned you from the hospital. I called the precinct, remember? You were supposed to come by at the end of your shift, but you never showed up."

It didn't really matter, but Dane couldn't control his need to confront the man and hear some kind of answer. It should all be secondary to hearing him admit to killing Dad, but he'd always known his priorities were fucked.

"You accusing me of something?" Phil asked, his eyes appearing jaundiced behind those lenses.

"I'm asking a question."

"Well, I don't like it."

"I didn't think you would."

"You got something to say, you just say it."

"I already did. I want to know where you were that night."

"Who the hell do you think you are? Asking me that! In my car! In my Cadillac while I'm driving. After I just been to the graves of your parents! And you're asking me that? You got something to say to me? You accusing me of something? This I want to hear! This I really want to hear!"

"It should be easy to answer, don't you think? It's not like you could forget a night like that, right? Or could you?"

"You got some nerve, Johnny! You got some goddamn frickin'—"

"I've got nerve, we both know that. What I don't have is an answer. You want to give me one?"

"Get out of my car."

"Can I still have the money? Five g's. Maybe I'll invest it."

"Get out of my car, you *strunzo* prick!"

"Sure," Dane said, and slid out of the Caddy. He smiled and let his cigarette hang loose from the corner of his mouth, hitting his father's pose.

Phil Guerra knew he'd messed up, showing heat like that. He sat looking at the dash for a minute, calming down. Then he held his index finger out, cocked his thumb like it was a gun, pretended to shoot Dane again, the same way he had the other day. Sometimes it felt like you were onstage all the time, in a very old play, hitting your mark and saying lines you'd said a thousand times before.

Dane walked inside and went to the kitchen junk drawer, grabbed a screwdriver and needle-nose pliers. Grandma was at the counter cooking *ziti*. She said, "You two have a good talk?"

He turned back for the door. "No."

"Where you going?"

"To make a point."

"Be home by six."

"I might be late."

"Six!"

The breeze could bring you back in time the way nothing else could. The smells in the chill air, the scent of impending rain. He tucked his chin against his chest and huddled against the wind. He walked with a fast stride over to the Guerra house.

Phil had parked the Cadillac in the garage but hadn't locked the door. Dane opened it, got in the car, used the tools, and got it started. He pulled out of the driveway slowly and waited in the street, his foot on the brake pedal, until he saw the front door open. Then he stomped the gas until the smoke of burning rubber rose up around car windows, cut loose on the brake, and peeled the fuck out.

He was feeling good, back behind the wheel, the horsepower working up into his chest to fortify his heart.

When you start moving you don't stop until it's finished.

He was moving again, finally. He drove over to the Monticelli mansion like the Caddy was leading the way. It was time to talk to the Don.

TWENTY

The forsaken understood the tactics of cruelty.

A pressure at Dane's side grew worse block after block until he thought maybe Phil had gotten a shot off and winged him. It came from the pocket where he carried the diamond ring he was supposed to give to Maria Monticelli. The pain intensified until he looked over and saw JoJo Tormino there beside him, his finger pressed into Dane's pocket.

"Give me a break, JoJo," Dane said. "I'll get to it. I've got a lot on my mind right now. Go visit my grandmother, I think she's got a thing for you."

But JoJo didn't buy that and shoved even harder. With love in his eyes and a tormented grimace, and all the regrets that a man with an unfinished mission might have, even under the mud, he stuck it to Dane.

They didn't turn over in their graves. They stood up and came after you, and they prodded you in your softest places.

JoJo opened his mouth as if to say something and suddenly Angelina was there, wearing a wild smile. She said, "Wow, you two really went at it in that swing! You deserve to have some fun, don't be ashamed of it."

"I'm not."

"You are, and you shouldn't be."

It was like living in a sideshow, where they watched your every move. You stared at them and they stared at you, gasping at the things you did.

The old ache revisited itself on him, his chest feeling huge and hollow, like he'd been embalmed, side by side in the morgue trays with all the rest of them. The mansion on the hill loomed above him, the sound of the heavy waves roaring in the bay.

"You still haven't come by to visit me," she said. "But that's all right, you've been having fun. I'm glad."

"It hasn't all been fun."

"No, but you've been doing okay so far. And I can see you're enjoying yourself now."

You really couldn't ask for more than that. Not from a girl you'd driven to the people who killed her.

"Your mother—" Angie slid closer, trying to curl across his lap.

"That's right. You said she had something to tell me. What is it?"

Now, the dead playing coy, she nibbled her bottom lip and let out a soft purr, the kind of sound he'd never heard her make when she was alive.

"You don't really want to know, Johnny."

"You're probably right."

"Are you going to kill my father?"

"No."

"Yes, you are. You're going to murder them all." A

titter eased free, thick with lust, like she wanted it done. "Send them to me."

Maybe he couldn't keep her sane in hell. Maybe he'd only driven her ghost out of its mind.

"My mother, Angie, quit sidetracking and tell me what she wants."

"She's finished with you, soldier boy. But I'm not."

He already knew that. She breathed against his ear, and he heard her mad desire there. The dark hair fell against him, floating in front of his mouth, stifling him with its heady scent, until he was nearly panting. He almost took his hands off the wheel. She moaned against his neck and he was hard and crazy and it didn't really matter a goddamn.

"I need you," she said.

"To do what?"

"Make things right."

He swung up the hill toward the Monti estate, gunning it hard, the Caddy's engine humming smoothly, rushing like his blood.

"We love you, Johnny. You're going to find that out."

It started to rain, and the water washed down the lengthy cobblestone driveway in heavy rivulets. There was a guardhouse at the front of the private gates to the estate, where he used to phone Vinny and ask him to come outside on summer days. Vinny would always say he had to stay in and practice, but every once in a while would sneak away, steal one of the patrol jeeps, and they'd go down to the beach.

Instead of Dane having to talk to someone or yell into a speaker, the gates opened as he approached. He drove right on up. Seemed like Phil Guerra was a welcomed guest.

Angelina drew closer, until he couldn't be sure where

she was anymore, on top of him or under him or sinking
farther inside. It got tiring trying to figure out which
ghosts you carried, and which ones carried you.

He pulled up to the Monticelli mansion. Looked
around for any overt action. Guns, goombas who'd read
The Valachi Papers too many times, with a bit too much
vino in them. Wanting to crack wise and throw down
with a machine gun. Or maybe they were all sleeping in
front of the television, empty plates in front of them on
the coffee table.

Dane cruised up to the door. Just a nice Italian boy
coming out for a visit. Maybe they were asking him in.

He parked, walked up to the door, and rang the bell.
Why not? Don Monti had manners, at least. Before he
did anything else, the man would want to talk. The
Monticellis liked to talk.

Georgie Delmare, the *consigliere,* met him at the door
bordered by two younger Monti thugs. He was surprised
to see Dane but hid it well. His chin stiffening only the
slightest bit. "Mr. Danetello. My, you certainly do come
seeking trouble, don't you?"

"Never my intention, Georgie, believe it or not."

"As Daniel told the lion. What do you want?"

"I think you know. Vinny here?"

"If he were, you'd very probably be dead by now."

"You popping off one-liners like the wiseguys now?
That was pretty good, I gotta admit. You gotta loosen
your shoulders a little though, you know? Work your
neck. Hey listen, there's this movie called *Under Heaven's
Canopy.* Watch for the scene with the chick with the
rocket launcher on the bridge. You can pick up a few
pointers."

One of the thugs glared at Dane, but the other had a
thousand-yard gaze going, probably thinking of Glory

Bishop and the look on her sweaty face when she pulled the trigger. *I'm gonna rock your world, baby!* A stupid grin started pushing his lips out of shape, but he caught himself in time and began glowering again.

Delmare stared at the Caddy, glowering, mouth open, then closing, then opening. "Isn't that Phil Guerra's Cadillac?"

"No, it's mine."

The tiniest change of expression, which in Georgie Delmare was pure shock. "Yours? But, no, I'm quite sure that it's—"

"Yeah, mine. Listen, I love gabbing with you, Georgie, but I want to see Don Pietro."

"That's quite impossible. Don't be ridiculous. Leave now and you might save your skin for a few days more. I suggest you leave the city immediately."

"The man taught me to play five-card draw when I was seven. I've had about five hundred meals here and attended every baptism, confirmation, and graduation in the family for the last two decades. Minus the last couple of years anyway. He'll talk to me."

"I don't think this is in your best interest."

Dane took a breath, feeling his impatience welling and about to break the surface. He'd always hated being edgy before, but now it felt kind of good. "You want to check out a real show of force?"

It perked up the legbreakers, who both sneered because they thought it was the thing to do. Dane wondered why no one bothered to teach them anything nowadays, content just to have muscle milling around without any purpose.

Delmare said, "You're a very foolish man, Mr. Danetello."

"Quit trying to sweet-talk me."

Stepping back, Delmare gestured for the thugs to

frisk Dane. They did a sloppy job of it, these mooks always afraid to touch a guy's groin or ass. You could smuggle a little palm-sized mini-Glock in your crotch and wipe six guys out without trying.

"If you won't listen to reason, Danetello, then enter. The Don is a very ill man. If he wishes to speak to you, he will. If not, you'll leave without any trouble. If there is trouble, I'll take matters into my own hands and abolish you as a problem for this family. Do I make myself absolutely clear?"

"Sure. Thanks, Georgie."

The *consigliere* led Dane through the foyer, the thugs strutting behind. They walked past glass cases and shelves containing Renaissance artwork, statuary, and shrines of Catholic significance. Family photos took up most of the remaining space on the shelves. Plenty of dour-faced people standing around frowning at the camera. Italians loved to show off the faces of their family.

"They always wore a lot of black," Dane said.

"Many of them have died violent deaths," Delmare told him. "Additionally, Catholics like to mourn."

"Don't I know it."

He was escorted into a broad living room that was dark with cherry paneling and burgundy carpeting, waves of rain slashing at the bay windows. More photographs abounded. A deep sense of anguished expectation spun in the air.

Don Pietro Monticelli still generated an overwhelming sense of power and confidence, even crippled in his chair, the years wearing into him like sandstorms cutting into rock. He had been one of the roughest, most intimidating bastards back in his prime. He sat smoking a thin European cigarette, fringed by Joey Fresco and Big Tommy Bartone, who were assembled on an uncomfortable-looking settee. Dane was a little shaken to see they were all drinking coffee and being chatty as the nuns of Our Lady of Blessed Mercy during a bake sale.

Delmare leaned down and whispered in the Don's ear. The old man waved his *consigliere* away and gestured for Dane to enter.

"John," the Don said.

"Hello, Don Pietro."

"You show great confidence inviting yourself into my home. Perhaps too much."

"I didn't invite myself in. I just rang the bell."

Dane stepped closer to the huge windows at the back of the room, watching as the streaming water battered the glass.

They all remained like that until Joey Fresco decided to tighten the tension and flex his attitude.

In the army, Dane had never learned to do as he was told and just make it easy on himself. He always spoke his mind and traveled in a straight line, and he didn't let an asshole officer's stripes keep him from saying his piece.

He felt acutely inadequate in the imagination department, and he knew what he was going to do now even though it was bound to cause a lot of problems all around.

Skinny Joey Fresco gave a grin. He put down his cup of coffee and a half-eaten anisette cookie and drew a pipsqueak .22. Dane almost burst out laughing. Joey used to go in for a .357 Magnum with a six-inch barrel, but it was a heavy piece of hardware and he hadn't needed that much firepower in a long time. So he'd gotten a touch soft and carried the much lighter snub-nosed Sentinel .22. It wouldn't stop a pissed off Sicilian with a couple of amarettos in him unless Joey walked right up and made a head shot.

"Joseph—" the Don said, waving Joey down.

"Please, Pietro, it's time."

That's right, beg to do Dane in, for the good of the world.

But it was all about being cool. That's why Joey carried the butterfly knife to clean his fingernails.

Now he put on the show and the two thugs followed suit, pulling their weapons. Each of them carried .44s. The Don appeared curious to see how things would play out, and Dane couldn't blame him for that.

Joey Fresco marched over, cocked the pistol, and pointed it at Dane's face. "So, how about this? How about if I give you a chance. Give me a reason not to blow you away right now."

"Here's one," Dane told him, and chopped the edge of his hand across Joey's throat.

The army had been all right for some things.

Joey flailed and Dane lightly plucked the .22 from his hand and put it in his belt. Delmare whispered, "Oh *dio mio,*" and Big Tommy let out a barking guffaw then finished his coffee.

The mood was warming up some. There was still a chance. The goombas liked to have their day broken up with a little activity like this from time to time. Joey was on his knees squeaking and choking, trying to suck in air.

"Put your weapon on the floor," one of the muscle boys said, both of them aiming their guns at Dane's chest.

"No."

"Do it."

"No."

"Now, or you're dead."

"Oh, you in charge?" Dane asked, hoping it would get under the Don's skin. You never really got away from the lessons you learned on the playground. The same petty insults worked now just like they did when you were seven.

Easing out a stream of smoke, Don Monti lifted his chin. He had the old-world slickness, the kind of unshakable aplomb that never revealed what was going on in his head.

Midsixties, slicked-back hair that drew up cruelly from a widow's peak, with sharply angular, craggy features showing great command and control. A widower for about ten years now, but he still wore his wedding ring. He had those nearly worthless legs crossed, hands cupped over his knee except when he raised the cigarette to take a slow drag. Smoke wreathed him like the offshore mists of Sicily.

Joey finally made it to his knees and Big Tommy and the others were helping him up, getting him into a chair. Delmare's lips were so flat and bloodless that his mouth looked like a paper cut.

The Don didn't appear to notice anyone but Dane. He asked, "How is Lucia?"

"She has bad dreams."

"We all do, and they grow worse as we age. Are you here to speak with me or my son?"

"I'm here to talk to the Don."

That left it in the air. Let the old man decide if he was the boss or not.

"I'm listening," Don Pietro Monticelli said. "Come sit with me over here. We won't be disturbed." As he spoke he gave the eye to his boys, who all backed off to the other side of the room, dragging Joey with them.

Dane sat in a Queen Anne wing chair without cushions, thinking about how sitting on furniture like this most of his life probably helped to cripple the Don. Dane shifted back and forth, sort of sliding around. Somebody had been at the cherrywood with an abundance of polish.

He couldn't keep himself from scanning the place, looking for Maria. His side still hurt from JoJo's prodding.

"Your house isn't in order," Dane said.

"You take too much for granted, John."

"No, I don't think I do."

"I once treated you like one of my own sons, here in this very home you affront. Even though you were a *cafone.*"

The Don putting Dane in his place, calling him a peasant. "You taught me how to play poker."

"Yes, I remember that. You had a natural talent for bluffing."

Dane said, "And for calling bluffs as well."

The Don tried to sit up straighter, but it didn't really work. Some of the old fire seemed to be trying to catch inside him. "Make no mistake. Despite the foolish bluster of too many of my men recently, what deeds need doing shall be done. Without hesitation, or remorse. This has always been my way."

"You also taught me how to shoot a gun."

Don Pietro nodded, smiling sadly but without much emotion in his eyes. "I thought you might be a police officer like your father. Or that you would have joined our business here, at some level, perhaps even as a trusted advisor. I never believed you'd . . . show so little interest in either of these ways of life."

"That was a very delicate way of telling me I'm a failure."

"Not so. Simply that you've chosen your own way

through the world. One I've never quite expected or understood."

"You and me both."

It made the Don chuckle under his breath. A few years back that would've been a sign that things were going to become ugly soon, but Dane just didn't get that feeling.

He wondered if the old man knew about Berto's predilections, and if they mattered to him at all. There was a time that something like that would've brought the ax down no matter who you were. If you were a made guy, if you were the big boss's son, that would only make it worse. You played around under the bridge with a pre-op tranny named Lulu, with 38D hooters and a seven inch pecker, and they'd find you floating in Sheepshead Bay with your nuts up your nose.

"What did you do in the military?"

"Wasted time mostly."

"And so you didn't learn any skills?"

"I was too busy being pissed off most of the time."

"Why is that, do you suppose, John?"

Smoke circled the Don, and the acrid, exotic stink hit Dane all at once. The man wasn't smoking a European cigarette after all. He was toking high-quality Colombian Gold.

"I didn't like always being told what to do."

"All that time in the army and you left with so little."

"I picked up a few things here and there."

The disappointment shone in the Don's eyes. He'd been thinking that maybe Dane had been a sniper, had learned how to plant bombs. Something he could put to use. Don Pietro was the type of guy who kept lists around, everything from the bookie accounts to Cayman bank numbers to anybody who'd ever crossed him up. Or maybe that had only been back in the day. The joint seemed to be doing its job. The man looked mellow.

"Your grandmother...Lucia...I see her sometimes, walking to the bingo parlor."

"Yes."

"A beautiful woman. She still cooks much?"

"Yes."

The hell was going on? Like this was a normal reunion where you play catch-up on all the silly trivia. Across the room the shooters were back to drinking coffee and eating their snacks, except for Joey Fresco, who fumed and sat hunched over, rubbing his throat.

It was time.

Dane stared the Don in the eye. "Do you hold me responsible for your daughter Angie's death?"

"Angelina, my Angelina," Don Monti said, and the grief was a barb that kept catching his tongue. He paused, evaluating his words. "She—she was too impetuous, my Angelina. Full of life but drawn to fire. I could not control her, nor did I make enough of an effort to do so." He drew another deep lungful. "Even her brothers were ineffective, as were the men assigned to safeguard her. I blame no one but myself for the troubles she endured. For the pain she brought to herself, and to this house."

Dane looked at the old man, sitting there stoned and in pain, those crooked legs hanging at such odd angles. When Dane was a kid he'd feared the Don the way he'd feared his father, the way he'd feared God. With a mixture of terror and pride.

"No," Don Pietro said, working the joint like it might be his last. "I do not hold you responsible."

"Then why don't you call Vinny off?"

"He would never hurt you. No, never. What he does, he does for *rispetto*."

"I don't understand," Dane said.

"You will see the truth, I think. One day soon. If you are strong and patient. I only hope you are worthy."

Maybe the weed had been spiked with some acid. Dane checked his watch. It was almost six. "I've got to go now."

The Don clasped his hand weakly and said, "Thank you for visiting. I enjoyed our talk."

The old man might not be senile, but whatever had once made him the big boss was gone. It wasn't a ploy. All the edgy madness and will to violence had drained away until there was somebody sitting in the chair who Dane didn't completely recognize anymore.

As Dane moved across the room, Joey reached out and said, "You listen to me, I want to say somethin' here, no matter what, you and me, if it's the last—" and Dane chopped him in the throat again. Joey gagged and fell to his knees, and Big Tommy barked again.

Out in the rain Dane walked to Phil Guerra's stolen car and stared at how brilliant the shimmering water on the Magi-laquer appeared. As if this was a giant piece of deep blue ice brought up from a thousand feet below the Arctic cap, frozen 10 million years ago.

He got in and started the engine, easing down the drive and back into the streets of Headstone City. He reached for his cigarettes and the nausea rushed through his belly.

Here it comes, he'd been expecting it. Vinny couldn't pass up a meeting like this.

Dane's scars began to heat. He tried to beat the sickness back but that only made it worse, and he rolled down his window fast in case he had to heave. He stuck his face into the wind like a dog.

At the next light he fell back against the seat and suddenly Vinny was in the car, holding his lighter out. In some other reality he'd picked Vinny up and they were riding together, and now Vinny was imposing that track onto this world.

Dane leaned in, puffed, and took a long drag. He grinned and said, "This the rainy day you were talking about?" but by the time the smoke rose to break against the crags of Vinny's disfigured face, he was already gone.

TWENTY-ONE

Such fierce laughter could only come from a precipice in the ugliest corner of the abyss. A sound set in the unbreakable amber of madness, hurling itself across the room into Dane's face.

He'd just stepped into Olympic Cab & Limo after dropping off a Japanese family of six out in Montauk, and that noise hit him so brutally wrong that he almost backed out again. It was the kind of highly contagious sickness that could be carried on the breeze. You started thinking mass infection. Germ warfare.

Eager eyes on him, Fran continued laughing for another few seconds before it ended like a whip crack. "You were specially requested for a pickup tonight."

Word had been getting around town about some of his exploits—the run through the hospital, the stolen Caddy. Fran sat there at the counter listening to the buzz across the radio, all the small, dangerous talk that circulated through Headstone City. Someone he didn't know was on there saying how Johnny Danetello wasn't long for this earth. The death pool had over five hundred bucks in it, and nobody had picked a day past November 4. They had started cutting up the boxes into morning, noon, and night.

"By who?" he asked.

"Your personality."

"My what?"

"Your personality. Your celebrity." Those teeth had a yellow shine to them that reminded him of gold rum.

"When?"

"Eight o'clock. Pepe wants to talk to you first."

Her callous voice came at him in a color now, the edges of his vision lighting up from one red instant to the next. He couldn't figure out what she'd gone through in her life to make her sound like that. He stared at her for another second, speculating what it might have been, and she said, "Stop fucking looking at me like that."

"Okay."

"You don't charm me."

"I realize that."

"I don't think you do."

"No, really, Franny, I do."

She had her hand under the counter again, grabbing hold of the nine iron. He leaned forward, kind of daring her, wishing she'd make a go of it. Maybe all she needed was to give him one good crack across the head, then they could settle into being amiable coworkers. "I'm waiting for the day you're found floating in the surf," she told him.

"I know; I'm just wondering why you hate me so much."

"Because you deserve it."

She believed it so honestly, with such affirmation, that

it almost made him believe it too. That he had done something so terrible in his life he should never be forgiven for it.

"What box did you pick in the pool?"

"Tomorrow. Do me a favor and drop dead, will you?" She stuck a toothpick in her mouth and started champing it to shavings. "At noon."

"Where's Pepe?"

"I don't know, but if you find him, tell him to get his ass back in here. Like I don't have enough to do, I have to cover his job too."

Dane went around to the garage parking lot and saw Pepe mixing it up with two enormous thugs.

For a guy weighing only about 120, Pepe was handling himself pretty well. He was fast and knew how to throw a punch, duck and weave and work from the outside.

It was a cold day but Pepe wore only a sleeveless T-shirt, his muscles corded and perfectly defined as he backpedaled and rope-a-doped, slugging each of the mooks in the chin with a one-two punch. A couple of quick raps, shoulders loose, then skipping back out of the way as they lunged.

Dane wasn't sure if he should get involved yet, because Pepe was smiling and having such a good time. He skipped around the parking lot like he was back in the ring.

Dane recognized one of the wiseguys from the Don's yesterday and the other from Chooch's when he'd shot the other asshole in the leg. There was a time when all the Monti family members had been made guys, top lieutenants who'd worked their way up the ranks pulling big heists nobody could pin on them. Now all these no-name slabs of meat.

He called out, "Need help?"

"You trying to insult me?" Pepe said, moving like he was listening to a nice salsa beat.

"I was asking them."

The thugs were trying to prance away without looking like they were running. They each had a bloody nose and a split lip and the beginnings of a shiner. The punk from the Don's looked at Dane and said, "You!"

"Me."

"I've got orders to pulp your ass!"

"Watch for the hook," Dane told him just as Pepe's left fist connected with the point of the prick's chin. It really was beautiful to watch, the supple way Pepe moved in and out and around with the quality of ballet. The thug's eyes started to roll and Pepe shifted and caught the other legbreaker with a right cross that threw the punk backwards like he'd been shot. Both Monti boys fell together in a heap, mostly unconscious and breathing shallowly, blood bubbling over their faces.

"They're not even as tough as the guy who came around last time," Pepe said.

"That one's name is Joey Fresco, and he's not even as tough as he used to be a few years ago."

"They got legit and they got soft."

"These two tell you the same spiel? It'd be in your best interest to do a favor for the Monti crew?"

"Yeah, but without the subtlety of that guy Joey shaving with his butterfly knife. These pricks, they just came right out with it, said they wanted me to fire you. If they were going to make a play, I thought they would've pulled it weeks ago, carrying some real firepower."

"Me too," Dane said. "I paid the Don a visit yesterday. It must've pushed a few buttons."

"Not any serious ones. They didn't even draw down

on me." His hands kept working in the air as he talked, like he still wanted to throw punches.

In the corner of the lot sat a maroon LeSabre with the passenger door ajar. "This their car?"

"Yeah, they pulled in while I was catching a smoke and just started staring me down. When that didn't work they called me spic, like I might break down and weep out of shame for my family heritage. They threaten to beat up some of the other drivers, but the guys just ignore them. Then this one here actually shoves me." Pepe grinned telling the story, his small hands moving in the air. "It was like junior high school all over again. I think they were working their way up to stealing my lunch box or giving me noogies. What the hell happened to the real wiseguys?"

"I don't know," Dane said. He frisked both the mooks and they weren't even carrying guns.

"Nothing?" Pepe asked.

"No. He had a pistol yesterday. Maybe they're scared of getting pulled over by the cops and found carrying."

"Does the Don know he's hiring such pathetic examples of la cosa nostra?"

"You know, I've got a feeling he does. But he's so sick and crippled that he smokes a lot of weed to help him with the pain."

"Really? Like any punk on the corner. That's sort of sad, ending up like that."

"I have to agree."

They wrestled the two legbreakers back onto their feet and helped them over to the LeSabre. Dane got the driver in and said, "Listen, tell Berto and Vinny to relax, I'm quitting Olympic. Oh no, my life is in tatters, how will I survive? The terror, the horror. Hey, watch your head now," and carefully closed the door. Pepe tapped the roof and the car pulled out.

"I have mixed feelings about all that," Pepe told him, still bouncing on his feet like he wanted to go another few rounds. "I kind of miss the old neighborhood, you know?"

"Yeah."

"A man is defined by the strength of his enemies."

Dane looked at him. "You quoting *The Art of War* now or what?"

"It's a line from *Under Heaven's Canopy*. One of those terrorists in the caves says it."

"I fast-forwarded through a lot of that."

"So did I the first twenty times, but then I finally let it roll."

Dane glanced over at the limousine in the garage, the back bumper all banged out and polished up again after the fracas with Big Tommy, and he felt a twinge of regret. He'd miss working on it. "I'll quit tomorrow, okay?"

"You don't have to leave on account of those mooks. Stick around if you want. Besides, didn't you want to build a stake?"

"Like you said, what do I need money for? Besides, something's happening."

Pepe gave him that long once-over. "What do you mean?"

"I'm not sure. Things are just coming into focus a little better."

Pepe made the same face again, but not nosy enough to ask if Dane had any kind of a plan in mind.

"What time does Glory Bishop want to be picked up?"

"What, you need an invitation from her now? Just go. Drop the limo off tonight or early tomorrow. Maybe I'll send Fran on the Montauk run from now on. She could use a little ocean air."

"By the way," Dane said, "I think she's insane."

"I've had some worries about that, but she's pretty stable most of the time. Like I told you, she's mostly a sweetheart, but she's got a fine-tuned instinct for criminal-type activity, you know? The action boiling behind the scenes."

"But she didn't know you were out here brawling with two mob dumbasses."

"I think she knew, she just didn't care much. She figured I could handle it." A worried expression crossed his face. "She doesn't get rattled most of the time. Except by you. You shake her up worse than anyone."

"Why?" Dane asked.

"She said you give her nightmares."

"Me?"

"She told me she dreamed of your eyes before she ever met you."

Tension tightened the muscles in Dane's back. "Jesus."

"Hey, I'm just explaining what she said."

Dane thought about it, wondering if Fran might have a touch of the burden herself. What Special Agent Daniel Ezekiel Cogan's blessed granny would've called special consideration under the Lord.

"I'll see you tomorrow," Dane told him. "Sorry for the trouble."

"No trouble at all, man, I had fun."

Dane climbed into the limo and went the slow way to Glory Bishop's place, hoping the extra time would help him to put everything into perspective. He cruised from Flatbush Avenue to Parkside, hitting the next round-about to Ocean Parkway, into the Prospect Expressway, merging onto the BQE, the flow of the cars around him always more consoling than being surrounded by people.

He slid into the Brooklyn Bridge traffic, another component of the burg, no different than any piece of stone or iron. Slowly he hiked from Greenwich Village to the Upper East Side, working his way through rush hour, enjoying the flux and drift.

Here he was doing nothing but killing time, even though it felt as if he didn't have that much time left.

A miserable whisper from the backseat made him look in the rearview. It was Aaron Fielding again, the grocer and fish seller, sitting back there whimpering. Dane wished he could hear the man's booming laugh just one more time, instead of all this sniveling.

Dane met the man's eyes in the mirror, and saw him raise an ashen, quivering hand, trying to clutch at Dane's shoulder. "Johnny, I need to—"

"What, Mr. Fielding? I'm listening."

"Johnny!"

"Tell me. I'll help if I can. I promise."

"I . . . I swear that I—"

What kind of confession was so important it would keep someone trapped in jail with you, in the cemetery with you, in the backseat?

"I never burned the fillet!"

The despair finally lifted clear of the old man, and Fielding threw his head back and smiled. A heavy, joyful laughter broke from him, resounding and pure, deepening and echoing beyond the confines of the car until the sound of his own deliverance carried him away.

Did you bring all your petty fears and worries with you right into the grave? Did they keep you awake during the long night of your interment? Were you compelled to confess and apologize and justify throughout the here-after?

A weak man became a martyr in his own mind. Did you do the same thing when you were underground?

The poor bastard, spinning in his coffin because every Friday afternoon Grandma Lucia would send Dane down to Fielding's market for the same order, memorized word for word. "Gimme two portions of shrimp, two of pota-toes, three fillets and don't burn them." A small joke preying on a corpse's conscience, even way down in the box.

Whatever the answer, Dane knew one thing now. The dead didn't have a sense of humor.

He pulled up to Glory Bishop's building and Special Agent Cogan was standing outside eating a *cannoli*, ri-cotta cheese on his tie. He grinned and approached.

TWENTY-TWO

Once, back when you were still driving a cab, you saw two guys beating a police officer in an alley with his own nightstick.

The cop scrambled on all fours trying to fight back, but they started kicking him until he rolled himself into a ball, his face to the brick.

Dane gunned it to the mouth of the alley, threw the taxi into park, and hopped out with the engine still screaming. He took his civic duty seriously, most of the time. What the fuck. The cop scuttled under the front end of the cab, and the two guys turned to face Dane, the one with the nightstick raised above his head, and the other picking up the vials of crack he'd dropped.

If you stared straight ahead long enough, they'd take it as a sign of fear and attack. The guy with the nightstick charged, bringing the club down, giving a warrior's bellow, and doing this little twirly jump he'd seen some stuntman do in a movie once.

Dane caught him by the throat with one hand and broke his nose with two short chops. The nightstick started to drop and Dane grabbed it in midair. A silly macho gesture because he didn't even need it, but it was kind of a cool move. This dumbass fell to his knees, clutching his face and sobbing. The other was still rooting around in the trash on the ground, picking up his drugs. Dane kicked out and felt the hinge of the mook's jaw shatter. Teeth collapsed against each other and his tongue slithered loose as if the muscles had been cut.

It was enough. The cop had blood on the back of his head and kept muttering, "Motherfuckers. Those rotten motherfuckers."

Dane leaned down and took his hand. He could not feel it. The cop was his father.

He didn't know what it meant. The man's ghost wandering around, talking to him finally? Or had Vinny's abilities somehow infected him, allowed him to warp things, tread another track, maybe even back in time? Or was he finally dead? Dane waited for Dad to speak. That same cold expectation he'd felt so many times before.

Without touching him, he helped his father into the back of the cab. His dad looked the way he had on the ten o'clock news the day of his murder. Not tough at all. Sort of soft, maybe a tad too nice for the job.

"I'll take you to the hospital," Dane said, knowing how stupid it sounded. The plates in his skull were vibrating.

"No, I'll be okay," his father told him, and said nothing more.

Blood dripped through the man's hair and soaked into his uniform shirt collar. His aftershave wafted through the taxi and made Dane grimace, thinking about his teenage years, when he used to splash on his father's remaining skin bracer while he learned to shave.

He drove his father home to Grandma Lucia's house. He led him up the front stairs and rang the bell. He hung back for a moment. His dead mother answered and gave a terrified cry. His father shushed her and said, "I'm all right, it's nothing. Let me get cleaned up and I'll walk to the station."

Dane thought that perhaps he'd been murdered himself, shot in the head, and was sitting around in limbo. He ran his fingers through his hair feeling for bullet wounds. There weren't any, and he stared at the closed door to his grandmother's house, where he lived, before he turned back to his cab.

He had slept in the backseat for two nights after that, and when he finally went home again, his grandmother slapped the crap out of him for not calling.

Dane was starting to feel like that again. Stuck in purgatory, waiting for the hand of God to reach down and smack him around.

Daniel Ezekiel Cogan walked over to the limo and asked, "You doin' okay there, son?"

"Sure."

Maybe it proved Cogan was wired into Olympic somehow, or maybe Fran was just telling everybody where Dane would be, at what time, hoping somebody would take him out when he got there.

Or perhaps Cogan really had managed to lie during his night ride and the feds did have Glory Bishop's place tapped. It put some tension between Dane's shoulders, all those possibilities.

"You waiting for me?" Dane asked.

"I thought we could talk together some more."

"Get in," Dane said, and Cogan did, impressed with the dashboard like he'd never been in a limousine before. "Where'd you get the *cannoli*?"

"A place called Warm & Wonderful up on 65th. I had one there in the place and I've been carrying this other one around for a while. I had the hankerin', you know? But these here aren't nearly as good as the ones from that Brooklyn bakery though."

"That shop is mostly bagels and whitefish. I'm probably the only Italian within a fifteen-block radius."

"Tha' right?"

You had to take your pride where you could. "What would you like to chat about?"

"Heard there was a little shake-up over at the Monticelli place."

Dane still couldn't figure where Cogan was tied in or what he wanted. Going after a mob family who'd lost all their juice seemed a big waste of time for the feds. Didn't anybody have anything better to do?

"I wouldn't call it much of a shake-up. I just stopped in to say hello."

"In your daddy's ex-partner's stolen vehicle."

"I was only borrowing it."

"He filled out a report."

"He got the car back, didn't he?"

"You put almost three thousand miles on it. Where the hell'd you go?"

"Nowhere," Dane admitted. "I just drove it around for a while."

"Like my cousin Cooter after the moonshine dried up."

That windblown, choppy hair hung at all kinds of crazy, clumped angles. The corners of his mouth were thick with chocolate. When he let out his weird, wide

smile, with those thick square teeth, he looked a little re-
tarded. Dane knew Cogan was affecting the bumpkin
appearance, but he'd never seen anyone go to such ex-
tremes before, just so folks would underestimate him.

"When you were in the pen, I almost paid you a visit."

Dane said, "I know. Why'd you want to, and why
didn't you bother?"

Cogan took another bite out of his half-eaten *cannoli*
but wasn't much enjoying himself. That Warm & Wonderful Café catered to the neighborhood wealthy, the su-
permodels and celebrities whose daily caloric intake never
broke five hundred. The café probably used skim milk and
a sugar substitute.

"I was thinking of cutting you some kind of a deal,"
Cogan told him. "Protection if you helped us take down
the crew."

"My grandmother could take down that crew. What
stopped you from making the offer?"

"I read through your file. It looked like you could
handle yourself all right. Like you said, they're not so
plucky anymore. I wanted to see what would happen
when you got out."

"Nothing's happened."

"That itself is the puzzle."

Dane had met a lot of cops—including his father and
Phil Guerra—who knew how to shoot the breeze and pa-
tiently chat with perps for weeks or even months before
making a bust.

But looking into Cogan's eyes, Dane couldn't get any
sense of what the man was after, except that he hadn't
come close to getting it yet. Even the night ride hadn't
given Dane much information, Cogan's soul just sitting
in the backseat bouncing around.

On the surface of things, Cogan certainly wasn't making great strides.

"What'd you go see the old Don for?"

"I wanted to say hello," Dane said. "It had been a while since I'd seen him."

"And your pal Vinny wasn't there."

"No."

"That's what's so surprisin' to me. How little you and Vinny been in the same place since you got out. So little interaction. You Mediterranean types run too hot or not at all. I would've thought you'd have walked right up to each other and started shootin' it out in the streets. But that's just not the way."

"No," Dane said.

"And nobody else has taken a run at you?"

Either Cogan wasn't as wired as it seemed, and he hadn't heard about Big Tommy Bartone and the chase through the hospital, or he was faking it. Testing Dane's honesty? Seeing how much Dane might be holding back?

You could make yourself nuts trying to second-guess every son of a bitch who got in your face. Dane figured telling the truth was always the best course, and it fucked the other guy up just as much as if you lied to him all the time.

"Big Tommy Bartone made a dash at me the other day. Sort of a half-assed one."

"Now, I did some checking on him too. He don't appear to be the sloppy type."

"He's not. At least he never used to be."

"Maybe he likes you too much to take you out of the game."

"I keep hoping someone will appreciate my charm."

"I wouldn't wait on that, son."

Special Agent Daniel Ezekiel Cogan, with pastry crumbs on his specially cut jacket, stepped out of the limo, the burden weighing on him, his gaze kind of shimmering with crucial knowledge, and said, "I enjoy our talks. I'll see you soon."

"Okay."

Dane watched him walk down the block and turn the corner before he got out of the car to go up and see Glory Bishop.

The doorman was back to making faces. Dane felt himself losing ground.

The elevator carried him too slowly to the fourth floor. Behind him he could feel two figures slumping against each other, not quite across the veil yet. Mako and Kremitz, in their comas, coming around again. They were both hanging on. Drawn to him as the source of their anguish, but not dead enough to prod him much.

The doors slid open and Dane stepped out, Mako and Kremitz shuffling along, their eyes closed.

They nudged forward just enough to annoy him, almost like they were trying to cockblock him, racing him down the hall. Dane started to say something but Glory's apartment door was already open, her shadow slanting across the carpet.

She waited there wearing a gaping crimson kimono, nothing beneath but a gold silk nightgown that tied at the shoulders and hips with cute little bows.

"Come in," she said, taking his hand. "Make yourself a drink."

"I don't drink on the job."

"You're not on the job, we're not going anywhere, if you couldn't tell."

That stopped him. "Why'd you book the limo then?"

"Maybe so you'd show up?"

Dane frowned, but moved to her. "What made you think I wouldn't show up if you just called me?"

"You never gave me your phone number," Glory said. Wary and cool, but with an edge to her.

She kissed him, and there was passion in it. He reminded himself she was an actress, and women could fake this kind of thing even without any training. She murmured against his tongue and broke away.

A stack of scripts lay spread out on the glass-topped coffee table in the living room, positioned in a way that made Dane think they'd been cleverly placed for appearance's sake. An electrical paranoia swept through his gut, and he really didn't know what to do about it. He turned and she said, "You look upset."

"I thought we might be going to another premiere or a fancy party."

"Would you want to attend one?"

"No," he told her.

"I'm not following you then. If you didn't want to go anyway, then why complain?" She smiled in a way meant to disarm him, but it only made him tighten up more. He couldn't get over the feeling that he was being watched, that there was somebody else here who wasn't dead.

"It's my last night," he said. "Working for the limousine service."

"What? Why?"

"I quit."

"You got another job?" she asked.

"No."

Probing now, her eyebrows arched into those inverted

Vs that only an angry woman can really do well. "You're not going back to stealing cars, are you?"

"No. Well, I don't intend to boost anymore. Not after the one I grabbed yesterday, I mean."

Shaking her head like she couldn't believe it. "So you have started stealing cars."

"Just the one."

"The cops might not look too fondly on that."

"I stole it from a cop. An ex-cop, actually. And I really don't give a shit how he looks on it."

"Is that why you seem so wired?"

He started toward the bar and then stopped. Liquor would only make things worse. "I feel it too. Sorry."

"Something the matter? Besides quitting the job and jacking a car, I mean."

"It wasn't much of a jack, and I brought it back a couple hours later."

"Police after you?"

"Nah."

She touched his shoulders and got his coat off. "You really have terrible taste in ties."

"I thought it was distinguished."

"Maybe for 1956."

"That's the look I was going for."

"Consider it a success then." She unknotted it and tossed it on the floor, undid the first couple buttons of his shirt, pressed her cheek to his chest, and took a deep breath. He brushed her hair back and kissed her again.

"Lie down on the couch," she told him, and he did. He liked the way she put a roughness in her voice, expecting no back talk. But focusing completely on him as she took his shoes off, shoved the sceenplays aside, got his feet on the table, and rubbed them for a while.

"Put a kimono on you and you get all geisha," he said.

"It's a side of my personality that doesn't come out much."

"I bet." One of the scripts had flipped onto the couch. He reached down and flipped through a few pages. *The Seven Angry Daughters of Valentino.*

"What do you think?" she asked.

"The title doesn't resonate."

He shut his eyes while Glory Bishop's hands worked over him, knowing he should be very happy here with her, but still finding himself thinking of Maria Monticelli. You couldn't restrain your brain, no matter who said you could. He opened his eyes and stared at the side of Glory's face as she unbuttoned his shirt farther and started to undo his pants.

She said, "Why are you looking at me like that?"

"Like what?"

"As if you don't know who I am."

You could hide some things, but never those of consequence. Dane grinned and pulled her closer and held on for a second like this moment truly mattered. Which it did, but maybe not enough. She let the kimono slide off her shoulders and she dropped on top of him, both of them keeping their eyes open while they kissed.

Somehow it made him angry and they began to struggle together, riding the wave of tension, as he pulled out those little bows on her nightie and grabbed her all over, squeezing hard. She moaned, and the noise didn't sound right. He shifted so he was on top of her on the couch and realized it was himself groaning, sounding weak.

Dane tasted blood. She was biting his lips and it hurt

like fuck, but he responded in kind as her nails raked over him. The best thing about sex is you could put all your hate where your love ought to be and still get away with it.

Afterward, unsated but more relaxed, they ordered Chinese food, drank a little too much, and had another go-round with much better results. He held her, stroking her thighs, as she nodded off.

If he could sleep, he might get over this caged feeling. It would probably be gone in the morning. He shut his eyes and slid his mouth against the muscular grooves of her back, but he could still taste blood under his tongue.

While she softly snored he searched the dressers and closets but found nothing out of the ordinary. He didn't know much about bugs but he checked out the places they were most likely to be hidden, the lamps and electrical outlets.

He sat down in the sex swing for a while and decided the thing was stupid enough when two people were in it, but when you were alone it was just pitiful.

Somebody knocking on the metal door from the other side of his skull.

He moved back to the sunken living room and sat on the edge of the couch, tired all of a sudden. Working against your own apathy took a lot of energy. He toyed with Glory's hair for a few minutes as she cooed in her sleep. He shifted slightly and spotted her cell phone on the far side of the coffee table, nearly hidden by the strewn screenplays.

It was open.

He picked it up and saw the tiny screen bright with his own face.

Jesus, she really didn't have much shame. A pole scene

in an action flick is one thing, but Christ, giving somebody else a show of her and Dane in bed really pissed
him off.

He held the phone up and stared at it. A surge of relief
went through him because, finally, the show was coming
together.

He whispered, "That you, Daniel Ezekiel?"

"Hellfire, son," the cell phone said. "You got me."

TWENTY-THREE

Look at this.

The boy with the sick brain leaning over in the corner and hiding his face, but holding his arm out to Dane like he wanted to be hugged.

The kid had tears on his cheeks and dried blood clotting the sutures thatching his shaved head. His hospital jammies were open. Bedsores spotted his back, covered with a thick salve that was stinking up the place.

Below him, crouched but staring wide-eyed, Dane's mother had her forehead pressed to the boy's leg, closer to him now than she'd ever been to her own son.

Well, all right, some things you have to get used to. Dark circles rimmed her eyes and her lips were thick with yellow froth. Dane almost fell over backwards but managed to stay on his feet.

She raised her chin and her mouth moved. He got a very strong sense that she did not wish him to approach. That would disturb the moment, the dynamics of this new bond they'd made in death. Him, his ma, and the ill child.

Dane wondered, thinking if he mapped his scars and those of the boy, how they'd line up. If they would connect and continue into a larger diagram, some kind of chart showing the measured slopes and ranges of their shared pain.

Stick them up close to each other, pressed cheek to cheek, temple to temple, and you could read the jagged routes of this brotherhood of head wounds.

He could feel his ma, struggling but feeble, trying to speak and growing frustrated with her lack of voice. She crept aside, head low as if she couldn't lift it. He looked at her hand where he'd rubbed his thumb over her flesh for hours, unable to stop, ill with that endless rhythm, and saw he'd left an impression there like a burn. Perhaps it was a sign of his love.

Dane let himself relax, pressing his envy as far to the side as he could. Maybe it would be enough, but it didn't seem possible anymore.

This new son of his mother continued to weep, shaking his head, still reaching out for something more. A family of deceased might not be enough for a lonely kid. Or for anyone. A tic in his cheek started up and quickly crawled across his face.

Ma, seated on the floor now with her knees drawn up, peered at him with misery and resentment. Dane wondered where the anger had come from, since she'd shown so little of it in life. Did the dead keep count of your mistakes? Did they catalog your sins? Indexed and cross-referenced, numbered in order of greatest transgressions. There, feel the heft of your faults and failures and crimes.

His mommy, what had he ever done to make her give him the eye like that?

The kid's muscles slowly loosened as he sank down to sit beside Ma. The thrum of Dane's pulse grew steadily more distant. The boy with the sick brain took a step forward. Ma opened her mouth to speak.

"Come on by, Daniel Ezekiel," Dane said, and shut the cell phone.

Glory Bishop was working with the feds. She'd probably helped them to corner her own husband and throw the net over him.

He turned around and she was sitting there naked, holding a Beretta Jaguar .22 loosely in her hand. All these people and their teeny guns they could hide anywhere. She must've had the gun clipped under the couch or stuffed between the cushions.

"You really think you need that roscoe with me?" he asked.

It made her grin with a little warmth, but not much. "No."

"You got something you want to tell me?"

"I'd like for you to put your .38 over on the table there."

"I didn't bring it with me."

For a second it looked like Glory might want to check his pile of clothes, forgetting that she'd taken them off him in the first place. "Was it really necessary to send him the whole show?"

"I didn't. You fell asleep for a while."

"C'mon."

"For a couple of minutes, Johnny. You've done it before, you just don't realize it. You talk in your sleep."

And Cogan thought he might say something interesting. "So you're partnered with the feds. To do what exactly?"

"Deal with the Monticelli drugs filtering into Holly-wood."

Jesus, back to that. "To help your husband get off easy?"

"I don't give a damn about that bastard. He lied and he used me. I'm trying to keep myself out of trouble and keep hold of some assets."

"How much trafficking money we talking about?"

"About two hundred grand a year."

When you broke it down that was less than twenty g's a month and hardly seemed worth the effort on any-body's part. More cash was changing hands on the corner of South Third and Hughes during the week, a block and a half from the 90th Precinct.

More likely this was really about the gunrunning coming up from south of the border. One of the serious revolutionary countries where the poppy fields took up half the nation. Guns, drugs, feds, and rebellion. It was the fed part that had fouled the equation. If Cogan had been CIA, then a banana republic government takeover would've been the first thing Dane had thought of. Well, maybe.

Glory Bishop was much sharper in some ways than he'd given her credit for, and a lot more naive too. This next scene was going to be a pretty ugly one.

He sat and tried not to glare at her, but he couldn't help feeling a touch betrayed. Somehow he'd grown to care enough about her to form expectations. She wrapped the kimono around herself and Dane asked, "You mind if I get dressed?"

"No, of course not."

Who would think that such a small thing as a .22 could ruin the mood? When events calmed down, he might have to ponder this one a little longer. But as it was, he'd barely zipped up his fly when Cogan walked in.

"Does that doorman give you dirty looks too?" Dane asked, continuing to dress.

"Naw, I'm on the lease."

"You the one that put up that goddamn swing?"

Glory had said the apartment didn't come from drug money. Couldn't fault her for telling the truth, when she did. So the place wasn't really bugged. Not technically. But Glory was in contact with Cogan, both of them keeping their eyes on Dane. But for what purpose?

"So it's not about the drugs. Or the movies. It's the guns."

"Yep," Cogan told him, no longer grinning. His hair combed. Everything in the open now. Two buddies who finally had all the bullshit out of the way and could lay it on the table.

Glory Bishop said, "Guns? What guns?" Feisty, but with a little girl air about her. Cogan came over and plucked the Beretta out of her hand, more daddy than boss or lover. "What are you two talking about?"

Dane finished dressing and sat on the other end of the couch from where he and Glory had gotten their final groove on. "Only in relation to a revolution."

"Tha's right."

"Which country?"

"Some Central America shithole I have a hard time pronouncin'."

Glory just kept standing there. "What•the hell are you both talking about?" Not even all that flustered. She'd always known something else was going on, and like Dane, she'd just gone with the flow, hoping everything would be revealed in the end.

"Start a war or stop one?" Dane asked.

"Tell you the truth, son, I'm not sure. That's for the fellas well above me. I'm just doing my job."

"I thought that sort of thing was the CIA's turf."

"It mostly is, but I suspect the Bureau is expanding. Interagency cooperation and like that."

"Oh holy shit," Glory said, cinching the kimono tighter around her waist, looking on the floor for her panties now, talking rapidly. "You motherfucker, Cogan, you rotten motherfucker. Jesus, when my husband was on trial, the things you said. All those threats you made . . . so determined to ruin my life, you fucker. You said you'd—"

"I said a lot of things, darlin', every one of them true. I needed your help, and I did what I had to do to get it."

"Motherfucker!"

"Why'd this guy take a fall in the first place?" Dane asked.

"He wasn't ambitious enough," Cogan explained. "He got sloppy. He wanted out of the deal, but we needed him. His company, the way the cash was cleaned, the way the weapons came on up out of Southern California. His contacts, the distribution, everything. But he kept trying to shut it down and pull out."

"He wanted to go clean and you wouldn't let him."

Noting the judgmental tone but ignoring it, Cogan said, "I told him to just keep on playin' ball, but he had to buck me. What makes a man do that, thwart his own government? He was a damn fool, and a traitor to boot, if you want to put a point on it. I figured Glory would step up when he went down."

"Rotten motherfucker!"

"So what do you want from me?" Dane asked.

"I want you to convince your friend Vincenzo Monticelli to help out his sister's career even more."

It started snapping into place then. "You want a new front man. Vinny Monticelli to take over where this guy left off. Grease the production company's wheels, that it? Smuggle the drugs and guns, keep putting the clean money into the business, make a few movies, put Maria on the screen, overthrow some pissant country."

"Tha's right."

"Man, did you go the long way around the block. Vinny wants me dead. So what makes you think I'll have any pull with them about where the family money goes?"

"Let's just say I got a hunch he'll listen to you. Some folks been declarin' that he's crazy. If so, I figure you might be the only one to talk any sense to him."

"Why?"

"You're kinda crazy too." Cogan showed his big teeth, almost getting podunk again, but not quite. The real smile this time, shining through. "I had a feelin' about you right from the start. You haven't exactly been lying low, son. Throwing down in Choochie's, going to visit the old Don right in his house. You've been shaking up that family like a hornet's nest. Sharpening the blade, getting the crew back into action. Kicking their asses into shape. You got spirit! Figured they'd take you on as a capo, then you'd have Vinny's ear again."

"Figured you'd put me to use."

"Just so."

Dane thought Special Agent Daniel Ezekiel Cogan might be out of his tree as well. The Right Reverend Matthew Colepepper probably had the right idea putting Cogan's mother in the asylum, but he shouldn't have stopped there. "You don't understand us Mediterranean types at all."

"Naw, probably not too well."

Glory drifted back toward Dane. "I'm sorry. I didn't know this rat fuck was playing me. I thought I was protecting myself."

"You were. It's okay," Dane told her. He thought about that day at the movie premiere, how she'd told him she was only attending as a favor to a friend. Cute, look at that, she'd told the truth again. Making contact with Dane under Cogan's orders. All because of Vinny, and nobody had even met with him yet.

Yeah, it was all pretty insane. Now that the mob was going legit, the feds wanted them to get back to the dirty dealing. The guy who wanted to go clean, they tossed his ass in the can.

"Why didn't you just ask Vinny yourself?" Dane asked.

"I didn't want to get that close to the situation, y'understand. Now, JoJo Tormino, he and I had been doing some talkin'. He was a bit sweet on Maria."

"He wanted to marry her, but he got iced before he could pop the question."

"I know it, and it was a damn sad thing to hear. Didn't figure him to go out the way he did. He was always cautious when meeting with me. Never took me to that bakery before, though, would've been nice if he had. He always wanted to meet in those there little strip mall coffee shops out on Long Island. He'd wear sunglasses, nervous as could be. That boy was headed for a heart attack."

Dane could imagine it, seeing JoJo and Cogan discussing the future of Maria Monticelli's acting career. Getting Vinny to invest in Glory's husband's production company. JoJo getting his ticket punched because he wanted the love of his life to get into movies and say dialogue like *Augh. Yeee. No please, I'll do anything you want. Wah.* Maria running away from Zypho, the monster with penislike tentacles trying to impregnate the all-female crew as they flew around the galaxy.

Dane frowned at both of them and felt a shard of hysterical laughter trying to shove itself up his throat. He swallowed twice to keep it down but he knew there was a sick smile on his face. "Even if I could get anybody in the Monti family to invest more of their time, effort, and money into drugs and the company . . . even if I could get them to launder the dirty cash and run out more guns . . . why the fuck would I want to? What do I get out of it?"

"Because it's what Maria Monticelli wants," Cogan said. "To be on the screen. And you love her."

There it was. The leverage that Cogan had been holding back.

Maria.

First JoJo. Now Dane. Everybody out of their head in love with her. Easily manipulated.

"How do you know that?" he asked.

"Vinny told my husband," Glory Bishop said, sounding embarrassed. "He always talked about you while they were doing business, while you were in prison. How you were the one his sister should be with. How you were the only one who really cared about his sister."

"He did?"

Cogan said, "I told you I had a feeling about you. That you were going to be his right-hand man. You're his best friend. All the other problems you've been having with the family, that's all the work of Roberto." Saying it right this time, not Robert-oh.

"So, you think because I love Maria, I'll talk to Vinny

and get him to do more drug trafficking with the Hollywood bigwigs, in which case more money and weapons will filter down to some South American shit-hole where a revolution is going on and the US government wants control?"

"Central America. Exactly."

"Okay," Dane said easily. "I'll do it."

"Now, that there's the way to talk, son!"

"Don't!" Glory shouted. "Johnny, are you nuts? After hearing this bastard's lies and seeing how he works?"

"Now, don't be like that, darlin'."

Dane and Glory stared at each other from across the glass table. A chasm had opened between them in only a few minutes and he knew there would never be any way for him to get back to the other side. Not that either of them would want to cross it anyway. Her eyes met his and there was a flicker of sorrow there, but not all that much, considering. They'd both had some fun and learned a few more things about the world worth knowing. All in all, it hadn't been a waste of time.

Cogan moved to embrace Glory, and she stood there allowing his hands on her. Angry, even disgusted with him, but they were still comfortable together. Her husband had gone away, what, nearly six months ago. Long enough for Cogan and Glory Bishop to forge one of those unhealthy bonds that could never be broken, no matter what happened. Just like the one between Dane and Vinny.

Dane said, "But I want you to do something for me."

Cogan tipped his jaw to the side, giving a wary smile. Like he'd known this was coming, the price he had to pay, and just hoped it wouldn't be too much. "And what's that?"

"I need a name."

"What name?"

Dane told him and Cogan spent less than fifteen minutes on Glory's cell phone getting the information.

Dane went to the window. He parted the curtains and saw two guys beating a police officer in an alley with his own nightstick. The cop scrambled on all fours trying to fight back, but they started kicking him until he rolled himself into a ball, face to the brick. Dane turned back to Glory Bishop and Cogan and saw they were holding on to each other again. He left them there for good.

TWENTY-FOUR

At dawn, Dane stopped by Phil Guerra's house and stole the Cadillac again.

He stopped over at his grandmother's house to check on her. She was up watching infomercials, sitting in her cotton nightgown with two crocheted blankets over her knees. Her lips were smeared black from eating licorice out of the candy dish. She said, "You think you can stop over at La Famiglia and pick me up some *sfogliatelle* and *cannoli*?"

"Sure, but they won't be open for another hour. What are you doing up this early? Trying to form a strategy to combat Mabel Guerra's psychological bingo attacks?"

"I had to pee and couldn't get back to sleep. That one, she sneaks gin and tonic in a coffee Thermos. They're going to ban her soon."

She glanced up at him with an expression like she wanted to say something else, but she held it back. All this holding back, it was driving them all *pazzo*. He knew she was having bad dreams again.

"So what happens to me?" he asked. "In your nightmares. Do I get chased out of the village?"

"No, you take it over."

It made him tuck his chin in. "What's that mean?"

"I don't know, but it worries me."

"Why?"

"Don't ask such questions. We do our best to understand these things even the priests won't help us with. We feel our way through the dark."

"Okay."

"Whatever you start today you need to finish."

Dane wanted to sit beside his grandma and hug her, but she shifted on the couch and pulled the blankets higher. He said, "I will."

"Go, then. You be careful."

He drove over to Williamsburg, down Bedford Avenue past the new ultrahip cafés, vintage clothing stores, and restaurants, heading to the projects. The neighborhood quickly gave way to abandoned buildings and burned-out blocks. He remembered his parents bringing him here to celebrate *La Festa del Giglio*, the Feast of the Lily, and Dane would watch the people carrying a fifty-foot-high obelisk covered in flowers topped with a statue of St. Paulinus down the streets. It seemed weird even by Catholic standards.

He found the address he was looking for and pulled over about a block away, behind a pile of garbage and rubble three feet high.

It took Dane about four hours to see how the setup worked. There were the lookouts, the dealers, the muscle, and the boss and his crew. The lookouts were perched on the corners and rooftops, keeping their eyes to the street, watching for police and potential buyers. Dane had been made immediately; but they knew he wasn't a cop, so they waited while he sat behind the Caddy's wheel.

The street action moved with well-oiled efficiency, honed by repetition. The crew used walkie-talkies, not cell phones where anybody could be listening. The scouts corralled addicts and sold to them within the safety of their secured alleys, the muscle protecting the exchange of money and making sure nobody hit the dealers. Every two hours a bag man would be sent up the block into an apartment with the take so far, retrieve more drugs, and get right back to selling. So far as Dane could tell, there were at least six dealers in this general area. Bag men farther out from the home base probably only made two drops a day.

Fredric Wilson appeared to be an all-around wing man. He sold some crack, dropped off a wad of cash, and spent a lot of time gabbing on the walkie-talkies. So far as Dane could tell, Fredric didn't fit easily into any particular slot of the crew. That was good, it would make things easier.

Dane took off his jacket, left his .38 in the Caddy's glove box, and strutted up the street, all the scouts watching him. Three approached him at once and didn't bother to hawk their wares since they knew he wasn't a buyer. They couldn't figure him out, which was also good. They remained silent until one of the thugs moved from a doorway and stepped up.

"I want to talk to Fredric Wilson," Dane said.

"Why?"

"We have business."

"Wait here."

It got more activity going, cars pulling out of alleys, doors opening and slamming. A few more faces peered at him through windows and from the fire escapes. The walkie-talkies squawked all over the fucking place.

Dane stood there on the corner with three kids not even in their twenties yet staring him down. They were nothing compared to his drill sergeant, and he let his face go placid. At the curb up ahead sat a silver Lexus, buffed out and the hubcaps shining so bright you couldn't stare at them for long. The toughs moved to the driver's door. It opened and Fredric popped out. He strutted up with a long-legged swagger.

He had on a fashionable silk-and-wool suit, posh, with a wide lapel and a lime-green tie knotted tightly. Dane wondered what Glory would've thought of that. There were diamond rings on six of his fingers, and a bump under his jacket that looked about the size of a SIG Mauser. He was one of those cats who liked to dare people to make a grab for what he had, hoping he'd appear so ready for it that nobody would make the move.

Dane permitted himself to feel the wind flowing around his shirt collar. This was gonna be all right.

Grabbing the knot of his tie to make sure it was still straight, Fredric approached Dane, his face clenched into an expression of contempt, but his eyes bright with the idea of easy cash. "What do you want?"

Dane slid into the guy's personal space, three inches away. "To talk to you."

"You a cop?"

It got Dane smiling like a mental patient. He had to put the brakes on his laughter before it became real. "You act like asking that question is going to keep you safe from the courts. Like a cop never lied on the stand.

'Your Honor, I told him I was a police officer, but he sold me the cocaine anyway.' Don't you know how lame it sounds when you ask somebody if he's a cop?"

"Who the hell are you, man?"

"I blew my horn at you once."

"What?"

"Outside your building in Bed-Stuy, the one with the red awning. You were there with your girlfriend Taneesha Welles two years ago."

"I haven't seen Taneesha in a while. You have business with her?"

"I have business with you, Fredric. Besides, Taneesha's dead."

That got the prick for about a half second. Fredric had known she was dead, but he'd forgotten. "Well, ain't that sad."

"It is. She died just like a friend of mine. Because you were selling bad shit."

Dane liked this crew. About ten guys were ringing him and Fredric now, killers to the core, but hardened and smartened by the life. None of them got in the way. They listened and watched, clever enough to wait and make up their own minds.

"The fuck you say, man?" Squaring himself, leaning in like the posturing would be enough.

"You heard me. You want me to repeat myself in front of your crew? You sold bad flake. You poisoned at least two people. Taneesha and a girl named Angelina Monticelli. I'm here to see you kick up for that."

Chewing his lips, trying to give the *malocchio,* the death gaze, but just not staunch enough to do it right. "You talk like we know each other, man, but I ain't never met you."

"You never budged from the house, that's why. Even

when a teenager was dying on your stoop. Maybe you
don't remember me jamming on my horn, but you
should."

"You crazy, fuckah." Fredric dropped out of his high-
class attitude and got back to sounding like a gang-
banger, with the moves now, arms akimbo, jumping
like some giant rooster. "You want me to put one in yo
head?"

"Pull that SIG Mauser and I'll have to stuff it in your
ear. You and I have had this meeting coming for too
long. We need to get past it."

"You talkin' like a guinea wiseguy now! That what
you is!" Leaping back and forth, like a dance, swinging
to his own rhythm.

"That's because I pretty much am one." It was time
to put the fear in him. "All those diamond rings flashing. You get put down, how long do you think it'll be
before somebody comes out with a bolt cutter and starts
taking your fingers?"

"What?"

"You're just daring them to try, aren't you? You
think everybody is a punk ass bitch except you. I bet
you flash those rocks in everybody's face all day long.
You tempt a man long enough and he's going to make a
grab. You're gonna look funny trying to pick your nose
with a stump."

There it was. The dark swirl of terror starting in his
eyes. "These are my men. This is my crew."

"And if you get iced, who takes over?"

Fredric quit moving around so much and tried to
keep his face impassive. But the only thing that ever
really rattled fuckers like this was the fact that there
was always somebody else willing to step into their

shoes. Fredric wouldn't be missed for a goddamn minute, no more than Taneesha Welles.

"I'm going to take you out of action, Fredric."

"Stop sayin' my name like that, man."

"I'm going to weaken you so much that your spot gets filled in a split goddamn second."

"Fuck you!"

"Nature abhors a vacuum, Fredric. You're going to the curb and no one is going to help you. Look at you. I been pissing on you for five minutes and you haven't made a move yet. You're going to lose those fingers of yours."

It was finally enough to get him reaching for his gun, proving to the others that he didn't have the guts to go hand to hand with an unarmed guy.

Dane pushed out with the flat of his palm and pressed Fredric Wilson's wrist tightly to his chest so he couldn't finish pulling the pistol. With his other fist he repeatedly cracked Fredric hard across the nose until blood spurted all over. Wanting to make the lesson last, Dane danced out of the way, driven by his frustration the day Angie died, but disconnected from it in a way, so it wouldn't impede him.

But Fredric wasn't a slouch. He was wiry and had good footwork, shaking off his pain and doggedly moving forward. He tried two quick jabs that Dane easily avoided, the silence around them thick and unnatural. In the army, during the training sessions, the squad used to yell and applaud and groan while watching somebody else take a beatdown, but Dane liked this a lot better. Everybody quiet and keeping to himself.

Fredric went for his back pocket, going for a switchblade. His face was filled with murder, the blood flowing from both nostrils and streaming against his teeth as he grinned and snapped the knife open. Dane quit dancing and settled back on the balls of his feet, hands at his sides, staring straight on.

The blade flashed out and Dane stepped in, chopping at Fredric's wrist twice in quick succession, feeling the bone snap on the second blow. Fredric let loose with a girlish squeal that hit a sweet note. Dane stooped and picked up the blade and handed it to the guy closest to him, who took the knife with a muted chuckle.

All right, so Dane could've ended it right then, but he wanted to prolong the moment, draw the scene out for more drama. Usually that would be a sign of weakness, but not now. It was important at this moment to show Fredric Wilson the folly of selling bad drugs to teen girls. Two haunted years needed to be paid for.

Tucking his broken hand behind him, Fredric moved in again, but his eyes were wildly searching for a way out. He wanted to race back to the car, but he realized there was no safety in making a run for it. Showing such fear and weakness was chum in the water. He scanned left and right, looking at the faces of the chicks on the stoops anxiously watching him.

"Her name was Angelina Monticelli, Fredric." Dane rushed forward, grabbed the prick's good arm at the elbow, and gave it a vicious twist. The snap was loud but not loud enough, so Dane yanked it again and felt the bone splinter up through the flesh. Fredric pulled a scream out from deep down under his balls, but Dane didn't want to hear it. He slapped a hand over Fredric's mouth and said, "Shh. Say her name."

Crying, Fredric dropped to his knees and vomited on the sidewalk. Dane grabbed him by the collar and pulled him to the curb and told him, "Say it. C'mon. Angelina Monticelli. Say it."

But Fredric Wilson had already passed out facedown in the gutter, blood and bile soaking into his green tie.

Dane turned to the muscle standing beside him. "Who do I contact to do some serious business?"

"My name's Cutter Bunk. You ever want to talk real money, you come to me."

Dane walked back to the Caddy and got in, pulled out, and swung around the corner heading back toward Bedford Avenue.

Forever fifteen years old and seething with a dark attitude. Smiling but with the annoying glint of superiority in her gray eyes shining through even more clearly now. That was okay, he was getting used to it. Angie's oversized black sweater and midnight-blue jeans made it difficult for him to see the subtle lines of her body. Black hair fell straight back over her ears, showing the slightest curl of bangs up front, moved by her breath although she didn't breathe.

JoJo Tormino sat in the backseat with her, staring at the side of her face like he didn't recognize her anymore. Or thought she was someone else.

Angelina leaned forward and said in Dane's ear, "Thank you."

"Sure."

"But you should have killed him."

"Maybe some other time."

"Will they really take his fingers?"

"I don't know. It might be a point of pride now, since I put the idea in their heads."

"I hope they do."

She climbed forward into the passenger seat, curling against him without touching. That familiar heat flooded into his guts and got him sweating, worse than usual because his heart was still hammering.

Could any woman alive ever do for him the things the dead could do? He started breathing heavily, nervous in the way that guns could never make him. Her bangs wafted again, brushing against his throat.

"You told me that my mother wanted to say something to me."

"She does."

"What is it?"

"How should I know?"

JoJo Tormino stared out the window. Unwilling or unable to speak. Funny how some of them had so much to say, and others so little. JoJo turned his gaze forward and caught Dane's eye in the rearview. He was going to start that whole prodding in the side thing again, Dane could tell. It was time to go give her the ring.

"Where's Maria now, Angie? In Hollywood?"

"Hell no, she's never been west of Jersey."

"But I thought Vinny was setting up her career?"

"He hasn't done a thing for her yet."

"So where is she?"

Angie smiled, like she knew what was coming next. "At our sister Carmella's house out on Begoyan Street. She's married to a podiatrist."

Dane didn't know Carmella all that well. She was older, the daughter of the Don's longtime *goomar,* a girlfriend he started hanging around with back in the late fifties. She didn't have much to do with the family, and Dane had only met her a couple of times at Monticelli functions a long time ago.

"Why's she there?"

"Berto is keeping watch over her."

"For what?"

"He thinks the Ventimiglia family might be taking a run at her."

Dane tried to track it but couldn't. With a touch of frustration he realized he still didn't see things the way the goombas did. After all these years it should be second nature, understanding their impractical moves, but he just couldn't ever get it into focus. "Why would they do that?"

"Because of JoJo Tormino."

"The Ventis think he died because of her?"

"Well, he did, pretty much."

"But she had nothing to do with it. The Ventimiglias work like that? Send a crew against a family member in payback? They've got to know JoJo loved her, right? So now they're gonna whack her?"

"They're the only rough family left," Angie said, her lips just under his ear. The Caddy veered a little over the double yellow and Dane had to yank it back. "I always hated those guys. Vito Grimaldi was constantly trying to paw me whenever there was some kind of get-together. Barbecues. Baptisms. Even at funerals."

"He a capo?"

"Yeah."

JoJo still had his bullet holes: the left elbow, left thigh, jagged melted graze along his jaw, and high in the chest. The sucking wound above his heart hissed and gurgled. How long could a dead man bleed? It got worrisome, having JoJo back there just watching, waiting, his spiritual peace all hinged on Dane facing a woman he'd wanted his entire life.

If only you could throw a corpse out of the car. It would make life so much easier.

"By the way," Angie said. "What did Mr. Fielding want with you? He no longer cries in his grave."

Dane told her, "He had a confession to make."

"Oh," she said. So beautiful, so much like Maria, that Dane had to rub his palms along his pant legs to dry them. "Oh, I know what that's like."

"Yeah, me too."

TWENTY-FIVE

The podiatrist's house stood so far out on Begoyan Street that you could see it from three blocks away. The front door had been painted a fierce turquoise, and there was a large wooden foot hanging from a pole on a pair of chains at curbside. The name DR. STANLEY WEIN-TRAUB arced along the heel in black-framed block letters. Classy.

Maria's sister Carmella had married young and gotten as far away from the Monticellis as she could: about two miles across Flatbush Avenue. Dane knew it was a whole different world here. You might as well be in Antarctica if you had to take a subway to get good *pasta fagliogli.*

But you couldn't really run from Don Monti, not even if you were his illegitimate daughter. You could only hope that family wasn't keeping an eye on you every minute of the day.

Like Angie had told Dane, they were watching the house.

Roberto Monticelli was out front in a sleeveless T-shirt, holding a cigar in his huge hand. He stood about six-four, heavily muscled but with a little spare tire around the middle and a double chin he'd never get rid of. He pretty much had only one eyebrow and didn't seem bothered by it. He kept his hair short but well moussed so that it appeared curly as razor wire.

He had surrounded himself with an atmosphere of self-importance, marred only by his extreme and total uncool. He wore a leather holster on his belt at the small of his back, housing a .44 Magnum. The barrel was so long that it hung out the bottom of the holster and made it look like Berto had a pipe sticking up his ass.

Dane used to be terrified of him—if you so much as said good morning to Maria in the school hallways, Roberto would stab you in the eye with a pencil.

It was sort of rough trying to visualize Berto under the bridge with transsexual hookers. Once you started bending your imagination in that direction, it just wouldn't stop. It made you wonder how long Berto's lifestyle had been curving like this. Since high school? Teenage son of a mob boss feeling up the tits of Bernadette, sucking her tongue, saying yeah baby baby, only to grab hold of Bernie's tool. Was it a turn-on right then or did he have to work it out for himself, struggling with his shame? Yeah, probably killed the first one out of revulsion, but the interest was implanted. He dumps the strangled body of Bernie but keeps seeing that swinging dick in his dreams. Gets him nauseous and aroused at the same time. No wonder he was always in such a bad fucking mood. Did he have one girlfriend he kept returning to, waiting for him beneath the bridge? How much was the standard rate for around-the-world with somebody you could do twice as much with? Like there weren't enough questions to make you crazy.

Seated in the Caddy, Dane scanned the area, looking for more members of the crew. Nobody else seemed to be around.

Dane knew what he was going to do now even though it was bound to cause a lot of problems all around. What the fuck.

Pocketing his keys and the .38, he slid from the car. Berto had seen the Cadillac go by, but showed no interest. It was a common sight to him.

Dane made sure he made some noise and slammed the door hard, stepping heavily across the street, kicking loose asphalt. He walked up with his arms loose at his sides, hands open. Roberto didn't quite recognize him and puffed intently on his cigar, blowing smoke in a thick cloud as if it somehow made him groovy, like one of the Old Mafiosi sitting around in their tomato gardens.

Dane moved up the flagstone walk and realized there wasn't any way to be hip with what he had to say, so he just let it out. "Berto, I want to talk to Maria. She here?"

Roberto fell back a step with a shocked expression, and for a second he looked like he might be having a heart attack. His features fell in and contorted and went a nice shade of blue, then purple, and then the immense, lunatic Sicilian rage was on him. "The fuck you say my sister's name!"

"Man, you have really got some serious hangups about Maria. But that's okay, you aren't the only one."

It was kind of fun watching Roberto turn so many

colors at once, the veins standing out in his temples, writhing and throbbing and clogging up along the contours of his neck. Dane was trying to stay focused and not let himself dwell on the fact that Berto had sent the hitters to off him in the can. "It's you. Soldier boy."

Dane sighed and figured, all right. "Yeah, okay, it's me, the soldier boy."

"And you strut right up to me? To my sister's house?"

"It wasn't much of a strut."

"After what you did?"

"You got a hangup about Angie too, don't you? Okay, I'm starting to see the picture now, why you've done the things you have."

It was easy to keep Berto off-balance, the guy puffing away like a maniac, making himself sick on the cigar. Dane tried not to think of what Freud might've had to say about the demonstration. "You know how much is on your head?"

"I've been out of the joint for three weeks. I walked up to your brother and his crew in Chooch's. I walked into your father's house. Except for one lame ass try by Big Tommy Bartone, nobody's done much to collect on your bounty. How much you offering anyway?"

Berto took another serious puff, sucked too much into his lungs, and had to suppress a cough. "Five grand!"

"You embarrass yourself," Dane said.

"Get out of my goddamn sight before I put two in your skull right now, you disrespectful prick! Your time is coming! I ought to kill you on general principle!"

There it was again. The threat but not the follow-through. What kind of wiseguy only stands there talking to the guy he's put a bounty on, when he's got a fucking Magnum hooked to his belt? Jesus. You'd think he'd be wailing Angelina's name, throwing his arms up to heaven. But no, just the same schoolyard bully shit he used to pull during recess.

"Really, can't we skip the goomba drama?" Dane asked. "Your boys screwed up on taking me out in the slam. Big Tommy messed up at the hospital. A few more of your muscle boys flubbed the hit on JoJo Tormino. I mean, really, three against one and he still manages to ice them all? That's just fucking sad. He's dead but so are they, if you care about cost-effectiveness and such."

"You son of a bitch. I don't care, so long as the job got done."

"Why did you come to the prison?"

"I want you dead."

"Sure. But why go yourself? Why didn't you just let Vinny send a lieutenant?"

Still flexing and puffing, getting his veins in those big hands to stick out but never making the move. "He wouldn't. He wouldn't pay anybody to hit you, so I did. You deserve to be chopped into dog food." His face burned with emotion. Whatever was going on, Berto Monticelli wasn't going to talk about it. "I'm gonna cut your liver out with a cleaver and—"

"Yeah, yeah. I need to speak to Maria. She around?"

"Vaffanculo!"

Okay, so maybe he should've handled it differently, more diplomatically, but JoJo had tapped him and this was the only way it was going to be.

Roberto's lips started to crawl over his face. Dane recognized the expression from back in the hallways. It was his way of grinning. He went for his Magnum, trying to jerk it out fast but unable to tug it free from the holster. The forward sight on the barrel was hung up on the leather and, as he fought to draw, yanking harder, it looked more and more like a puppy's tail twitching back and forth. Dane figured that Berto had never pulled a gun while looking a guy in the eye, so he had no clue how to do it.

The mood kept shifting but things weren't quite totally tense yet. Dane could do a few things here. Go for the throat, work the inner thigh, even knee Berto in the crotch if it came down to that. Dane's father had taught him how to disarm a perp, toss him down, and twist him up. Maybe that was the way to go. He thought it was about time to try a few moves, but the weight of the ring in his pocket felt heavier than before, his promise to JoJo so loud in his mind. That wearisome indifference was back and dulling him. He took a few seconds to sigh, scratch his head, and let loose with an "Uyh."

Finally, with a grunt of satisfaction, Roberto Monticelli got his pistol loose from the small of his back. His face bloomed with an ecstasy so ideal that he nearly glowed with happiness.

He cried out, "You're dead, you *strunzo!*" and started to bring the .44 around.

Dane slugged Roberto Monticelli on the point of his chin and knocked him back into the fervently turquoise front door.

Simple, sure, but the gun had barely cleared the holster and Berto hit the middle six panels of the door hard. A crack appeared in the wood. It vibrated roughly enough that the brass knocker clapped a couple times. A sweet scent of lilacs floated in from somebody else's yard. The big foot on the lawn appeared to be angry—ready to kick a lot of ass—in the slashing sunlight.

With a viciously slick grin twisting his mouth, the butchery so clear in Berto's eyes that they were black with hatred, his tongue lolled good-naturedly in his mouth until the Magnum went off behind him.

It blasted fragments of his spine into, and out through, his own heart. A burst of blood and gristle shot across the flagstone stoop.

Dane stood there staring, thinking, Un-fuckin'-believable.

There it is. I just crossed the final line. I'll never be able to get back to the other side again.

The door opened and he looked into the horrified faces of Carmella Monticelli, her podiatrist husband, and some fat broad in baby-blue orthopedic sneakers.

Dane blinked and found his voice, said, "It was an accident. Kind of. I'm sorry. Is Maria here?"

Nearly as beautiful as her sister, but lacking the nameless extra quality that sent the lightning down into his soul, Carmella's lips worked silently. She kept gawking at her dead brother on her front step, bits and pieces of his major organs having blown out onto the lawn.

"Where is she?" Dane asked.

"Vinny took her home a couple hours ago," Carmella whispered, just as the podiatrist threw up on his welcome mat, and the fat lady started hopping around on her bad feet, shrieking.

TWENTY-SIX

It rattled him a touch. Dane quickly pulled away from the curb and drove back to Grandma Lucia's house. This was a turn of events that some people might describe as pretty bad. Seriously fucked, even.

But there was something else going on, and his scars began to warm. He checked around for Vinny but didn't see him anywhere. Dane clicked on the radio, waiting for the music to change to the voices of the dead, berating him, reviling him. It didn't happen. He said, "JoJo? Angie?" Struggling to remember his father's face. "Dad?"

All that blood, the guy's heart practically exploding out his chest and wobbling through the air, but not a drop on Dane. He sat behind the wheel fingering the ring, suddenly realizing just how small the rock was when you got down to it. All these wiseguys, tripping over themselves with new scams and enterprises, but what the hell did they do with their cash?

He lit a cigarette and got onto the highway, staring at the cracked, discolored, cement wall surrounding the cemetery. The shadows of the extravagant gravestones flashed out across the lanes. Cold patches warning you of what was coming. He took the exit and drove through Outlook Park and into Headstone City.

There was still only the one pattern he could move in through the neighborhood, this direction, with the faces of the deadly seven sins glaring down at him from the sides of the brownstones. They seemed to be having a deep dialogue.

Could you ever be forgiven for what you've done?

His mother said nothing. His father didn't run out in front of the grille. The Caddy hummed as he went along, the decades of power and beauty working into Dane's chest. He made a turn and rolled through the cemetery, taking precise curves, never hitting the brake, smoothly swinging past the leaning gravestones trying to make a grab as he went by. He drove out through the gates and parked in front of his grandmother's house.

Were you supposed to have done it? Did they want you to do it? Had they been waiting for you to take the step?

Dane had the storm door open, sticking his key in the lock, when the screech of tires drew his attention back to the street. A smudge of black motion coming from the driveway. They'd found him already.

Dane dove inside as Joe Fresco called out with an amiable, "Hey, hold up!"

Uh-huh. Dane slammed the door shut, threw the dead bolt, and drew the well-oiled .38 from his jacket pocket.

Who was in charge of matters now? Vinny or the Don? Or were some of the boys starting to cut loose?

The Monticelli mob liked to send their crews in teams

of three. It was a stupid ploy. They were already getting in each other's way as they came up across the lawn. Joey seemed to be running this part of the show, with a bit too much composure. It would've been easier to take him out if he was raving, like back at the Monti mansion.

But Joey had it together now. He'd be tougher to drop. Dane tried not to think about what the inside of a trunk might feel like while you were waiting for somebody to fire up a blowtorch.

Grandma Lucia plodded out from the kitchen. She'd spent the morning dyeing her hair again. Christ, he had to turn away. "Why do you do that to yourself?" he asked.

Her presence pressed against him like the turbulent massing of a hurricane. "Where the hell's the *cannoli*!"

"Look, I got a situation here—" He rushed to her, took her elbow, and led her out of the living room and back into the kitchen.

"You piss somebody off?" she asked.

"You could say that."

"Who?"

"I accidentally killed Roberto Monticelli."

She let out a long-suffering sigh that went, "Uyh—" Really sounding deeply irritated, it was a talent she had. In all these years he hadn't quite gotten it down right.

She smacked him in the back of the head with fingers like iron. "*Stunad!* What'd you do? Run him over, the way you drive?"

He pushed her toward the cellar. "Go wait for me."

"I've got *pesto funghi* on the stove."

"Leave it, we'll have it later."

"Don't talk to them. Those Monticellis like to talk." She opened the cellar door and left it open, the basement steps creaking as she moved into darkness.

"Just keep your hot pink head down."

"It's magenta, I told ya!"

Joey and his thugs forced themselves against the front door, shouldering the dead bolt. All three of them were at it, nobody coming around to the back of the house to cut off an escape. He heard them shouting, Joey still trying to sound smooth and natural, a pal come around to watch a ball game. "Hey, Danetello, c'mon, I just want to chat. Have a sit-down."

So it was going to be like that.

"Yeah, about what?" Dane yelled.

"About our conversation the other day."

"Which one specifically?"

"From the other day!"

"Oh, when I punched you in the throat a couple times?"

"Yeah!"

The hitters fired several shots, sort of playing around, shooting up the door, having a good time. Dane had to admit it felt like the ending of some movie where nobody gave a shit anymore, they all just go rushing headlong into hell. The door burst open.

Joey and his boys were in the living room now, chattering like they were sitting around a bar waiting for somebody to buy them a beer. Joey called out, "Hey there. How about if we just relax and have a nice discussion. Defuse this situation before it gets any worse. How's that? How'd that be?"

"Sure," Dane said, and they opened up on the sound of his voice, firing into the other side of the wall. Splinters and chunks of plaster spewed all over the kitchen as he squatted lower behind the refrigerator. Joey Fresco was back to using his .357. Grandma was right, they liked to get you talking.

Three guys but nobody moving up on him, no one spreading out any covering fire. The rattle of a glass caught Dane's attention.

Son of a bitch.

One of them was actually in the candy dish.

Sometimes you had just enough guts and technique to get you where you were going. He thought of Maria, his promises met and those unkept, and he spun into the doorway and aimed at the nearest hitter, easing back on the trigger of the .38.

It took Joey's lieutenant in the thigh and whipped him around so that he faced the opposite direction. Dane didn't even get an impression of what the bastard looked like, of who he was, this man he was killing. He fired twice more and nailed the guy both times between the shoulder blades, a splash of blood soaring against the plastic-covered couch pillows.

Look at this, look at where I am now.

And it's only going to get easier.

Dane had screwed up, the scene was too large in his mind. He'd lost his cover, jumped out too far, and had nowhere to hide. No choice but to continue leaping forward to the end. He fired twice more at the other hitter and missed both times, and he only had one bullet left. He was saving it for Joey, who was chewing on Grandma's black licorice, the .357 held too low. The thug was closer, already aiming his .45 at Dane's chest.

The *pesto funghi* had started to smoke, filling the room with a sharp odor of overcooked sauce that still managed to make Dane's stomach growl.

This was bad. His hand flashed out and caught the thug by the wrist, pulling him forward so the barrel of the .45 actually passed over his ribs. The guy wasn't fast enough to pull the trigger in time, and nowhere near light enough on his feet to stay balanced.

You had to count your good fortunes when they occurred. The hitter threw his arms out like a little kid walking on ice, sliding on Grandma Lucia's plastic runner protecting the carpet. After thirty years of walking on that goddamn thing, Dane was finally happy it was there.

He brought the .38 up, pressed it to the prick's cheekbone, said, "This isn't about you," and shot him through the head.

Joey spit out his licorice.

He wasn't as good with guns as he used to be. He'd grown lazy as he'd been promoted up the family chain, and he wound up putting too much faith in the men around him. Joey held his .357 out in front of him but had too tight a grip on it, the way second-rate drivers would grip a steering wheel in a high-speed pursuit. The gun angled slightly downward. Joey was used to his snub-nosed .22, and the weight of the Magnum was throwing him off a hair.

Ten feet separated them. Dane aimed the empty .38 at Joey's heart. He just might be able to bluff his way out here, if he had enough slickness to get by. Joey Fresco probably hadn't counted the shots. He was getting older, more insecure, not keeping his mind on the business at hand. His suit jacket had stuffed shoulder pads to lend him some extra size, but they appeared as stiff as a French general's epaulets.

"With a Magnum, I can miss you and still punch a hole through your chest," Joey said.

"Drop it. I'm trained. I can put out your eye from a thousand yards."

"Yeah, they teach you that in the army?" Joey asked. "Special Forces? No wonder you handled those two so easy. Am I right?"

"Yeah."

"You do any assassination stuff?"

"All the time."

"Down in Nicaragua?"

It was becoming fairly apparent that the men of the Monticelli clan were about as upright and stable as the Tower of Pisa.

Dane said, "How about if you just drop the gun, Joey?"

"Hell no, you killed my boss."

"Yeah, but it was an accident. Besides, the Don is really your boss."

"Him and his sons. I took an oath."

"I didn't even pull the trigger on Berto. He did it to himself."

"I don't give a damn."

"You should."

Sirens blurted in the distance, too far away to do any good for the next three minutes, which were the important ones.

"I mean, I don't mind that you took that *finocchio* out of the game. Far as I'm concerned, he was giving us a bad name. Nobody respected our crew anymore because'a what he did down there under the bridge. It was bad for our reputation. We were planning to whack him soon anyway, so you did us a favor."

"Then let's call it even."

"Can't do that. There's some things a guy has to do, you know? Of course you do. Well, this is one of them, am I right?"

No arguing that particular point.

Joey let out a wild noise like a mongoose in heat and lurched forward as if he were going to stab Dane with the gun instead of shooting him. Then he stopped, grinned, and settled back, wanting to relax and enjoy the moment before it passed him up. Maybe he had counted the shots. Dane held the .38 higher, aiming at Joey Fresco's eye, hoping it would be enough to scare the stupid mook off.

Murder moved in and out of the room. Dane thought about jumping, rolling, trying some funky shit in midair to get back into the kitchen and hide, but he felt it would just look too ridiculous.

He wanted to do a lot of things, but couldn't put them in any order. Speak with his mother. Kick Cogan's ass. Make Phil Guerra confess. Look Vinny in the eye.

Shout Maria's name, fall down on his knees and let it all out in one long howl, but even that was denied him—what, he was going to live his last few seconds reenacting Tony's death scene from *West Side Story*? Start calling out for Riff? Bernardo and Chino? Fuck. It's really over.

But sometimes the angel of mercy shows up in disguise. Grandma Lucia came trundling out of the kitchen with her slippers slapping the bottoms of her feet. She carried an eleven-gauge pump, holding it the right way, braced against her shoulder.

"Jesus, Grandma!" Dane shouted.

Wide-eyed, Joey shouted, "What the fuck is up with your hair, lady!"

"Shaddup!"

"Listen up, Lucia! I lived through three hits from Benny the Penny Castigliano, and I survived Catholic school. You ain't got the brass to take me out! You're kiddin' me, right?"

But no, Grandma definitely wasn't kidding. She yelled,

"Va fa napole!" squeezed the trigger, and blasted Joey Fresco's ass fifteen feet across her living room.

They watched him hit the wall and knock the 3-D blessed heart picture of Jesus askew.

Go to hell, for sure.

"Goddamn," Dane said.

She took a slow gander over the room but showed little reaction and no remorse. The photos on the shelves seemed to be in shock, Dad's smiling face a little perturbed, Mom wearing a startled grin. Grandma stood the shotgun upright beside the armoire that housed her good china and her thimble collection. She flitted into the bathroom and started spraying germ killer and potpourri room freshener.

"Why didn't you shoot?" she asked.

"I was out of rounds."

"You need an automatic. I meant to tell you before."

"I think you're right."

"Is this all because of that dead girl?"

"Not really."

"Her sister? That Maria, right?"

"Yeah, in a way."

"I thought so. I always knew you'd been hit by the thunderbolt." She clutched his shoulder, chucked him under the chin so he'd meet her eye. "You don't have much time. You can't stop now. You've got to finish it."

He'd been thinking the same thing.

There was no other way out of it. They'd just keep taking runs at him until he was dead unless he took the fight to the Monticellis.

The sirens sounded to be about the same distance away. There were probably enough cops on the Don's payroll to keep them running in circles for the next half hour.

Grandma retreated back to the cellar and came up with an unopened box of .38 bullets and a handful of shotgun shells. He'd been in the basement maybe ten thousand times and had no idea where the shotgun might've been hidden.

He took the ammo and reloaded the pistol, grabbed up the shotgun, and started for the door. But something was still nagging him.

Turning at the last second, he asked, "Hey, how's everybody know your name anyway? You used to fool around with Don Monti back in the day, right?"

"Don't talk dirty. Now go and end this thing. And when I send you to the bakery from now on, you think you can just get a few *cannoli* and some *sfogliatelle* and come home again without causing so much trouble?"

"Next time," Dane said.

TWENTY-SEVEN

Walking through ICU past the gray wasted faces of families of the dying. His mother lay in a small room surrounded by machinery that loomed over her like gods of steel.

Her kidneys had failed and she was yellow and bloated with toxins. The machines forced her frail chest to continue breathing. They surrounded her, winking, watching, livid with screens everywhere so he could witness the gradual slowing of her pulse and her steadily decreasing heartbeat.

His mother had something to tell him.

The kid with the twisted head from across the hall was lying in the bed with her, saying Mama, Mama. Crying the way Dane should be crying but couldn't. Hugging her, his sutures and busted skull bones pressed against her breast.

Dane sat and watched the jagged raw red scars across the frontal lobe moving, reaching, wanting to leap the distance and crawl against Dane's flesh, digging down into his brain. Lying up against his own scars, connecting, mating, reproducing. Crashing in the metal doors and taking over.

What did you dream, Mama?

I dreamed an angel with golden wings as shiny as coins sat with me on the end of the bed. I watched the television for a while, but it wasn't on. I bled in the toilet.

You wanted her to tell you more about the angel but her mouth was sealed with tape around the tubes that forced breath into her lungs. You understood the men who went berserk in this situation and killed their loved ones. You could stand the sound of the buzzing and dripping and clicking around them, all designed to extend pain?

Dane couldn't speak and sat rubbing his mother's hand with his thumb. The rhythm seemed to calm him for some reason, while his shadow grew beneath his feet.

The boy with the sick brain spoke with a beautiful voice, in English and other languages Dane didn't know but could, for the moment, understand.

"Why are you here?"

"Because my mother is dying."

"Hebben u gezien de engel met gouden vleugels?"

"No, what kind of angel is it? Is it death?"

"C'est un ange signifiée pour vous."

"Why is she seeing an angel that's come for me?"

"Parce que vous êtes béni." The kid hissed his words, full of a promising but terrible emotion.

"It's not a blessing. This is a burden."

"You have no idea of what real sorrow is," the boy told him. "Her sleep can never be pure. She will always struggle, restless here and elsewhere. Weeping for you, and later in hell."

"Fuck off, kid!"

Thumb moving back and forth on your mother's yellow, bloated flesh. The machines speaking in ancient rhymes that haven't been translated in millennia.

The boy touched your scars, matching them against his own. You're glad that he keeps on talking.

"*Was wünschen Sie von mir?*"

"I don't want anything from you."

"*É bonita. Eu quero-a. Você não merece uma mulher tão maravilhosa. É minha. Mãe. Mãe.*"

"She's not your mother. She's beyond you now."

"*Mère. Mère.*"

"She's my ma."

"*Mia madre. La mia madre!*"

"She's my mom."

Thinking about how easy it would be to snap the boy's neck, Dane waited for somebody to come save him. He waited for his ma to save him.

The kid's head came further apart, the sutures and staples pulling away.

Or maybe that was only Dane.

It was hard to tell, especially now.

Dane pulled the Caddy back up into Phil Guerra's driveway and the garage door opened. Phil stepped out holding a 9mm aimed at him.

Living up to his name. Bringing the war right out into the street to Dane, who dared to snatch the '59 dream car. Twice. The 9mm reflected in the fiery Magic-Mirror acrylic lacquer finish. The chrome grill blazed like a smelter's forge.

Phil was digging the moment. Getting a chance to stand there with his gun out, probably seeing himself in black-and-white, up on the screen with Bogie and Robert Ryan. He still moved pretty good even with the

extra weight, easing out onto the driveway and making
sure he was clear in case Dane tried to gun the engine
and run him over.

"You don't want to ruin your spacious, curvy windshield," Dane told him.

"Get out of my car, Johnny!"

"No. You get in."

"I'm not kidding here, you punk!"

"I can see that, Uncle Philly. It's been a bad day all
around."

Phil leaned down and peered at Dane. The 9mm bob-
bed for a moment, then pointed downward. "What've you
done, Johnny?"

"Climb in, I'll tell you all about it."

"Nobody drives my car but me, damn it!"

Grinning at him pleasantly, Dane said, "Nobody but
you, me, and the twenty guys that owned it before you.
All the mechanics and grease monkeys and shop owners
over forty-five years. You shouldn't be behind a wheel.
You're going to flatten somebody someday soon, some
lady pushing a carriage in a crosswalk. I'm a driver, you
know that. Let me drive. Come on, Phil, just a quick one
around the neighborhood, then it's all yours again. Don't
be a prick like your father just because he never let you
behind the wheel when you were a kid."

That touched a nasty nerve. Phil grimaced and his
eyes swirled. He'd at last gone all the way to the wall,
and Dane took a weird sort of pride in that. "You got
balls talking about my old man."

"We all speak our piece eventually."

Look at him now. His rug hung too far to one side,
like he'd been sitting in the garage with his head leaned
up against the workbench, waiting through the night for
his car to come home.

Phil slipped up to the door and carefully maneuvered it open like it might be wired with explosives. He pointed the gun at Dane's chest and, in a lingering manner, his face crumbled. The hard veneer cracked loose and he seemed on the verge of walking away. "What's the shotgun in the backseat for?"

"Persuasion."

Phil really had been a pretty good cop once. He was careful enough to keep the 9mm trained on Dane the entire time he was getting in.

"You been smoking in here? Jesus fuckin' Christ!"

"Sorry," Dane said. "That was rude, I apologize."

He meant it, and Phil understood that, his expression softening even more. It didn't take much to start a blood feud, and equally little to let it slide. The 9mm dropped into his lap, then down between his knees.

Dane drove leisurely around town, teaching Phil Guerra how it was actually done. Without all the frenzied squealing turns and near misses. The screaming pedestrians and Chinese delivery guys.

This was how you drove a '59 Cadillac.

The rocket tail fins and jet pod taillights cleaving through the asphalt ocean. Grille glittering like the eyes of every mook who'd never ride in such a luscious and exquisite car, never climb into a saddle as sweet and flawless. Massive front bumper churning aside all doubts and fears, debts and misgivings.

Phil felt it too. He visibly calmed, the corners of his mouth relaxing, and after a deep breath let out a singsong, throaty hum.

Smooth and effortlessly. Dane looked at Uncle Philly again, with the fake silver hair and the perpetual false tan. The years dug into him as a testament to resilience. The expensive leather shoes, jolly fat cheeks, thinking what his father might've looked like now if the man had lived this long.

How would he have taken to retirement? Would he have phoned Dane in the joint? Could a cop like that come and see his own son? The myth of his old man would always be too great for Dane to comprehend fully. That wreck of a spectre sitting in the center of the bed, his pulse leaking, those eyes unfamiliar.

"I knew you never should've come back to the neighborhood," Phil said. "I still have that money waiting for you, if you want it."

"No thanks."

"I told you and I told you that it wasn't the safest place for you!"

"What can I say?"

Dane didn't feel the need to bring up the fact that it was obviously safer for him than it had been for Berto Monti or Joey Fresco or JoJo Tormino.

"Why'd you do it?" Phil asked. "Snuff Roberto Monticelli?"

There wasn't much point in denying culpability anymore. "He wanted it that way."

"They won't rest now. That crew."

"They're all slow, lazy, and stupid."

"They have money and numbers."

"That's not enough," Dane told him. It was obvious, but hardly anybody saw it. He turned, wondering if Phil might make a move, try to take Dane down himself and get in good with the boss. But the 9mm didn't come up into sight again.

Uncle Philly, sitting there, was just an old man, with his hair slipping down farther over his left ear. None of the brass or fire anymore, not even the usual, natural belligerence. The guy's shoulders so slack it looked like he might slump over and go to sleep with his head resting on Dane's arm.

They parked in the same spot where Dad's crusier had been found, the man inside, his temple leaking endless dreams. Five police cars were out in front of Grandma Lucia's house down the block, but they hadn't barricaded the street and no cops approached the Caddy. What shitty police work.

"Why did you kill my father?" Dane asked.

Phil's lackluster expression seemed more beaten down than anything, like this was only another wearying subject. "What the hell is this now?"

"I want to know."

"Johnny—"

"Was it because he found out you were in the Montis' pocket? Is that why you did it?"

"Found out?" A dismal, steady titter almost worked up into a chuckle. "He always knew that. So what? You think your dad was clean? Hey, he didn't take as much as most guys, but he took his share. We all did."

"Like you said, you ought to get something out of twenty-five years besides a gold watch."

"Yeah. But . . . Johnny, you been thinking I killed your old man? Since when?"

"What do you think?"

"Since it happened? That been on your mind all this time? Ah, Christ, kid, what put this *pazzo* idea in your head?"

So easy to just grab the pistol, put it to Uncle Philly's temple, and pull the trigger. Put Dad's soul to rest and keep him off the bed. A son has obligations he can never neglect, no matter the cost. Any resolution was better than none. Dane's chest started to hitch, his hands tight on the steering wheel like a second-rate driver.

You couldn't get away with saying this was an accident. That this was somehow self-defense.

Here, you're going to mess up this exquisite '59 Caddy with viscera and fluids.

You're about to willingly become the thing you hate most.

"You poor twisted kid," Phil said, and Dane's scars began to burn.

The flickering image of Vinny appeared all around the Cadillac, wearing a black Armani suit and an open leather overcoat. In several spots at once—holding a cigarette, hands in his pockets, clutching a gun. It was just beginning to rain, but Vinny was already drenched like he'd been in the storm for hours. Dissolving and solidifying, finally, into one figure, he stood there outside of the passenger door, grasping a .38.

Dane reached into his jacket pocket for his own gun and it wasn't there anymore.

Vinny had it. In some other track he'd gotten into the car, wrestled with Dane, and managed to grab hold of the pistol.

Now he was out there, pointing it into the Caddy. Grinning with those dentures. The fake eye with emerald flecks watching. Another boy with a sick brain.

TWENTY-EIGHT

You wait so long for the moment to come, imagining what it'll be like and how you'll feel about it, and when it finally arrives you feel nothing.

Staring at the man who, out of everybody in the world, still knew you the best.

Teeth bearing down on the tip of his tongue, Dane let out a soft, loose growl.

Vinny fucked around for another minute, aiming the barrel first at Dane's face, then at Phil's, then back again. Letting out a soft hiss of empty laughter every so often, like it was a game he'd played so often it had driven him crazy with boredom.

With an easy glide, Phil's right hand started to work down into his lap, reaching for the 9mm.

"Don't," Dane told him.

The water dripping down his face, funneling through the dent across his brow, Vinny let the wind flap his overcoat open behind him, trailing in the breeze whistling

through the cemetery gates. He motioned for Phil to roll
down the window, then looked inside and told Dane,
"He killed your old man."

"I'm not so sure anymore."

"It's true. If you want, I'll help you bury him. We
could drive down to the Jersey Shore. Or we could do it
right here, inside. No one will ever find him."

Phil started to protest several times, but he fudged his
words. He wasn't so much scared as he was doing his best
to play the situation right, but he just didn't know how.
"Look—look, Vincenzo, this, this here, it's—look . . .
I'm . . . I'm not—"

"Tell him that you killed his father, Phil."

"No."

"Do it. Make it right after all these years."

"I didn't shoot my partner," Phil said flatly, staring
straight ahead through the windshield, so if Vinny did
pull the trigger, he'd have to shoot Phil in the temple.
Dane looked over and saw that he was telling the truth.
Phil Guerra hadn't killed Sgt. John Danetello.

"Let him go," Dane said.

"You certain about that?" Vinny cut loose with another hollow giggle, only a dim echo of real emotion.

"Yeah." Dane turned to Phil and said, "I'm gonna
keep the Caddy for a little while longer, Uncle Philly.
You'll get it back soon though, I promise. Now take a
walk."

Phil climbed out. With more emotion than Dane
thought possible, the man said, "You two have had this
coming for a while. Good luck on settling it."

This was the kind of thing that Cogan enjoyed about
Brooklyn. Only here could you point a gun at somebody
and nearly bury him in somebody else's plot, only to
have him wishing you well two minutes later.

"Shut up, you dirty rat bastard prick," Vinny snarled as Phil backed down the street. The wind took his toupee and hurled it into the street. Vinny laughed and cocked his chin at Dane, still not climbing in. "He really did put one in your dad's head, you know."

"Yeah?"

"Yeah. If he hadn't, he'd go run over to those cops in front of your house and call them down here. But look what he's doing." Vinny craned his neck and let out a merciless laugh. "He's ducking and pretending not to see them."

"Maybe he just wants us to finish it without anybody else getting between us."

"There's always somebody in the middle."

Even now. There was someone else there, in the back-seat. Dane couldn't stop sweating, his hair almost as wet as Vinny's. He hoped it wasn't his father, appearing just to tell him what a foul-up Dane was, letting a killer go free.

He checked the rearview. It took a while but he eventually recognized her from the night of the accident. It was the girl Vinny had laid down in the Jersey dunes, who'd been pissed that he'd offered her cash afterward. The one who'd called the cops.

She said, "Kill him. He murdered me. After he got out of the hospital, he came back and found me and stuck a knife in my back. Eleven times. He took his time. He dumped me behind the same dune where he fucked me. Kill him."

Vinny clambered into the Cadillac. He shoved his dripping hair back off his forehead, then plied the fabric on the seat. "This is that Fleetwood Sixty metallic shit."

"He got screwed by the restorer."

"Did a nice job otherwise."

Dane started the car and drove back around Head-stone City as if experiencing it for the first time. Sensing more beauty here than he'd seen the past couple of weeks, and feeling even more at home. This town took your marrow but replaced it with steel.

"Please, kill him now," the girl said, smelling like the morning tide.

"I heard Fredric Wilson is dead," Vinny said. Letting it out without any emotion.

Dane looked at the side of Vinny's scarred face. "So you knew his name the whole time."

"Of course. I wondered when you'd take care of that."

That put things in perspective.

Dane finally realized that Vinny was harder and stronger than him. He'd never be able to beat Vinny, ever, at anything. He didn't have the fortitude it took to do the things that Vinny was capable of. "And you never went after him? The guy who sold your sister the poi-soned flake?"

"It was your debt. I figured you'd eventually handle it."

"And you didn't put the contract out on me. It was Berto. But you didn't lift it either."

"Appearance's sake and all that. Besides, I knew he wouldn't be able to find anybody worth a damn, the cheap fuck. Five grand. He was degrading himself. That disgusting *finocchio* prick, always down at the bridge looking for drag queens, he's lucky one of the other made guys didn't catch him. They'd have broiled his nuts with a blowtorch for a weekend."

"Joey said they were getting ready to ice him."

"They should've moved faster."

They passed police cars prowling the neighborhood. Some of the cruisers going by with their lights flashing, but none taking a second glance at the Caddy. The rain came down a little harder but Dane didn't need to turn on the wipers yet. Watching the world through the smears and dapples, even Vinny got into it, the poetry of their town. Holding his palm up to the lightly throbbing water on the other side of the glass, Vinny said, "Every once in a while, it breaks your heart."

"I'm not doing what you want anymore," Dane told him, wincing at how weak it sounded. There was always one person you'd always be inferior to, no matter what you did.

"Don't you get it, Johnny? Nobody pushed you. Everything you've done is because you wanted to do it. You stand or slump on your own."

"What do you want?"

"*Rispetto.*"

"You're not respected enough already?"

"I'm talking about you." The fake eye fixed, seeing deep into Dane's brain, peering through the fractures that would never completely heal. "I told you. I had something special in mind for you. What's mine I give to you, Johnny. You're taking over. You're going to finish what you started. You're going to kill my father and take what's his."

"You've completely cracked."

The radio began to murmur and cackle with the voices of his parents, his father in there sort of laughing, nobody crying at all. His mother, sounding happy, her hands coming together in excitement.

Dozens of others, maybe hundreds, all his relatives going back twenty or thirty centuries, to the Sicilians who revolted against Roman, Carthaginian, Norman, and French rule.

"The Don is dying," Vinny said without sorrow. "He's

got cancer. Pancreas, liver, and prostate. He's rotting inside. All the damn doctors can't believe he's held on this long. He should've been dead more than a year ago. Only weed helps him with the pain. But he's making the effort to keep going for one reason."

Vinny stopped and waited for Dane to play his role and ask the question. You could only improvise for so long, and then you had to go back to the script.

"Why?"

"He wants to go out with a bullet in his head. The way his father did. And his grandfather. And his uncles, and everybody else in my family going back about a hundred years or more. You'd be doing the old man a favor."

"He's your father."

"And I love him. That's why I want you to do this. For me. I'd do it myself, but that's not how it happens. I don't have that choice. You're going to take over the business. After I'm gone."

"Where are you going? You going to produce movies in Hollywood for the rest of your life? Working with the feds? That why you've been laying the groundwork?"

"There is no groundwork."

"So how's it going to help Maria into the movie biz? How's it going to be an advantage?"

"It isn't."

Like talking to a slab of concrete in the street. "Then why do any of it?"

"For you," Vinny said, and he was serious.

"What the hell does that mean?"

"To help you set it up for Maria. To win her over. To show her how much you love her. Everything I've said, you're going to do it all for her and yourself. Nobody else."

Dane thought about it for a minute and realized, So at

least one of us is totally insane here. Maybe both of them. But that didn't matter much now, at the end of things.

"Don't feel bad, man," Vinny said. "It's supposed to be this way. I saw flashes of it the day we went through the glass."

Dane looked around and noticed he had parked back in the same spot, in front of the gate where his old man had died. Where he was supposed to die too.

"Death is nothing," Vinny went on.

The girl in the backseat lay down with eleven knife wounds in her kidneys, stared at the roof of the Caddy, and let out a cry fashioned from the incomprehensible loss inside her, a scream from the bottom of such intense anguish that Dane had to cover his face.

On the radio, his mother was giggling.

"We beat it a long time ago, when we went through the windshield," Vinny continued, certain that Dane would come to believe it too. "You didn't know that?"

"Jesus Christ."

"Here, watch."

Dane thought, Here it is, I'm about to be put down with my own gun.

Vinny yanked the .38 up in a beautiful move, showing just how incredibly fast he was. No one could ever have a chance against him. He pressed the barrel between Dane's eyes. "This won't hurt at all. Trust me."

An enormous blast like the truest name of God roared up from every corner of the world, as the night folded itself into all the contours of your worst fears. Dane's head flew to pieces.

TWENTY-NINE

Death is nothing. We beat it a long time ago, when we went through the windshield," Vinny said. "You telling me you didn't know that? Here, watch."

Vinny yanked the .38 up in a beautiful move, showing just how incredibly fast he was, no one could ever have a chance against him. He pressed the barrel under his chin and gave a grin that made Dane start to groan.

Dane leaped forward and grabbed Vinny's hand, twisting it backwards so he'd drop the gun. But he wouldn't let go. Somebody pounded on the doors of Dane's skull, wanting to be let in, or out. There was hardly any room to move. Dane chopped at Vinny's collarbone, once, twice, hearing it snap. It just made Vinny yelp and tug harder until the .38 was pointed at Dane's gut.

The bullet took Dane low in the stomach and punched him backwards against the driver's door. He hit hard, the window cracking beneath his head. He felt everything rip inside him and slosh to the left. He opened his mouth and red foam bubbled over his chin. He was going to die with no style at all, but at least he was still behind a steering wheel.

"You stupid, lousy prick," Vinny said, still smiling, shaking his head, with his busted collarbone poking up a half inch through his raincoat. "You got shit and black blood coming out your belly now. That means you're finished."

Vinny coughed and panted, pressed a hand to Dane's clammy cheek, and told him, "Don't do that again. Right?"

THIRTY

"Death is nothing."

"It's something," Dane told him.

"We beat it a long time ago, when we went through the windshield," Vinny said. "You telling me you didn't know that?"

"No, I don't think I did."

"Do you now?"

"I'm not sure."

"You're the *pazzo* fuck."

Dane thought that maybe he understood what it had been like for Vinny all along. He felt the draw, the separation of himself heading down toward another life. He stood on one path and looked around, then saw there might be another slightly better chance for happiness if only he made a choice that took him there. There. There.

"Don't do it, Vinny."

"Look, there's nobody in the middle anymore. Here, watch."

On the radio, Dad mumbling about the rules of the road, always wearing your seat belt, being courteous to your fellow driver. The girl in the backseat lay down with eleven knife wounds in her kidneys, stared at the roof of the Caddy, and let out a cry fashioned from the incomprehensible loss inside her.

Vinny yanked the .38 up in a beautiful move, showing just how incredibly fast he was. No one could have ever had a chance against him. He pressed the barrel under his chin and gave a grin that made Dane whimper, thinking, How will I explain this to Maria?

Vinny pulled the trigger and took off the back of his skull, fucking up the beautiful interior of the '59 Caddy. He managed to heave a sigh of satisfaction as he flopped into Dane's arms.

They stayed like that for a while.

THIRTY-ONE

Despite it all, having crossed so many of these lines you never thought you'd step over, tears still clinging at your beard stubble, it felt proper to finally have a clear and unswerving purpose. This is what you've always wanted.

On his way out to the Monti mansion, with Vinny's body in the trunk, most of the inside of the Caddy cleaned up, Dane passed St. Mary's and spotted a bright blue hot-air balloon hovering about three feet above the lawn. Vinny had mentioned it back in Chooch's. But what did something like this mean, what symbolism could you find, when a piece of the sky was hanging down in back of your church?

About forty people clotted the front doors of the rectory, trying to keep warm. A handful of the elderly, a group of teens, a few six-year-olds, and even a couple of the modern nuns who didn't completely cover up in black head to toe.

A priest he didn't recognize stood looking at the basket, scared to let the kids get too close, with the rising wind, and the increasingly heavy rain coming down. Dane had the feeling God was presenting him with one last chance to get out of this—hop in the balloon, cut the ropes, and just drift away.

The priest caught his eye and immediately understood something was wrong. His gaze filled with alert apprehension and meaningless concern as he walked over to the car. "Is there some problem?"

"What is this?" Dane called. "The Jesus Jamboree?"

"Don't you read your *Papist Gazette*?"

Goddamn, did they really print such a thing? Dane smiled blandly, the growing agitation working inside him trying to get out. He checked the rearview to see who might be in the backseat. Without humor he said, "The neighbor's dog got it off our stoop this week."

"It's our St. Mary's Redemption and Atonement Gala."

No wonder you only had a handful of people wandering around wearing puzzled expressions. "You might consider spiffing up the name next year."

"I'll think about that. Why don't you join us?"

"Sorry, I'm on an errand."

"We've got grape juice and *biscotti*."

Dane let out a chuckle that grew a little too wild, reminding him of Joey's mongoose sounds. He swallowed back the rest of it. "Bread and wine? You bless them so the WASPs are taking communion without knowing it?"

"There's been a lot of police prowling the area today. A good deal of talk."

"There's gonna be a little more." Dane reached into the glove compartment and grabbed the envelope with ten grand in it that JoJo Tormino had given him. "Here.

To help you hire a couple of horses for next year, and a merry-go-round. A cotton candy maker, maybe pay somebody who tells pope jokes. Bobo the Catholic Clown, that'll get a crowd in. Instead of a funny pope hat going up and down, his goes side to side. You'll make a killing."

"I think I know who you are. Perhaps you should come in."

"Another time."

As he pulled away from the curb, the storm kicked up another notch and the wind tore at the surrounding woodlands of Outlook Park.

He swung up the hill toward the Monticelli estate and the gushing rainwater washed down the cobblestone driveway in a thick, pulsing torrent. He picked up his .38 off the seat and held it in his left hand, thinking he might have to reach out the window, plink a few guys, and crash through the private gates. You couldn't get away from the movie rolling in your head, your name leading the credits. The pressure pushed at the metal plates in your skull, trying to cut loose.

The guardhouse appeared empty, the gates already open. There were occasional shouts and the squealing of tires as their Jeeps buzzed around the various paths on the grounds. Everybody in a panic over Berto and Joey, looking for Vinny, but nobody watching the door.

Dane drove up and still didn't get the reception he'd been expecting. Nobody stopped him. There were no police cars asking questions at the Monticelli residence. His sense of farce was beginning to overwhelm him.

Dane grabbed the shotgun off the backseat and walked up to the front door. It was unlocked and he let himself inside.

His entire life had brought him right here, to this moment.

Everyone, in his own way, had to be in on it, a part of the continuing process. Georgie Delmare, the *consigliere,* tucked away someplace in the house, thinking about how the business would have to be transferred into other names, already working on the new tax reports. Big Tommy Bartone, probably sitting in the next room, feeling old and waiting for a war. Any war. Dane turned the corner and looked up the staircase, seeing no one on the landing. He moved down the hallway, and there, sitting alone in the living room, anticipating this meeting, sat the dying Don.

The debility and pain in his rough features had almost given away to placidity. He saw Dane and immediately lit a joint, rushing his first drag. He took it in deep and let it out in a thin stream so his eyes clouded.

"Hello, John."

"Hello, Don Pietro."

"You've been working very hard lately."

Dane nodded. "I'm showing an interest in life."

"I'm glad. You're going to put my house in order?" Saying it with just the barest lilt of a question, putting a little dare into it.

"If I can."

Would the Don be surprised to learn Grandma had blown Joey's ass to hell? Or would he have expected that? Knowing how powerful Lucia could be. Dane figured they'd probably fooled around some back in the forties or fifties, listening to Sinatra, Jerry Vale, and Mel Torme.

"I knew if you were strong and patient, you would find the truth. The truth meant for you to find. That you would discover your nature."

"I just wanted to talk to Maria."

"That would be pointless now, don't you think?"

"No. It's my only objective."

The Don held on with great resolve against his own cancer, still the boss of the family even with his rickety legs and shivery hands, stoned out of his gourd. They both looked around the room at the old photographs of brutal men who'd died violent deaths, their blood soaking down through the ages into the flesh and the concrete of Headstone City. Dane was as much a product of any of them as he was his own parents.

Voices moved through the halls, coming closer. Dane snapped up, holding the shotgun, the .38 within easy reach, stuffed in his belt.

The smart move was to take out the muscle first, the guys with the guns, but Dane just didn't see it happening that way. The Don was the only one left who wanted to end it with some honor, meeting the void with his head up.

Dane had always held a fierce respect for him, but now he just wanted to hug the man, draw him close, and perhaps say a few of the things he'd never been able to say to his own father. Maybe because he owned the neighborhood, or because he'd been instrumental in providing Dane's small world with at least one beautiful thing.

But he also felt a mild but crude hatred. For having given up so easily on centuries-old traditions of order and command. For degenerating what should've been a class act. For letting down his guard. For keeping Maria from true love.

"Thank you, John."

Dane stepped up, drew his .38, and put a bullet into the center of Don Monticelli's peaceful face.

It only took ten seconds for a couple of interchangeable thugs to appear. They let out hisses of fear and confusion but didn't yank any weapons. They glared with open mouths, unsure of what the hell else to do.

These fuckin' kids, they all needed a lesson.

Georgie Delmare walked in, his bland eyes showing only a little more emotion than usual, but not enough to shake his perfect composure. Big Tommy moved down the corridor to stand beside him. Big's perpetual sneer had vanished, his lips welded together like scraps of tin. They both stared at him, disregarding the Don slumped in his seat.

"What about Vinny?" Tommy asked, and his voice damn near broke.

"He wanted to prove to me he wasn't afraid of dying."

"So?"

"So he wasn't."

Sgt. John Danetello's son was taking over the Monti crime organization because he was bored and needed something to do. Because already there were plenty of scores to settle.

"I'm going to need your help," Dane told them. "First thing we do is dry up the drug trade into Hollywood through the company once run by Glory Bishop's husband."

"What's his name?" the *consigliere* asked. He'd seen his masters dead in their chairs and beds before, and he'd survived them all. He served whoever was at the top of the heap at any given hour.

"I still don't goddamn know. But the feds are all over it. We're going to sell plenty, just not through

Hollywood. There's a crew in Williamsburg we can put to use."

Fuck Cogan and his little wars in Central America. Dane was going to start his payback with that son of a bitch.

"You bringing in the *mulignan*?" Big asked.

"They're already in. We're just going to take some of their pie. Hollywood is wide-open for other things. I think we'll front a few independent film makers."

Georgie Delmare grinned with interest, his thoughts moving fast. "Who?"

Dane remembered all the stacks of shitty scripts on the floor beside Glory Bishop's bed. The one where the serial killer runs across the river and doesn't get wet. Lots of topless broads capering around. "I don't know yet, give me some time. But start setting money aside. And get a list of the best-looking whores and strippers on the payroll."

"There aren't many."

"Yeah, yeah, because you're so legit now, I know."

Big Tommy glanced over at the Don, looking contented there in his seat. "You really taking over, Johnny?"

You could only do what's given you to do. Dane thought about his grandmother's dream. About how Dane didn't get chased out of the village, but wound up running it.

Here we are, doing what we're meant to do. "Yeah."

"You're not even a made guy."

"That doesn't carry the weight it used to. You people held true for about a thousand years, but the last fifty have gone all to hell. I killed four people today. I think that qualifies me."

"Not even close," Big told him, hitching up his

shoulders and getting some bravura back. "You did Berto?"

"It was sort of an accident."

"The other families won't accept you, Johnny. Even this crew here."

"That doesn't matter." He glanced at the toughs, who he'd never be able to distinguish apart. "If they want to make a run at me, let them. You're welcome to try too."

Dane tightened, holding the shotgun in one hand, setting himself. He shifted so he could swing on Big and take his head off with no trouble.

Big Tommy Bartone wasn't an idiot though, not anymore. "You want to live like that, Johnny? Never relaxed? Always on your toes?"

You could do worse. Dane thought about his life up to this point and how he'd walked through so much of it without giving a damn about anything. Like Vinny said, they'd already met death and gotten tangled in the veil. "It's something to do."

Delmare said, "The police will be here soon asking questions about everything that's happened today. You need a cover story for why you're not at home."

"Call the Marriott in Mount Laurel. I'll hole up there for a few days, then come back. I'll tell the investigators I had to hide for fear of retribution."

"Who do we say whacked Roberto?" Tommy asked.

Delmare liked using his mind, letting his instincts run. "Joey Fresco. Joey did it all. He had bad debts catching up to him. He used to visit the Ventimiglia casinos a lot and owed them at least twenty large. We say he was a traitor who went to work destroying our organization from the inside." Delmare gestured with his chin toward the Don. "He did this. And Berto. He also murdered Vinny. We lay it all at his feet, and we implicate the Venimiglia family in doing so." Staring into Dane's eyes now. "You were Vinny's best friend. Joey Fresco knew you'd come after him, so he tried to ice you in your grandmother's house. But you were faster and killed him."

"Actually, she did."

"Holy fuck," Big Tommy said. "I gotta meet this lady."

Dane asked, "Does this place have a large kitchen?"

"What?"

"Is there a lot of room to move in the kitchen?"

"The hell are you doing talking about the kitchen for?"

"Just answer me."

"Yeah, it's huge."

"Good, my grandmother will like it."

He imagined Grandma Lucia moving into the mansion, settling in upstairs, an old-world *cafone* peasant woman surrounded by all this wealth. So long as Dane had the strength to keep it all.

He'd get Pepe over here to act as his capo, help sharpen up these poor examples of *la cosa nostra*. Who knew, maybe even Fran, with all that awful hate inside her, could be put to good use. If not, then he'd have to kill her. He didn't want somebody like that walking around anywhere near him in this town.

Delmare stared over Dane's shoulder. Dane turned and looked down the corridor.

And there she was.

Maria Monticelli.

With her insanely black hair coiling and twining to frame her dark and eternal eyes, the luscious angles of her body shown off to perfection. Her blouse open one button too far. The hem of her burgundy skirt caught over her knee to give an enticing view of what he'd dreamed about most of his life. If this wasn't love, it was the next best thing.

This is what you've always wanted.

She moved from the bottom of the staircase, looked at her murdered daddy in the chair. She said nothing, but took another step closer. He breathed her in. His chest was constricted with the insane excitement of being so close to her again.

Of course you would murder men for her. You'd have to be crazy not to.

He drew the bloodstained box from his pocket and opened it, held the diamond ring out to her.

"What's this?" she said. "You . . . you're asking me . . . ? You—?"

"Yeah."

Those lips, drawing him in, as if he'd traveled a thousand miles but somehow the journey got easier with each step. Leading him to stand before her. The funny guy who wasn't so tough.

She said, "Everything you did today, Johnny. What they've been saying. About my brothers . . . and my father—my daddy?"

"Yes, Maria."

Everybody just stared at him, maybe waiting for her to give the order to kill Dane.

Dane scowled at one of the toughs. Just another kid really, no more than twenty or so. Dane said, "You. You just got promoted. What's your name?"

"Nunzio."

Jesus, all these old-world Italians and their names from the Olive Oil villages. "All right, Nunz, I want you to take the Don out of here. Use the Caddy out front. Vinny's in the trunk."

"Holy fuck," Big Tommy said.

"Bury them wherever you get rid of bodies, Big. The Meadowlands? Fresh Kills?"

"Yeah, Staten Island. There's no room behind Kennedy Airport anymore."

"Go take them." Gesturing to the muscle. "Both of you help him. Remember the spot though. In a couple of weeks we'll drop a call to the police, have them found and brought home. Give them a big funeral." They deserved that, and both of them would've understood this had to come first. "Afterward, I'll have a list of more to do. And your salary's just been doubled."

"Everybody in the organization?" Delmare asked.

"Everybody in this room. Get the troops together in the morning. I got a few things I can teach them."

"Do you mean military tactics?"

"Yeah."

"What are you planning to do?"

"To pay a visit to the Ventimiglias. We're going to take out Vito Grimaldi."

"But why? They haven't done anything. By implicating them with all these recent crimes, they'll be smeared in the media and under continuous investigation for months. There's no reason to take a stand against them."

Dane looked at him. "They're the last rough crew around."

"Yes, that's right."

"So that's the reason, Georgie."

Everybody grateful now. The two thugs with the same expression on their stupid faces—giddy, sensing major changes ahead. They grabbed the Don's body and hustled him down the hallway and out the door. Big carried away the blood-smeared chair, and that was the only evidence that the Don had died in his own living room. Georgie nodded and left for his office.

Dane turned to Maria and saw real fright in her eyes.

He stepped closer and saw the lust there too, the reverence.

Rispetto.

She was looking at him as if noticing him for the first time since he was a child, and she was.

It made his pulse hammer and the sweat flood down his back. He took her gently but assuredly, encircling her waist and drawing her to him. She held her ground for an instant, then flowed against his body, squirming there, then yielding.

"Do you still want to be an actress?"

"I never really cared much about that," she said. "It was something to dream about until something else better came along."

He thought of her on the screen, sharing her with the world, ten thousand theaters filled with squirming men, guys at home with their VCRs all freeze-framed on her. "Good," Dane told her. "I need you here."

"You need me." Her face softening even more, so beautiful that he could barely control himself.

"I always have."

"I've been waiting for you, Johnny."

JoJo had been right. We all got one thing in the world that we love more than anything else. That makes us do what we do and makes us who we are.

He led her upstairs, kicking in doors until he found her bedroom. As he kissed her throat he saw the photo of JoJo Tormino behind her, on the night table. He eased her down on the mattress, reached over, and slapped the frame to the floor.

She unbuckled his belt and he said, "JoJo loved you. I promised him I'd tell you that."

"I don't give a shit," she whispered, and Dane rolled her back on the bed and was on her.

The boy with the sick brain happily bounded forward from a corner of the room, perhaps finally ready to tell Dane whatever it was he'd been trying to say. An angel with golden wings as shiny as coins sat on the edge of the mattress, supplicant but silent, a burning sword in its right hand. Dane lay with his love and let out his first real laugh in thirty years against her throat as he waited for the kid so much like himself to again mutter all the grievous, joyous, secret languages of the profane and fitful dead.

ABOUT THE AUTHOR

TOM PICCIRILLI is the author of fourteen novels, including *November Mourns, A Choir of Ill Children, The Night Class, A Lower Deep,* and *Coffin Blues*. He's had over 150 stories published, and his short fiction spans multiple genres and demonstrates his wide-ranging narrative skills. He has been a World Fantasy Award finalist and a three-time Bram Stoker Award winner. Visit Tom's official website, Epitaphs, at www.tompiccirilli.com. Tom welcomes email at PicSelf1@aol.com.

Don't miss

Tom Piccirilli's

exciting next novel
coming from
Bantam Books
in Fall 2006.

Read on for an exclusive sneak peek
and pick up your copy at
your favorite bookseller

Killjoy wrote:

Words are not as adequate as teeth.

Incisors are incapable of lying. If I pressed them into wax or paper or fish or flesh you would know my meaning, the constraints of form, and every trivial fact there is to be found. Words are deficient, even impractical, when attempting to convey the substance of true (modest) self. Deed is definition. We are restricted by mind and voice but not in action, wouldn't you agree? That we can never completely express that which is within. That sometimes the very act of feeling isn't enough to encompass all there is to feel. Frenzy is trying to explain your behaviors to yourself. I suspect I have yet a long way to go at the art of becoming human.

Remember Schlagelford's great treatise on the fear of non-existence. He spent some thirty-seven years of his adult life with his left hand clamped to his left thigh (trouserless, of course). Despite his grip cutting off all circulation in that leg until it withered, blackened, and eventually had to be amputated (and the hand, no more than a frozen talon, had grown useless, and continued to squeeze the phantom limb), at which point he gripped his right thigh with his right hand and had to write his last major work, The Season of Femoral, *with quill champed between teeth, still he was content.*

Satisfied in his knowledge of personal existence in a world without enough promise or structure.

Do you ever feel that way, Whitt?

Do your hands shake?

The mama cultist told Whitt about the dead ballerina, a god named Mucus Thorn-in-Brain, and the starving baby that had been stolen out of the back room.

She and her two lumbering middle-aged sons smiled at him. Whitt tried to smile back but the muscles in his jaw were so tight that he barely managed a grimace. It got like that sometimes, when he was forced to hold himself in check. Luckily these people were so caught up in their own mania that they hardly even noticed him while they prattled on incessantly. They gave him a cup of herbal tea that smelled like turpentine and he left it on the scratched table in front of him.

Except for the murders, they were about the same as any other cult members he'd met. Considering his narrow range of interests and social obligations, he'd actually met more than his share. Whatever the hell a man's share of cultists should be in this world.

The woman, Mrs. Prott, who introduced herself as the High Priestess of the Cosmic Knot, spoke with near hysterical excitement about a new god being born in the back of her son Merwin's heart. Merwin, who had awful surgical scars covering his forehead, grinned stupidly and petted his chest like he was stroking a luscious woman's hair.

The other son, Franklin, was blind and kept flexing his hands like he wanted to leap out of his chair and tear something to pieces.

Whitt feigned interest in Mrs. Prott's continuing sermon and looked at her star charts, notes, magazine articles, and photographs of the multitude of people who played some role in her ever widening tale of religion, murder, and secret government experiments. She kept tapping a spot between her eyes, saying they'd shot her there and her brain had leaked out, which was why she sometimes got mixed up. Whenever she said the word "government," Merwin would stop stroking his invisible lover's hair and thump his head.

The house had been the dumping ground for members of the group for years. Whitt got up and wandered around while the woman talked, rifling through stacks of newspapers dating back three, four years. He saw himself on the front page of more than one, laid out mostly in the open, as if waiting for him.

A metal shelf unit held two dozen upside-down mason jars, each sealed with contact cement, and sprinkled with a handful of salt. Words, possibly names, were scrawled in black marker on old yellow masking tape: *Hogarth. Pedantry. Airsiez. Colby. Terminus. Kinnick. Insensate. Testament of Ya'al. Ussel. Dr. Dispensations. O'Mundanity.*

She kept on preaching. It threw him off a bit, this lady's willingness to discuss such matters so openly, in her strange manner, as though she were telling only basic, incontrovertible truths. Speaking in a happily lilting voice, like she was overjoyed to find someone who actually had interest in her life, no matter why. Whitt nodded like an idiot, and she nodded back. Was it only loneliness that drove people to such extreme acts?

"And she came to you for help," he said, sitting back down, trying to keep mama on topic. "The ballerina."

"For the truth, yes. And for love. Everyone, always in such need of love. You see, she also had quite the nervous disposition. Emotionally she'd been tormented by her parents, who never responded to her with affection of any kind. They merely drove her ever more forcefully toward the perfection of her dancing. Into the arms of boys. That's what the child was. A symbol of her desperation."

"And you murdered her," Whitt said.

Telling it while fluttering her hand at him as if he were absurd, so silly. "What do you mean? Who?"

Whitt forced his breath out in a stream that blew ripples across the stinking tea. He remembered to make the effort to smile again. "The ballerina."

Head eased back, Franklin rolled his blank eyes up and let out a guffaw. It came from down low in his belly and the depths of his hate. Whitt wanted to hear what the guy's voice sounded like, but so far Franklin refused to make any comment beyond that sick laughter. If any trouble started, Whitt would take out the blind guy before anybody else.

Mrs. Prott said, "Oh yes, that one. The dancer."

First thing you saw when you looked at Mama Prott was the jiggle of turkey neck. Even when she wasn't turning her head, that neck still flapped, vibrating with her breathing, always catching your attention. Whitt couldn't get over it.

The woman boiling with gaiety, heavy and earthen. Someone you wanted to hug, really. Her expensive, chic clothing was mismatched and too tight. He figured she'd stolen them from ladies with taste in order to pretend she had some fashion sense herself. Lots of jewelry, most of it fake but some pieces worth more than this shit hole's entire mortgage. She wore men's wedding bands on both thumbs.

Franklin's hands opening and closing in perfect timing to Whitt's pulse.

Mrs. Prott smiling, her teeth dark and crooked. "Well, no one actually killed her. You cannot destroy that which is *obdurate. Insensible.* You can only transform it. She wasn't human." Doing the fluttery finger thing again. "She was *other,* and the purifying light of Mucus Thorn-in-Brain struck her down when she tried to steal my breath one morning."

"I see," Whitt said.

"She climbed on top of me while I slept and tried to kiss me so she could steal the soulwind from my lungs. You can't call it murder to set right the karmic cosmic wheel again."

"I thought it was a knot."

"A knot that spins and spins like a wheel across the great ecclesiastical galaxy."

"Okay," Whitt said. "So what happened to her?"

"The only way to defend ourselves from a soul thief is to stab it thrice in the heart, with the point of the blade aiming north. Then the throat must be cut so its evil incantations will dribble to the floor instead of being raised to the cosmic masters. This is the transformation that must take place. Conversion. Reformation. Then the genitals must be removed or the seed may infect another vessel and give birth even in its dying throes."

"Dying throes," Whitt repeated.

"And we wouldn't want that. We could not bear that."

"No, we could not."

"More tea?"

"Please."

That blank gaze of the blind man landed on Whitt with a certain amount of weight. Franklin's fists grasping nothing. The other brother with his hand on his chest. Whitt whispered, "Government, government," and watched Merwin clunk his thatched head twice.

Mama Prott handed Whitt a series of graphs and charts that had been modified from the zodiac. Strange uses of Cabalistic symbols, Teutonic characters, numerology, and scatterings of nonsensical pseudo-sexual terms, with an emphasis on bodily fluids and naughty bits. Phlegm in Hair. Whore's Bait. Orifice Eye. Mucus Desisting the Efforts of Knee. Failure of Urethra. The handwriting so crimped that it would take hours to decipher it all.

Pulling out one particular sheet, stained with pinkish fluid. "Here, here it is," she said, "proof that the girl was other. That the Sect of Purification and Consummation acted in protection of all the earth and humanity."

"So you're a branch of a larger—" What should he call this thing she believed in? He didn't think she'd take offense at the word *cult*, but calling this a cult lent it too much credence. "—persuasion."

"Yes. We have nineteen more members back at the other house, where the majority of our communicants live, and where we hold our official ceremonies."

"Which house would that be?" he asked.

Pointing at the far wall, the mis-sized rings on her fingers jingling slightly. "The one on Carver Way, where most of the important rituals are held. This one here, we use it only every so often, to store our belongings. You're very lucky to have found us here this morning."

"Yes," he said.

It took another half hour of finagling, but Whitt finally got the ballerina's name out of her: Grace Kinnick. It was one of the names on the jars. What did the Protts think they had in there? Captured souls?

"And the child?"

"Stolen. That's why we need your help. The beget . . . the offspring . . . of the soulthief is still in its genuine form. It can be dealt with now. Sent back into the celestial continuum where it can once again rejoin with the great astral identiform."

"Sure."

"We have to have the child before midnight Friday night. You said you know who has it now?"

"That's right, it's with a friend of mine who

works for social services," Whitt lied. He grinned at Merwin. "A government agency."

Merwin rapping himself in the head again, looking scared that somebody from the Pentagon might come take away more of his brain. And Whitt sitting here making a game of it. He had to have a little fun here so he didn't go wild and start crossing the hard line, becoming what everyone told him he'd become.

"Oh, it's dangerous to have the beget loose like this," Mrs. Prott warbled, the neck going gangbusters. "Magic circles must be precipitated, the proper guiding influences invoked before the evisceration and following rituals."

Whitt said, "So the baby is *other*. Genuine. It's blood-tainted. And must be struck down by Mucus Thorn-in-Brain. And returned to the cosmic knot."

She broke into a delighted squeal that went on for too long. "Yes, exactly. Oh, you are adept. A true sensitive. You have the gift, do you realize that? I've never seen an aura quite like yours. You're exceptionally dark and very powerful."

"How often have you done this?" he asked. "Purified these . . . evils."

"Oh, we don't keep accounts of such things. This is a spiritual war we fight. There are many casualties sprawled across both sides of the veil."

"Fourteen," Franklin said, a wet chuckle easing

from his chest. "The ballerina was number four-teen."

That voice, obscenely joyful, yet frothing with its hate. Whitt shifted to the edge of the chair in case he had to dive. Thinking that maybe now Franklin was about to use those hands. "What do you mean?"

"The ballerina was number fourteen," Franklin repeated. "The baby, it would've been fifteen."

Mama Prott smiled at her boy. Whitt thought about the dead, probably buried in the yard, hidden in the house. He stared at the spot between her eyes, where she said they'd shot her and her brains had leaked out, and wondered if he could drop, roll aside, draw his .32, spring to his feet and hit the target, the way he'd been practicing.

"So, Mr. Whitt, can you help us retrieve the offspring?"

"Yes," he said. "I consider it my reverent duty."

"Glorious! We'll be holding services this afternoon at the other house."

"On Carver Way."

"Yes. Please join us so we can sanctify and protect you from harm. You'll never regret your initiation into that which is Mucus Thorn-in-Brain and the clarity and peace you'll feel afterward. We'll brighten your aura yet."

That thick neck wobbling. The blind guy glaring. The other one grinning, his scars thick and shining like leeches.

"I look forward to it," Whitt said.

He drove off, parked around the corner near a sump that doubled as a dump site, and waited until the woman and her sons left in their SUV with out-of-state plates. More stolen goods. Spoils of the dead. He returned to the house with a pick-axe, shovel, and flashlight and stepped in through the broken back door that had been tied shut with the elastic from an old brassiere.

He left the tools on the stoop while he searched the house for any other squirrelly cultists that might be hiding under a bed somewhere. Except there weren't any beds. The three upstairs rooms looked poisonous, toxic, the old paint peeling in strips and the plaster gouged by fingernails. He found bullet holes and dried spatters that could've been any of the bodily fluids the Protts seemed to groove on so much.

Whitt grabbed his tools again and looked for the cellar door. He found it hidden behind the metal shelving stacked with all the upside-down jars of trapped souls.

The old stupidity and lack of control overwhelmed him for a minute. He took great pleasure in smashing the glass containers and releasing Hogarth and Ussel and Airsiez and the rest. He held on to the jar with the ballerina in it and pressed it to the side of his head, knowing how insane it looked but feeling an urgency to will her to peace, if he could. You never knew what you could do when you put your mind to it. Finally he hurled the container against the wall with the rest of them and went into the basement to dig.

The body was in the corner of the dirt floor about three feet down, missing its genitals and wearing orange sneakers, just like Killjoy had said.